PRAISE FOR  RL,

BOOK ONE IN TH RIES

"MAGICAL AND BRILLIANT! *THE ABSINTHE EARL* IS A FAST-PACED ROMP THAT EXPERTLY WEAVES TWO DIFFERENT WORLDS INTO AN ADVENTURE NOT TO BE MISSED. SHARON LYNN FISHER CRAFTS CLEVER DIALOGUE AND CREATES CHARACTERS TO FALL IN LOVE WITH."

—LORRAINE HEATH, BESTSELLING AUTHOR OF THE SCOUNDRELS OF ST. JAMES SERIES

"ANYONE WHO LOVES A GOOD SUPERNATURAL STORY, ALONG WITH A HEFTY DOSE OF IRISH LEGEND AND ROMANCE, WILL ADORE THIS NEW SERIES."

—*BOOKLIST*

"WONDERFULLY WRITTEN AND WONDERFULLY ROMANTIC, SHARON LYNN FISHER'S *THE ABSINTHE EARL* SWEEPS READERS INTO A POWERFULLY REIMAGINED VICTORIAN IRELAND WHERE A STRONG QUEEN RULES AND THE WORLD OF FAERY IS JUST A HEARTBEAT AWAY."

—MARY JO PUTNEY, *NEW YORK TIMES* BESTSELLING AUTHOR

"THE ENVIRONMENT IS LUSH AND IMAGINATIVE, WITH EVERYONE APPEARING TO HIDE THEIR OWN SEDUCTIVE, DARK SECRETS. IT'S A WORLD THAT COMES ALIVE WITH MYSTERIOUS, FOGGY MOORS, DANGEROUS PEAT BOGS, AND GORGEOUS GREEN HILLS."

—*KIRKUS REVIEWS*

“DANGER, INTRIGUE, ACTION, AND PASSION—*THE ABSINTHE EARL* HAS IT ALL! THIS BOLD BLEND OF HISTORICAL ROMANCE, LEGEND, AND FANTASY TAKES READERS ON A THRILLING RIDE THROUGH AN ALTERNATE IRELAND THAT WEAVES FOLKLORE RIGHT INTO THE WORLD WE KNOW. ORIGINAL AND CAPTIVATING!”

— AMANDA BOUCHET, *USA TODAY*
BESTSELLING AUTHOR OF THE KINGMAKER CHRONICLES

“FANS OF GAIL CARRIGER AND LEANNA RENEE HIEBER WILL SAVOR THIS PROMISING SERIES OPENER.”

—*PUBLISHERS WEEKLY*

“CHARMING AND FILLED WITH INTRIGUING CHARACTERS, DANGEROUS ENEMIES, AND HIDDEN DESIRES, *THE ABSINTHE EARL* HOOKED ME FROM THE START.”

— MARIA V. SNYDER, *NEW YORK TIMES* BESTSELLING AUTHOR

“I SUGGEST READING THIS CAPTIVATING NOVEL IN A VERDANT WOODLAND, SITTING IN THE SHADE AGAINST A STOUT TREE TRUNK AND PERHAPS SIPPING A BIT OF ABSINTHE.”

—HISTORICAL NOVEL SOCIETY

PRAISE FOR *THE RAVEN LADY*, BOOK TWO IN THE FAERY REHISTORY SERIES

"The mix of Irish and Icelandic mythology, fairy lore, and steampunk magic make for a delightful read in *The Raven Lady* by Sharon Lynn Fisher. I thoroughly enjoyed following the intrigue, subterfuge, and building romance at play between Finvara and Koli. I highly recommend to fantasy readers who appreciate an inventive take on magic and folklore."

—Luanne G. Smith, *Washington Post* and Amazon bestselling author of *The Vine Witch*

"Fisher returns to the queens, elves, and fae of eighteenth-century Ireland of *The Absinthe Earl* . . . Readers will be drawn in from the very first word of this fantasy romance, which has plenty of action and an appealing give and take between Koli and Finvara."

—*Booklist*

"From cozy mystery to gorgeous fairy romance, we are *in love* with [Sharon Lynn Fisher] and the next installment of her Faery Rehistory series!"

— Annie Carl, owner of The Neverending Bookshop

"The world-building draws from Irish mythology and fairy lore to fun effect . . . There's plenty to enjoy in the magical moments and expanding world of the series. Fisher's fans will be pleased."

—*Publishers Weekly*

· THE FAERY REHISTORY SERIES ·
THE
WARRIOR
POET

ALSO BY SHARON LYNN FISHER

THE FAERY REHISTORY SERIES

The Absinthe Earl

The Raven Lady

The Warrior Poet

STANDALONE NOVELS

Ghost Planet

The Ophelia Prophecy

Echo 8

Before She Wakes: Forbidden Fairy Tales

SHARON LYNN FISHER

Published in 2021 by Blackstone Publishing
Cover design by Bookfly Design

Printed in the United States of America

First edition: 2021
ISBN 978-1-9825-7280-8
Fiction / Fantasy / General

Version 1

CIP data for this book is available from the Library of Congress

Blackstone Publishing
31 Mistletoe Rd.
Ashland, OR 97520

www.BlackstonePublishing.com

Dedicated to Irish poet William Butler Yeats
June 13, 1865–January 28, 1939

"He is a whimsical fellow but writes devilish well at times."

—A. H. Bullen, Yeats's publisher, in a 1903 letter to Sir Sidney Cockarell[1]

1 Cited in *A Yeats Dictionary*, Syracuse University Press, by Lester I. Conner

And may no restless fay with fidget finger
Trouble his sleeping; give him dreams of me.

—William Butler Yeats,
"Anashuya and Vijaya"

GLOSSARY OF IRISH TERMS AND NAMES

absinthe: Anise-flavored alcoholic spirit also referred to as "the green fairy;" drinking absinthe allows some people to see into the fairy world.

Battle of Ben Bulben (AD 1882): Fought between the Tuatha De Danaan, allied with the people of Ireland, and their enemies the Fomorians.

Battle of Connacht (AD 882): Fought between the Tuatha De Danaan and the Fomorians—final battle before Diarmuid and Far Dorocha created the seal between Ireland and Faery.

Battle of Knock Ma (AD 1883): Fought between the king and queen of fairies—Finvara and Koli—and the Icelandic king of shadow elves.

Borabu: The horn of the warrior poet Oisin, used to call the Fianna, the warriors of the Tuatha De Danaan.

Connacht (KAH-nucht): Region and ancient kingdom in the west of Ireland.

Dana: Celtic deity, mother of the Tuatha De Danaan people (also referred to as Ana/Anu/Danu).

Diarmuid (DEER-muhd): A legendary warrior of the Tuatha De Danaan; in this series, ancestor of the character Edward Donoghue, Earl of Meath.

Diarmuid's seal: A centuries-old boundary between Ireland and Faery, created by Diarmuid and the fairy Far Dorocha, and broken before the Battle of Ben Bulben.

Duncan O'Malley: See entry for **Finvara.**

Elvish: In this text, Old Norse, the language of the Icelandic elves.

Faery: In this series, the domain of the fairies; also refers to the collective races of fairies.

Far Dorocha: In Irish mythology, a malevolent fairy who serves as the steward of the fairy queen and is known for abducting mortals; in this series, a foe of King Finvara and betrayer of the Morrigan and the Irish people; also called "Doro."

Fianna: The warriors of the Tuatha De Danaan.

Finvara (fin-VAHR-ah), King: The fairy king of Connacht and a Tuatha De Danaan immortal; in this series, the ancestor of Duncan O'Malley, and the name Duncan takes when he becomes fairy king.

Firglas: Irish woodland fairies and guardians of Knock Ma; literally "green men."

Fomorians: Ancient seafaring foes of the Tuatha De Danaan; often portrayed as a race of monsters; sometimes referred to as the Plague Warriors.

Gap, the: A space-like void between the overlapping worlds of Ireland and Faery.

Gap galleon: A type of sailing ship that can travel inside the Gap, between Ireland and Faery, and inside Faery.

Grace O'Malley: Sixteenth-century pirate queen of Connacht; in this series, ghostly captain of the Gap galleon that served in the Battle of Ben Bulben and ancestress of Duncan O'Malley, Edward Donoghue (Lord Meath), and Queen Isolde.

Hidden Folk: Icelandic equivalent of Irish fairies; includes elves, dwarves, and trolls.

Horned God, the: Irish deity who is the protector of trees, plants, and animals; also called "Uindos."

Isolde, Queen: The Queen of Ireland, descended from the mythological figure Queen Maeve; cousin of Duncan O'Malley (King Finvara) and Edward Donoghue (Lord Meath).

Knock Ma: Connacht court and stronghold of the fairy king Finvara.

Koli Alfdóttir: Half-mortal daughter of the Icelandic Elf King; also descended from Gunnhild, a Norse queen and sorceress; married to Finvara, Irish king of fairies.

Lady Meath (née Ada Quicksilver): Englishwoman descended from Cliona of the Tuatha De Danaan; a scholar of fairy lore who married Edward Donoghue, Earl of Meath.

light elves: Icelandic Hidden Folk; in this series, descendants of the Norse god Loki; *íssfólk* in Elvish.

Lord Meath: Irish earl, Edward Donoghue, descended from Diarmuid of the Tuatha De Danaan; cousin of Queen Isolde and Duncan O'Malley (King Finvara); married to Ada Quicksilver.

Morrigan, the: Irish goddess of war; crow shapeshifter; also called "the battle crow."

Niamh (NEE-av): Faery woman who was the lover of Oisin; in this series, descended from the Tuatha De Danaan.

Oisin (AWSH-een): A Fianna warrior, poet, and historian of the Tuatha De Danaan; lover of Niamh.

shadow elves: Icelandic Hidden Folk; in this series, descendants of the Norse god Loki; fought with the Fomorians against Ireland in the Battle of Ben Bulben; fought against Ireland in the Battle of Knock Ma.

Tír na nÓg (TEER-na-NOWG): A Celtic otherworld also called Land of the Young or Land of Promise; in this series, a part of Faery that serves as the afterworld for deceased fairies and Tuatha De Danaan.

Tuatha De Danaan (Too-AH-hah day DAHN-uhn), abbrev. Danaan: Ancient supernatural people of Ireland often associated with fairies; people of the Celtic goddess Dana.

Notes: With regard to the Tuatha De Danaan, this series conforms to the naming conventions and spellings used by W. B. Yeats.

For more information about the fairies' return to Ireland, the Battle of Ben Bulben, and the first Battle of Knock Ma, see books one and two in the Faery Rehistory series, *The Absinthe Earl* and *The Raven Lady*.

PROLOGUE

NIAMH

AD 882

"My love?" Space and time fold like silk between us, yet I still taste the salty warmth of his chest.

You must let go.

The words are not a request from *him*, whose voice I long to hear, but a command from the one who has answered my prayer. The Morrigan says that to be reborn, we must forget. We must forsake our immortal forms, destroyed in battle with our ancient enemy. Forsake golden eternity in the Land of Promise.

If it means feeling his arms around me again—his heat, his flesh, his bones—it is worth the price.

I sigh and release his image from my mind, severing the connection that binds us in death.

Yet I wonder . . . Will he recognize my new earthly form, or

I his? Will it be as it once was between us, the Tuatha De Danaan warrior and his Faery lady?

There is no knowing, only waiting. And only the goddess knows how long.

THE VISITOR

NEVE

Portland, Oregon—Modern day

A falling sensation and a soft squealing noise jolted me from a vivid daydream. I glanced up in time to see the glass door of the bus fold closed before the metal beast hissed and lurched forward. Through the window, fogged on the inside and rain-spattered out, I watched my stop recede into the trademark Northwest gray.

Not again.

More and more, my daydreams were nudging me out of reality. And not just the dreams, but the strange compulsion I felt to get them down on paper.

Of course, reality was relative. As both an artist and a bookstore employee, you could say I made my living from *un*reality. But the daydreams of the last few weeks—day*mares*, most of them—were something new, and they had begun to trouble me. They waited for quiet moments to ambush me—brushing my teeth, sipping my morning half-decaf, riding to work.

I got off the bus at the next stop and sank onto the covered bench, looking at the notebook I'd been clutching as I missed my stop. I opened to the newest page—the frantically scribbled lines didn't even look like my handwriting.

By the light of the triumphal fire, I can see myself reflected in my enemy's dead-dark eyes. Hair the color of summer wheat fans out in a corona around my face. Blood streams from a gash across my forehead, stinging my eyes and marring my vision.

My love lies dead beside me. The beasts have clasped our hands together in mockery of our union, yet I am grateful for this gift.

My enemy's slow grin looses a drop of saliva, and it splatters onto my cheek. His low growl of pleasure vibrates in my chest.

We are finished. Our people are finished.

"Darkness shall swallow you all," hisses my enemy, as if completing my thought.

"Shall not." Ignoring the fangs and talons inches from my face, I turn my head—my love yet lives! His beauty has been defiled by the weapons of our enemies, but his eyes smile.

My heart sings, though I know there are only moments left to us, and my tears stream freely. I feel his breath as he whispers again, "Shall not."

His fingers press my hand as our enemy's blood-slicked sword descends. In the moment before our last, I hear the call of Borabu, the horn of the Fianna.

My heart thumped heavily. I fought an urge to rip out the page and toss it into the trash bin beside the bench. How could I have written such a thing—not ten minutes ago—and have no memory of it?

I drew the tip of my finger over the final word, smearing the graphite of the soft pencil. *Fianna*. That, at least, was a clue. A proper noun that might be a real thing.

I slapped the notebook closed, but my gaze caught on the cover. I'd embellished it with drawings, refrigerator poetry tiles, and polished fragments of mirror glass. The eyes that looked back at me from those glinting slivers seemed to know something I didn't.

Get a grip, Neve.

Stowing the notebook in my shoulder bag, I rose from the bench. The rain had stopped and the walk back to my neighborhood would do me good. On the way, I could collect materials—a nice, tactile activity to reground myself in reality.

Until I reached the art supply shop my haul was pretty thin—the metal spring from a ballpoint pen, a swatch of purple rubber from a popped balloon, and a discarded Popsicle stick, stained red except for the inch that a child's fingers had held. I pinched the bare wood, imagining that I was sealing in whatever essence of the child might remain. It wasn't something I believed in so much as *felt*. And the image of a curly-headed boy that rose to mind . . . I wasn't sure whether that was fact or figment.

Inert as the other two items now were, they still possessed a kinetic quality: the purple rubber, shrapnel from a recent explosion, and the spring, the mechanism that allowed the pen to open and close. Balloons were linked to celebrations. Pens to literature and learning. It was because of these connections the items were more than trash to me, regardless of whether they'd ever make it into one of my art projects.

Sometimes I felt like an overeducated magpie.

The owner of the art supply shop had a goodie bag ready for me—scraps from the last week's painting and collage classes. But that wasn't what produced the find of the day. *That* I stepped on as I was leaving, in front of the shop window—a small plastic figure, a knight holding a sword and red shield. I dropped the toy into the pocket of my jacket and walked another block down Belmont before turning onto my street.

My apartment was on the top floor of a faded, funky, late-Victorian-era house that was quintessentially Portland. An enormous weeping willow served as guardian, dominating our yard and brushing the garage of the new construction next door. The gentle giant still groped blindly for its twin, which had been destroyed by the same fire that consumed the neighbor's original house. In the twin's place stood ornamental cherry trees, just as the home had been replaced by something sleek and energy-efficient—solar panels, rain collection, rooftop garden. Appealing in its clean lines and muted colors but lacking a soul. That wasn't something you could install.

I had nothing against modern structures, except when they tore down buildings like mine to put them up. And, given time, they would grow a soul. Living left a mark. My boss's modern Pearl District apartment, strewn with potted plants and piles of shells and stones she'd picked up on her trips to the Oregon coast, had a brightness and vitality mine could never have. Young, fresh energy, unjaded by time. No ghosts. No regrets. A lot like my boss.

I picked up my mail from the box downstairs and climbed to the third floor. Dumping my stuff by the front door, I creaked across the hardwood to the kitchen. As I opened the fridge for a can of seltzer, my gaze lingered on the artsy alchemy-themed label on the bottle of absinthe that Noah, my former roommate, had given me for my birthday a couple of months back—the same night I'd asked him to move out.

Cocktail o'clock, I decided. I eyeballed a shot measure into a wine glass, dosed it with simple syrup and a squeeze of fresh lime, and topped it off with seltzer and a couple of ice cubes.

Then I grabbed my notebook from my bag and headed out onto my tiny terrace. My beloved "porch" rocking chair had flaking powder-blue paint and was cranky in its rhythm. It reminded me of home—not this apartment, but *home* home—which I was always trying to forget. It wasn't so much that I liked paradoxes as they seemed to like me.

I sank into the rocker and took a sip of my drink, enjoying the fizzy sensation in my nose and throat. Here was the notebook again, in my lap, when I had meant to give it the cold shoulder. It seemed to have become another of the things I was unsuccessfully trying to forget.

I touched the word "fire," which I'd spelled with fridge-magnet letters and a wooden Scrabble *F.* The other words were elements too—earth, air, water. And I'd added drawings representing each. I loved making my own notebooks, and I'd decorated this one before knowing how I'd use it.

Opening the journal to the first page, I studied the charcoal sketch of my first daydream—or really more of an image that had come to me suddenly and then refused to go away until I got it down on paper. A man and woman knelt with their torsos and cheeks pressed together, like a figure against a mirror, their hands holding a bow and arrow that pointed skyward.

On the next page, using colored pencils, I'd sketched the face of a man. He had longish, wavy brown hair and a beard, and eyes a shade lighter than his hair. He was frowning. Or maybe just thinking. Next to this drawing was something I can't easily explain. A sort of menacing shape moving off the page, but actually nothing more than a grayish smudge. In that spot I had sketched and erased something so many times I'd made a hole in the paper, and then outlined the hole with a pencil. I could *see* this was what I had done, but I had no memory of doing it.

Setting my drink down, I lightly touched the hole—and

jumped. Somehow there was more threat in that absence of drawing than if it had been there.

I turned another page to find line upon line of cramped writing . . . every one the same.

The blood-slicked field was no bed for the body I had worshipped.

I shivered and touched my chest, feeling for the locket my mother had given me for my twelfth birthday—a locket I no longer wore. It had come from the gift shop where she'd worked for a while as an assistant manager, in the small town of Poteau, Oklahoma, where I'd grown up. Silver and heart-shaped, with embossed edges that I'd soon rubbed away, it enclosed a clipping of my mother's hair. She told me it would protect me from the nightmares that had begun to plague me. Until now I hadn't connected them with the daydreams, but the nightmares, too, had been violent.

The old wood of the rocking chair gave a protest like a cap gun going off as I got up. I carried the journal to my little book bindery, which was just a couple of tables set up beneath the living room windows. One table was a production space for the creations that actually helped pay the bills—the literature-themed "junk journals" I sold through Etsy. The other table was dedicated to the larger art book projects I submitted for gallery exhibitions and even occasionally sold.

My art and this space were sacred to me. Maybe they could help me understand the weird shit that was happening.

Maybe my subconscious was trying to give birth to a new project.

First, I folded eight signatures—smaller sets of pages that, when sewn together, made up the book. Half of the pages included a pocket, so I'd have a place to store any scraps and bits that were relevant to the subject of each two-page spread. I punched holes in the signature gutters and stitched them together with waxed linen cord.

My books were more about form than function, so I often left my bindings exposed. In this case I was making a dummy for an eventual book—I'd use it to plan out content and graphic placement. I loved the freedom of prototypes, made for no one but myself, and *meant* to contain flaws and rough content. I'd kept the prototypes of every art book project I'd worked on, so I never lost connection with my creations even if they were turned over to others. I was protective of them to the point of superstition—I kind of believed if anything happened to them, the end product would lose some of its impact. I was safeguarding the soul of the work.

After assembling the signatures, I dug through a box of interesting boards I'd collected over the years. Normally I'd use something plain and prefab for a dummy, maybe embellish it later, but it didn't feel right for this. I took out two thin panels of reclaimed wood that each had some remaining strips of dark red paint. I had bored holes along one edge of the boards, and applied a sealant to keep the shabby chic perfection from wearing away—I didn't let the irony bother me. There were creators who could make a living off of art that was *supposed* to break down over time, but I wasn't one of them.

Positioning the signature spines so they were recessed about an inch and a half inside the spine edge of the covers, I used card stock and glue to bind everything together. Then I stitched thicker red cord through the holes along the spine of the covers, adding beads and other objects from my bins of supplies as I worked. On impulse, I fished the knight figure out of my pocket and used fine linen thread to suspend it inside the recessed area. I carefully tucked and glued the thread behind the cord stitching so you would have to look closely to discover how it was held in place. *Magic.*

This ready receptacle made me feel safer. Like I had a chance of taking control of whatever was happening to me. I began removing pages from my notebook, using a knife to cut out drawings and blocks of text and slip them into the pockets of the dummy. On each page I jotted down ideas about the design and the materials I would need, or made a quick sketch.

Finally, realizing by the stickiness of my eyelids that I'd lost track of the time, I straightened and rubbed my low back, sore from so much hunching over. After a couple minutes of tidying my workspace, I went to bed.

But as I lay there, staring at the glowing green galaxy overhead—plastic stars that Noah and I had pressed into my ceiling one New Year's Eve after splitting a bottle of cheap champagne—a strong urge came over me. Hopping out of bed, I went to the dresser and opened the carved box where I kept the few items of jewelry I owned. My fingers shook as I took out the locket, a little tarnished thing that felt cool on my palm. The day they called about my mother's suicide—only a week after I left Poteau for Portland—I'd taken it off for good. How could a talisman from a woman afraid of her own life protect *me*? I'd been angry—I didn't want a damn locket, I wanted my mom. I'd *always* just wanted my mom, but she'd been caught up in navigating the hellscape of her own mind.

A tidal wave of guilt slapped against me and I dropped the locket back in the box.

I can't do this right now.

I lay awake for hours. Sometime before sunrise, I woke with my heart racing and skin clammy, my mind pelting me with a question.

What if it's happening to me?

Schizophrenia could run in families. My mom's doctor had assured me that my risk was only slightly higher than the average person, and I had worked hard to put it out of my mind. But these recent episodes had brought that anxiety back with a vengeance.

I sat up, pulling one of the blankets around my shoulders. Would Noah be up yet, I wondered?

Stupendously terrible idea.

My former roommate was also my former best friend. We worked together at the bookstore, and we'd shared the apartment for three years. All of it had ended on my birthday, when he'd told me he was in love with me. At the time it had felt like the ultimate betrayal, and I hadn't spoken to him since he'd moved out.

Sighing, I threw off the covers and got up to make coffee.

I slapped at the light switch in the living room for a few seconds before I recalled the bulb was out, and then I fumbled for the floor lamp. With a click, light washed over the room—

And the stranger standing in the middle of it.

Stumbling back to the bedroom, I slammed the door behind me, its antique hinges voicing the scream that I had stifled.

But the doors in my apartment had no working locks. Holding onto the old brass knob, I glanced at the nightstand, cursing to discover that my phone wasn't there. I must have left it on my work table.

My gaze shifted to the window. *Three floors—no way.*

"I'm calling the police!" I shouted.

I held my breath, waiting for a reply. My hammering heart was the only thing I could hear.

Closing my eyes, I pressed my forehead to the door, picturing the intruder—a man with dark hair who was wearing an extremely outdated suit, maybe a costume? Halloween was only a couple weeks away.

Then it dawned on me . . . *He's not really there.* It was just another of the bizarre dreams. In a minute I'd scribble it down, forget the whole thing, and finally freak out when I came to and found it.

Groaning, I turned and pressed my back against the door and slid down to the floor. My throat tightened, and my gaze fell to the inside of my right wrist, where I'd gotten a fanciful Victorian clock face tattoo during my steampunk phase in art school. It read midnight, or noon, and was making me feel a little like Alice in Wonderland right now—which was not helpful.

"Lady?"

I launched to my feet. "I called 911! The police are coming!"

Then came a rustling noise, followed by indistinct muttering, and I looked around for something to shove in front of the door. There was nothing close enough.

"Do you hear me?" I demanded, searching instead for something to hit him with. The only thing in reach was an ankle boot. I grabbed it anyway.

"I do, lady," the man replied. "I beg your pardon. I'm a stranger to your . . ." He paused a few seconds. "To your country. I have no intention of harming you, and I very much regret having frightened you."

What the hell? He sounded like a *Masterpiece Theatre* historical drama. And Irish. Definitely Irish.

"What do you want?"

"I—I'm not entirely sure." There was real confusion in his tone. "If you could be so good as to tell me *where* I am, I might be able to make a guess about why I'm here."

Was he drunk? High? "This is the Belmont district."

"The Belmont district of . . . ?"

"Of *Portland*."

"And the year?"

No, no, no. I started to wonder whether someone was messing with me, or playing an elaborate prank. But who? Noah had been angry when he left, but he'd never do something like this.

"This is *not* funny," I said.

Another pause. "Bear with me, if you will, lady."

I shook my head, but replied, "It's twenty—"

Then came a heavy thud. "Hello?" I called, straining for another sound that would give away his position. I pressed my body against the door. Had he knocked something over walking toward me? "Are you still there?"

Silence.

There was definitely something wrong with him—something I recognized. Whether the result of illness or substance abuse, he was deep in delusion. Though my mother's delusions . . . they had been stream-of-consciousness, peppered with whimsy and full-on nonsense. Despite his old-fashioned way of speaking, the man in my living room sounded rational.

Or the man that *had* been in my living room. No doors had opened or closed, and no floorboards had creaked. Was he still there, waiting to pounce? Had he passed out?

Holding my breath, I turned the knob slowly and pushed the door open a crack.

I couldn't see the spot where he'd been standing, so I pushed it open farther, wincing as the hinges made a popping sound.

Nothing. Raising my boot and taking a few steps into the living room, I glanced at the front door—it was closed. The south-facing windows were open to let in the cool evening air, but the screens had not been disturbed. I could see the small guest bathroom was empty, and checking the second bedroom, found nothing.

On my way to the kitchen, I noticed something on the floor in the middle of the living room—a piece of paper. There were often bits of paper around my apartment, but this one made the back of my neck tingle. I knelt, staring at it for a moment before picking it up.

I realized immediately that the crumpled sheet wasn't something of mine. There were several paragraphs, and they'd been written with a nib pen. I had quite a few old-fashioned writing implements, mostly used for calligraphy, so that alone was nothing unusual. But the handwriting was barely legible cursive, and the paper looked expensive—not the kind I'd use to dash off a note.

It was hard to make out in the low light, so I dropped the boot and took the paper to the kitchen, flipping on the overhead.

> *How much time has passed in this barren cave of twilight consciousness? Would I have chosen this had I known [illegible]? Had I known I would wait like no other has waited, feeling the cold, keen edge of our separation? And when I wake, she will be lost to me. Even the memory of her [illegible]. I will be lost to myself.*

Next there was a smeared section and I paused, struck by how similar in style this was to the stuff I'd been sleep-writing lately. In fact, if it hadn't been for the difference in paper and handwriting, I would have assumed it was mine. I skipped down to the next lines that I could read.

> *And yet the alternative is cruel . . . Never again to feel the warm flesh that knit so perfectly with mine. Or kiss the silken lips that breathed purpose into my body. I count this loss greater than the loss of kin or country.*

My hands shook as I set the paper on the counter.

I turned my back on it and started my morning ritual—grinding the beans, pressing the filter into the dripper, pouring boiling water over the grounds. I usually did this in a trancelike state, but this morning I was wide awake. I consciously focused on each step, giving myself some distance from the sequence of shocks.

When I finished, I dosed my cup heavily with cream and then drank the whole thing while staring at the paper.

As I set my cup in the sink, I also set aside the question of whether I was mentally ill. I was or I wasn't. Freaking out about the possibility was wreaking havoc on my capacity for problem-solving. I closed my eyes and made myself a promise that should any thought of harming myself enter my head, I would go to a hospital.

So, presuming the man in my living room was real, could he be hanging around still? He'd seemed mostly harmless, and I had questions. Starting with why the hell he had broken into my apartment, obviously. But also, had he written those things, and if so, what did they mean?

Grabbing my phone, I went to the door and padded downstairs in my T-shirt and boxers. From the building's porch, I peered up and down the street. The sky was gray with dawn, but the streetlamps were still on. The only person I saw was a neighbor on an early morning run with her dog. I found myself in a strange position—unsure whether to feel relieved about the disappearance of a home intruder. Should I call the police? Probably, but imagining the story I'd have to tell, I couldn't bring myself to do it.

As I headed back up to get ready for work, I considered calling in sick. At the same time, I felt like I needed to keep focusing on normal things. I showered, dressed, and ate breakfast. Read news headlines and scrolled my Instagram feed. Finally, I tucked the stranger's note into the project dummy I'd made, stuck it in my bag, and hurried to catch the bus.

Even for a Monday morning the store was quiet, and I walked around in a drowsy fog. The customers that did appear in the aisles were like ghosts to me . . . or maybe it was the other way around. I was startled when a woman spoke to me, asking where she could find Octavia Butler's *Kindred*. For a moment I could only stare at her.

More caffeine required.

Normally my workplace was grounding for me. Even the name, Powell's City of Books, made me feel ensconced in a fortress of stories and knowledge. Holly Golightly had said about Tiffany's: "Nothing very bad could happen to you there." That was it exactly. Noah had teased me for being obsessed with that old film. It wasn't really obsession—more that I was fascinated by Holly's lifestyle (despite the troubling symbiosis between her and most of the male characters) as well as her odd backstory. Holly and I both had a hillbilly twist in the cocktails of our past. Sometimes those old ghosts came back, called you by your true name, and busted all the dishes to make sure they had your attention.

I managed to make it until lunch and then ordered a fully caffeinated latte from the ground floor café. I was sipping my drink in the break room, leafing through my new prototype, when I noticed someone standing on the other side of the table.

My eyes followed a pair of faded jeans up to a green T-shirt and finally to a smiling face and a crown of spiky dark-red hair only partly subdued under a gray fisherman's beanie. Noah looked sheepish, like he knew I might not want to talk to him. Our last meeting had been charged with hurt feelings and resentment. We both worked here, so we'd seen each other in passing, but it was the first time we'd been face-to-face since I'd thrown him out.

"Hi," I said, hoping for neutral but sounding stiff instead.

"Could I sit for a minute?"

I blinked at the chair across from me. Was this a good idea? Without a doubt, I was relieved to see him, and I desperately hoped we'd be able to resume our friendship at some point. But was two months enough?

"Sure," I replied, because I couldn't stomach saying no.

He sank down in the chair and set his energy drink on the table. "It's good to see you. How have you been?"

"I'm good," I said too quickly. "How about you?"

He studied me and then nodded. "Okay."

He spun the soda can between his fingers. "You sure you're good? You look tired."

Sighing, I folded my arms on the table. "Yeah, I'm just not sleeping great."

God, I had missed him. As an introvert, I didn't have a lot of friends, but the ones I did have were close and trusted and necessary. Losing one was a significant life event. Especially as the result of a betrayal—which was how it had felt to me.

"Sorry to hear it," he replied. His gaze settled on my book. "Is that a new project?"

"It is," I said, closing the cover.

He sat up straighter. "I'm sorry. I didn't mean to—"

"It's fine," I said, shaking my head. "It's . . . this one is personal."

"Sure," he said. "Probably why you're not sleeping."

Noah knew me better than anyone. He knew that when I started a new project, I stayed up late and forgot to eat. "You need carbs," he'd say, dragging me out of the house and down to our favorite food truck. We'd sit at a picnic table and dip Belgian frites in blue cheese dressing. Even if it was raining.

Look what you did to us. I bit down on the flare of anger.

"Do you want to talk about it?" He was half-wincing as he asked. This wasn't "just like old times" and he knew it.

But hell yeah I wanted to talk about it.

I poked at the knight figure embedded in the book's spine.

"What's that?" he asked, eyes following the motion of my hand.

"Archetype," I murmured, feeling the rubbery tip of the tiny sword against the pad of my thumb.

Noah gave a soft grunt. He was used to my obtuse answers.

Glancing up, I said, "Something I found. It reminded me . . ." I sighed in defeat. "It reminded me of the weird dreams I've been having."

He lifted his eyebrows, which were the same mahogany color as his hair. "Different somehow from the weird dreams you always have?"

I sipped my cold coffee. "Different in that they happen when I'm awake."

"Ah."

"They're like flashbacks, except someone else's. Someone who died violently, a really long time ago."

I watched his throat work as he swallowed. "Have you talked to anyone about them?"

I smiled, but it felt off. Thin and uncomfortable. "I'm talking to you."

He sank back in his chair, playing with his drink can again. "Your head has always worked in mysterious ways, Neve. It's one of the things I—that I've always loved about you. But I can't help wondering if the new dreams somehow have to do with me moving out . . . I mean not that everything has to be about me, but just, you know, with loss."

It wasn't a horrible theory. I missed our Sunday evening walks to the pub. I missed the sound of his guitar in the apartment, especially in the morning. He used to sing to me when I was worrying about something. That Bob Marley song with the three little birds. He didn't even *like* Reggae.

And yet somehow, I never noticed he was in love with me. Maybe I hadn't *wanted* to notice.

Being an introvert wasn't the only thing that had kept me from forming very many relationships. Was it possible I felt for him what he felt for me and I had buried it because I was afraid?

Afraid to let him become like family because family disappears—my mother, who'd mentally disappeared years before her suicide, and the father who'd left shortly after I was born.

Of course, he *was* like family and he *had* disappeared. But in my gut, I knew I wasn't feeling the loss of a breakup. Just a deep, dull ache over the end of our friendship, and the knowledge that too many things might have been said for us to get it back. That pain was very real, even if it didn't mean I was in love.

I nodded. "You could be right."

And the man in my apartment? In the predawn hours, his visit had seemed to mean something. But in the clear fluorescent light of the break room, it seemed more like he was a man who'd missed his meds, or had too much fun at a Halloween party and got lost on his way home. I'd only started being careful about locking the door since Noah left. I'd *thought* I locked it, but maybe I'd forgotten.

Too much time in my own head. It all seemed so obvious now.

Noah was waiting, and I dragged myself back into the conversation. "Thanks for listening to all of this."

He smiled and shrugged. "Lots of practice, right?"

I smiled too, feeling grateful both for his help and for the fact he hadn't reopened the conversation that had dealt a death blow to our friendship.

Maybe it didn't have to be a death blow.

He stood up and slid the chair back under the table. "I've gotta get back," he said, "but if you need to talk, or you get worried about something, *text* me, okay? I won't read anything into it, I promise."

"Thanks, Noah," I said, meaning it.

By the time my shift ended, the low clouds had broken and dispersed, revealing a starched autumnal sky. The sun sank behind the downtown towers, and I soaked up the last rays of coppery light while I waited for the bus.

Early fall had always been a productive time for me. A time for sloughing off the long and languid days. Summers in Portland were practically chilly compared to where I'd grown up, but still warm enough to slow everything down. I hadn't worked on anything new in more than two months now. The quickening I felt in my body at the crispness in the air told me it was time.

On the way home, I shelved my half-hearted low-carb diet and bought a baguette and a piece of coconut cake at the French bakery on Belmont Street. When I got to my apartment, I also shelved the new book. I needed to take it easy on myself—let myself grieve over Noah—not find new ways to obsess about what was going on in my head.

I made a sandwich with ham, two kinds of cheese, avocado, and a thick smear of aioli. Then I poured a glass of wine and settled in to watch my favorite baking show. I was personally useless at baking—an art form with so many unbreakable rules was, for me, a literal recipe for disaster—but I loved to watch people who were good at it.

As I snuggled into the couch pillows, it struck me that this was the first time I'd practiced any self-care in weeks. As usual, my anxiety had taken over before I even knew what was happening. The indulgence felt so good that when I finished my wine, I burrowed deeper into the nest of pillows and closed my eyes.

I woke to the sound of breathing. Not mine, because *something was pressing so hard on my chest that I couldn't take in air.*

My eyes snapped open and I found myself staring into a ghastly crater—a large, stone-rimmed hole in the middle of my living room ceiling. The inside was lined with what looked like living *tissue*, fleshy and red.

Air gushed from the opening, plastering my hair back against the couch.

This is a dream. It'll be over soon.

Then why can't I breathe?

I writhed, desperate for air now. The gust abruptly subsided and the whole room slowly heaved, as if the house itself was inhaling—it sounded like a pack of snarling hell hounds.

The pressure on my chest released and I gasped. The air was foul. *Smoke and rot.*

The inhalation grew stronger—so strong that loose sheets of paper on my worktables flew into the hole in the ceiling. Pillows from the couch followed. I hooked an arm over the back of the couch and called out for help, but, like everything else, my shout was sucked up into the ceiling.

Most of the books above my workspace were gone. I watched the new prototype fly off the shelf and then somersault and flap around like a bird in a tornado. When its drunken flight path sent it right at my head, I foolishly let go of the couch to block the blow—and screamed as my body lifted toward the opening.

UNDER BEN BULBEN

WILL

Connacht, Ireland—1888

Sitting up, I took a deep breath and held my head in my hands in an effort to ease the vertigo.

"Mr. Yeats! Are you well?"

I met the worried gaze of my housekeeper as she bent over me—I was sprawled on the grass in my garden.

"Indeed I am, Mrs. Marsh," I replied though, in fact, I was not.

I had time traveled again. A woman's face was in my mind—a woman I had badly frightened. When she had uttered an impossible reply to my question about the year, my heart had heaved and the room had spun. Suddenly I was back in the Gap, the boundless void that made it possible to travel between worlds.

So far in the future—I could hardly take it in. Even the idea that the future was actually a *place*, like a village or county.

I stood up on shaking legs and moved to take a seat at the nearby table.

"Careful now, sir," said Mrs. Marsh, assisting me, "you've taken ill."

"Only a dizzy spell," I replied, smiling at the well-intentioned woman in hopes she would leave me alone. I needed to think more than I needed to be fussed over. "A pot of tea, Mrs. Marsh, and maybe something to eat?"

She straightened and smoothed her apron, giving a nod of approval. "Of course, sir. You haven't eaten since breakfast and I'm sure it's to blame for your . . . for your *fit*. Now just you sit tight and I'll be back with a plate of cold chicken."

The poor woman had eyed me askance on more than one occasion, and this wasn't likely to improve that situation. Yet she took good care of me when I would let her. I knew she was suspicious of bachelors in general, but in my case it had more to do with *who* I was rather than what. Not the fact I was a poet, though that was bad enough. It was my long association with "the gentlefolk" that unsettled her. The events of five years ago at the court of Finvara, the fairy king, had made it impossible to keep that aspect of my character a secret.

I was the Irishman who had led an army of trees to destroy Finvara's foe—the Elf King, ruler of the Icelandic shadow elves. Like most stories of its kind, it was an exaggeration. But everyone believed it, which had resulted in me being left in peace at my grandparents' cottage in the shadow of Ben Bulben, a high, flat-topped rock formation in County Sligo. Believing in fairy folk was one thing; consorting with them was quite another.

It was *not* general knowledge, however, that I had passed through an alchemist's portal and emerged with the ability to time travel. Though until now I had traveled only once—many centuries backward—to enlist the aid of an ancient forest in defense of Knock Ma, King Finvara's stronghold. (Yes, *centuries*. Apparently, you must give trees a shocking amount of advance notice.)

I had known that it was about to happen again, or at least suspected, having woken this morning to the telltale sound of a ticking clock inside my skull. In both instances, my time traveling had been involuntary. The first time, there was an obvious and desperate need—saving Knock Ma, and Ireland itself, from the Elf King. This time I hadn't even a guess as to why it had happened.

Mrs. Marsh reappeared now with my tea, and after she had arranged everything, she hesitated, watching me—no doubt assuring herself there would be no further fits. She was a good woman whom my grandmother had hired to keep house for my two younger sisters when they lived here, and she respected my need for quiet. Though I wasn't sure how much longer she'd remain in my service were she to witness me departing our plane of existence.

My request for the meal had been partly a ruse to give me a few minutes to compose myself, but the tea and sustenance eased my vertigo. It was time to contemplate the possibility that I had not come to the end of my adventures, as I had believed, when I refused invitations from both the queen of Ireland and the fairy king to remain at court, choosing instead to complete my schooling and retire to the countryside to write.

So why might I have been suddenly called more than a century into the future? After Knock Ma was saved, I had dared to hope I would never leave my own time again—that there would be no further need for it. I had no clear idea of *where* I had traveled on this second occasion. The woman had said "Portland," and there was an island by that name in the English channel. Yet her accent made me think she might be American—I had met Americans during my studies at the Dublin Metropolitan School of Art. There was a town called Portland on the country's northern Atlantic coast. Had I traveled, then, to America? Did the reason have something to do with the lady?

I was not entirely sure the person I met *had* been a lady, though the tone of her voice—and indeed the shape of her body—had indicated she was. She had been dressed like no lady I'd ever seen—in what appeared to be a mix of men's and women's *undergarments.*

Nothing she'd told me had helped me to understand why I had traveled there. Attempting to recall what I'd been doing just before my departure, I stood up and dug through the books and papers piled on the other side of the table. I flipped through the pages of my notebook and discovered that despite my intention to work on my memoir, I had made no progress there.

I lifted another notebook, one I had begun to fill with the contents of the vivid dreams I'd been having over the past few weeks, and discovered there was a page torn out. I scanned the ground around the table and patted my pockets. Mrs. Marsh never disturbed my things—*I* must have torn it out, maybe inadvertently when I was yanked out of time.

These dreams again. Might they be connected to my sudden time traveling?

I had seen much in my youth, born a fairy seer and having spent many childhood days playing in the countryside around a fairy gate. When barely more than a boy, I had served as crew and scribe onboard the fairy ship of the Irish pirate queen Grace O'Malley. I'd been present at the Battle of Ben Bulben—which took place on this very ground—when Faery, allied with the Irish, defeated the ancient enemies of the Tuatha De Danaan. And I'd aided the fairy king and queen in their battle to retake Knock Ma from the Icelandic shadow elves. It was fair to say my dreams had been vivid for as long as I could remember, and for very good reason.

Yet these new dreams had been different. They might occur day or night, and in them I was never myself, but a warrior of old. I was always wandering, often riding a white horse through what seemed to me to be Faery. I was always looking for someone—a woman I had loved—but never found her. I chased her like the moon chases the sun—devotedly, but without hope of success. My own body betrayed me in these dreams, burning with desire for a woman I had never known. The yearning and sense of loss was so real and so heavy, the feelings would persist for an hour or more after the vision had passed.

Twice I had woken in another room of the house. In the evenings I'd begun taking a dram of absinthe to stave off night-walking, as the Earl of Meath had done to prevent his ancestor, Diarmuid, from taking over his body while he was sleeping. But the absinthe only made the dreams more vivid.

The more I thought of it, the more I felt that the dreams and the time traveling *must* be connected.

When I had traveled the first time, Ireland had been facing an enemy invasion. Now I considered whether I had a duty to inform Ireland's queen, Isolde. Inform her of what exactly, though? That I had traveled forward in time and seen a half-naked woman? Without more information, it would be a waste of her time. Having served in her court, I knew there was little she hated more.

The only way to obtain more information, it would seem, was to wait and see if it happened again.

I tried to go back to my memoir but found I could not focus. My thoughts kept straying to the American. Even the brief glimpse I got of her before she disappeared behind the door had been enough to make me curious. In addition to being strangely—and barely—dressed, her light hair had been mussed and loose around her shoulders, and I now wondered if perhaps I'd roused her from sleep. She had clearly thought me an intruder, and for all practical purposes, I was. It occurred to me now that the commotion should have woken a husband or other family member. A woman of her age was not likely to be living alone and unprotected, whatever her station in life.

A sense of dread took hold of me—a feeling that I should not have left her. Yet what choice had there been?

At last, I abandoned all efforts at writing. Rising from the table,

I decided to walk over the battlefield below Ben Bulben. Leaving my books and papers and hopefully my disturbed thoughts behind, I crossed the apple orchard and stepped onto the plain.

For October the weather was mild, and the birds still busied themselves harvesting seeds and insects in the grasses. Gazing over the meadow, now bathed in golden late-afternoon light, it was easy to forget that Queen Isolde's army, allied with Faery, had clashed with the Fomorians here only six years ago. The bloody imagery still haunted my dreams.

I fervently hoped that my visions and my trip to the future were no harbinger of a return to conflict. Relations between Faery and Ireland were finally on a reasonably comfortable footing. With the death of the elf king, and his daughter's regent, Ulf, installed in his place, Ireland's northern enemies had become allies. Queen Isolde had designated the precocious, silver-haired daughter of Lord Meath, the queen's cousin, as her successor, securing the throne. The fairy king and his elven wife had been blessed with a mischievous and far-too-clever son with glinting blue eyes and raven-black curls. It was the great hope of the children's relations that a future union between them would strengthen the bond between their peoples—assuming they could be persuaded to cooperate. There'd been no hint of more clouds on the horizon . . . until now.

When my loop of the battlefield was complete, I started back to the cottage, brushing a hand over the silken seed heads of the tall, dry grass alongside the footpath. They were very close in color to the American woman's hair.

The sounds of tinkling bells and canine yapping drifted over from the neighbor's field, where herding dogs were marshaling their flock home for the evening.

On the heels of golden light
Rides the cool and velvet night

I had loved the time I'd spent wandering between worlds, but the soft and gentle beauty of this place made my heart ache. It was the only place that felt like home.

I opened the door to the cottage to find the lamps already lit and a warm fire waiting. The watchfulness of my housekeeper was almost palpable—despite the fact she was attentively sweeping the hearth.

I was in awe of the unobtrusive fastidiousness of the lady. Empty tea cups and glasses seemed to evaporate. My various papers and stacks of books never collected dust, nor did my desk or typewriter. Jackets left on chairs vanished and reappeared in my closet, and muddied shoes kicked off beside the door were always clean and dry the next time I went to put them on. The fire in my study was lit by the time I woke each morning in all but the warmest months. Fresh flowers from the garden brightened every room from May through October, and I'd not once seen a wilted bloom or fallen petal.

So the fact that I'd caught her at work was significant; she wanted to keep an eye on me without my noticing. The matron had a good heart and I was fond of her, so I let her think her stratagem was working.

The aroma of roasting lamb and rosemary filled the cottage, indicating my one other domestic hand was readying the evening meal. My suppers were simple, early, and generally solitary, and afterward, I spent most evenings in my study writing and nursing a glass of whiskey. I often lost track of the time and rose from my work long past the time good Christians were all abed, as my grandmother would have said.

The pleasant autumn walk had cleared my head and the excellent supper renewed my energy. Mrs. Marsh built up the fire in my study and I settled in an armchair to outline the next chapter of my memoir, which would begin my journey with Captain O'Malley on the highest point of Ben Bulben.

But it wasn't to be. The fire was warm, the chair comfortable, and after the day's excitement, the whiskey acted like a soporific. I soon lost the thread of my narrative.

The ticking sound in my head woke me. I sat up, blinking in the low light. My eyes fell on the last line I'd scribbled on my notebook.

The past will swallow her.

The ticking grew louder, and I trained my focus on the room—the fireplace, the desk, the typewriter—trying to hold onto my place in time, if only for a moment. But a shadowy veil fell over everything and I felt the floor go out from under me. My stomach dropped too, and then I was falling in starry darkness.

Pain shot through one knee as I landed on a hard floor. I closed my eyes against the spinning sensation, trying not to retch.

A violent disturbance—and horrible stench—made me open my eyes. There was a *monstrous hole* in the center of the room's ceiling, like the gaping wound of some beast. It was sucking the air out of the room. I saw the American woman—she was trying to anchor herself on the back of a sofa as loose objects around her were swept up and into the hole.

She's going to be next.

"Lady!" I shouted, but the eldritch roar of the thing drowned out all other sound. She hadn't seen or heard me.

I launched to my feet, ignoring the pain in my bruised knee. The hot, sucking wind was whipping me too, and it got much stronger as I drew nearer the opening. The moment before I reached her, she let go of the sofa to block something that had flown at her face—a book. She grabbed it as her body lifted toward the ceiling.

Lunging, I caught her around the waist—but the force of the suction pulled me up with her.

For the love of God, let us get away from here!

The wind and noise cut off suddenly—the livid tissue overhead was replaced by the relative tranquility of the Gap. I tightened my arms around her, afraid of what would happen to her if we became separated—it was possible to drift forever in the Gap.

In her panic and confusion, she fought me, and I muttered a feeble, "I'm sorry."

Our impact with the floor of my study broke us apart.

The lady rolled over and looked at me, her gray-green eyes wide with shock. She wrapped bare arms around bare legs, her whole body trembling. She was like a lost, half-wild creature—the state of her wrung my heart. But I dared not speak yet, even to comfort her, for fear of making things worse.

Her gaze moved around my study and she shook her head. "Not happening," she said, despair in her voice.

She closed her eyes tightly, and the color of her complexion faded from sun-kissed fair to verging on pale green. I scrambled for the waste bin next to my desk and slid it toward her.

I watched in sympathy as she braced her hands against the bin—knuckles white—and emptied the contents of her stomach.

Then she wiped her mouth with the back of her hand and said, "I don't think I imagined that."

"No, lady," I assured her. "You did not."

NEVE

My rescuer—or kidnapper—got up and grabbed a blanket from the back of a nearby armchair. Then he moved to a table containing an assortment of liquor bottles and sloshed some amber liquid into a glass.

He came toward me, and I scooted back. "Who *are* you? Where am I, and how *the hell* did I get here?"

He frowned, and he knelt down right where he was, a few feet away. It was a weird thing to do, but my panic receded a little when he was no longer standing over me. The guy was definitely my middle-of-the-night visitor—still costumed, still Irish. Warm brown eyes and a neatly trimmed beard could also be added to the list. Now it occurred to me that something about him felt very familiar—maybe the way it would feel to run into your grade-school crush twenty years later at the grocery store.

He placed the folded blanket and the glass on the wood floor in front of him.

"My name is Will Yeats," he said finally. "Forgive my reticence. I have no objection to telling you where you are, but I fear it will come as a shock. And as to how you got here . . ." He shook his head. "That, you are unlikely to believe."

He gave the glass of booze a push toward me.

"I don't drink whiskey," I said. I had gone to a distillery once with Noah and my boss, Rebecca, for Noah's birthday. The memory alone was enough to sour my stomach for a week.

"It's brandy," replied the man in a gentle tone.

I wasn't sure there was much difference, and I never accepted drinks from men I didn't know.

"Your name is Will Yeats?" I said. "Like the poet?" Maybe it explained why he dressed the way he did.

His eyes widened. "Is it possible that you know me, lady?"

I stared at him, unsure what he was asking me. "You've been to my apartment twice now, though I don't think that makes us friends." He looked even more confused, and then it struck me what his question had implied. "*Are* you a poet?"

"I am, in fact."

I reached for the blanket. When I shook it out and wrapped it around my shoulders, the scent of lavender wafted out. Not perfumy laundry soap lavender, but light and fresh, like when you picked it and rolled it between your fingers.

I glanced around again at what appeared to be an office, or more like a study. There were books everywhere. Embers in the fireplace popped and glowed a molten orange. Comfy reading chairs were arranged in front of the fire, and an actual *typewriter* rested on the gleaming wood desk. If you looked up "hygge" on Wikipedia, there would definitely be a photo of this room.

I pressed my nose into the blanket, pulling it tighter. "Okay, I'm ready."

His dark brows lifted.

"Tell me where I am. I would also really appreciate it if you could tell me whether you saw the giant throat-tunnel in my ceiling, because I think I might be losing it."

Will ran a hand through his hair, and the front part flopped right back down into his face. It was a disarmingly boyish gesture, though I guessed he was close to my age. The old-fashioned getup he wore suited him. It looked expensive and fit him well, not like a costume at all.

He let out a quiet sigh and stood up, taking a few steps toward the desk and gazing out the window at the darkness.

Finally, he said, "County Sligo." Then he turned to look at me.

I shook my head in incomprehension.

"In the west of Ireland," he added.

I froze, then placed a trembling hand on the floor. *What* had he said?

He watched me like I was a cat he thought might dart into the bushes.

Glancing up at the window, I could make out a line of trees and low wall in the moonlight. A steep hill loomed a short distance away. The vertigo had returned and I placed my other hand on the floor, feeling the uneven surface of the wood pressing into my palms. *Breathe.*

"I'm afraid there's more, lady."

More?

"The year is 1888."

He waited for my reaction, but I had gone numb. I nodded so he would continue, and hopefully say something my mind could make sense of.

"I have come to you twice now by traveling into the future. I did in fact see the tunnel in your ceiling. I believed that you were in danger, so I brought you back here—though in full disclosure, I'm not sure exactly *how*. As to the why of the tunnel, or of my traveling to your time in the first place . . ." He shook his head. "I can't yet say. I'm trying to understand it myself."

He folded his arms and stared at the floor. Blackness crept in at the edges of my vision.

You are NOT fainting.

No, just losing my mind. It really was the only thing that made sense—that I was ill like my mother and hallucinating all of it.

Except also it *didn't* make sense. Schizophrenic delusions could explain throat-tunnels and imaginary people for sure. But cozy rooms with lavender-scented blankets and brandy? And the voices my mother described—they'd never been soft or kind.

Will Yeats had maybe the softest, kindest voice I'd ever heard.

Still, my poor brain flailed for a rational explanation—had I somehow been *drugged* by the ridiculously good-looking and not-at-all-creepy Victorian poet guy?

I covered my face with my hands.

For now, assume it's all real. The throat-tunnel and everything else. What questions does that leave?

I looked up at him. "Have you been having strange dreams, Will?"

A DELICATE MATTER

NEVE

My question had startled him. "I *have*. How did you know?"

"I found a piece of paper after you left the first time—there was some writing on it, a story about a man who had lost someone. It reminded me of some stuff I've been writing lately. Was it yours?"

He stepped closer, but I could see he was restraining himself. Trying to keep me from seeing his eagerness. "I believe it was. Miss—" He broke off, frowning. "Could I ask your name?"

"Sure. It's Neve."

He looked puzzled, as people often did when I told them my name.

"Neve Kelly," I said, giving him another chance to catch the pronunciation. My mother had always pronounced it "NEE-av," but I'd been called "Nehv" so many times by teachers and receptionists that finally in high school I gave in.

"May I also know where you come from, Miss Kelly? I guessed America by your accent, but I've been struggling to accept the idea that my travels could have carried me so far beyond my island."

I raised an eyebrow. "But the time traveling part didn't worry you at all."

He smiled, and *heaven help me*. It was a crooked smile, with a slight lip twist and one eye half squinting. Sparkly things danced in his eyes—or maybe I imagined that part.

"I wouldn't say that," he replied.

"Well, you guessed right. I live in Portland, Oregon."

"Ah." He rubbed his lips together, thinking. "Oregon is on the Pacific coast?"

"That's right."

"And will someone there be wondering what has happened to you?"

I eyed him, confirming he still looked more concerned than sociopathic. "Eventually," I said. He didn't need to know everything.

Possibly noticing my hesitation, he only nodded and folded his hands behind his back.

It occurred to me maybe I should be worried about how harmless he seemed. How comfortable I felt talking to him. It was often a tactic of people with bad intentions, wasn't it?

If he *wasn't* a sociopathic kidnapper who'd slipped me a hallucinogen and told me a wild story for unknown nefarious purposes, he'd want to help me, right?

"Can you take me home, Will?"

He frowned. "Is that what you want?"

Yeah . . . so it was complicated. Obviously, I wanted to go home, but I did *not* want to be digested by my ceiling.

"If I did want to go back, would you take me?"

He ran a hand through his hair again. "I would try."

I couldn't help it, I believed him. The guy was freakishly believable.

I slumped and stared into the fire.

Finally I reached for the brandy glass and poked my nose into it—I could have gotten drunk off the fumes. I sipped. It was pleasant and warming, so I kept going, letting it flow over my teeth and gums, rinsing away the lingering foulness from earlier.

Clearing my throat, I said, "Throat-tunnels aside, I'm thinking my being here isn't a great idea. It could cause changes to the future, right? My family immigrated from Ireland. Maybe I'll screw that up somehow and my whole life will be different when I get back to my time. Or maybe I won't even be born."

I winced at how ridiculous I sounded even to myself. Everything I knew about the potential pitfalls of time travel had come out of the science fiction and fantasy section of the bookstore.

"Your family is from Ireland?"

I looked at him. "My mom always said they were. I don't know if any of them are still there." *Here.*

"Do you know what year your mother left?"

"It happened way before she was born. Irish ancestry in America is pretty common because of the famine."

His expression flattened. "Famine?"

Alarm bells went off. Had it not happened yet? Was I already messing around with the timeline by telling him about it? He'd said the year was 1880-something. I was pretty sure the famine came before that.

"The Irish potato famine?" I said.

WILL

I stared at her, feeling faintly ill. I knew of the famine—*An Drochshaol*, "the hard times"—from the alternate-history books in the Faery library. It had been Queen Isolde who discovered the existence of multiple timelines—of the various realities parallel to our own. In our Ireland, a great famine had been averted when Lady Meath—then Miss Ada Quicksilver—had persuaded the bog king to help her find and destroy the source of a pestilence that threatened all of Ireland's food crops. Was it possible that tragedy had only been postponed? Or, was it possible that I had not only traveled to another time and country, *but also to another reality?*

"Are you staring at me like that because you've never *heard* of the potato famine?" she asked, looking uneasy.

What could I say? If she wasn't aware of the existence of alternate timelines, I was not about to enlighten her after the shocks I'd already delivered. Though if I was right, it could mean the possibility of her altering her own future was less of a concern.

"Not at all. Forgive me, I was lost in thought. Your concern about altering the future is a valid one, but I'm reluctant to attempt returning you to your own time when you seemed to be in peril there."

She tightened the blanket around her shoulders. "Yeah, I did."

I went for the bottle of brandy and held it up to her. She shook her head, and I poured some in another glass, swallowing it before continuing. "Could we talk for a moment about the dreams you mentioned? I don't mean to change the subject, but if I could better understand our connection, maybe we'd have a starting point for unraveling this mystery."

She nodded. "They're daydreams, mostly. It feels like they come out of nowhere, and when I snap out of it, I've forgotten where I was and what I was doing. Not only that, I always end up writing—"

She paused, eyes sweeping over the floor around her. Her gaze came to rest on an object I hadn't paid attention to since our arrival—the book I'd seen her grab. It was peeking out from under the edge of the blanket. She pulled it into her lap.

"You've written your dreams down in that?" I guessed.

"I made it to collect my notes and drawings. I hoped it might help me figure out what's been happening to me. I think I almost died because of the damn thing."

"Might I look at it?" She glanced up, and I saw the wariness return. "Or . . ." I gestured toward my desk. "I've written my dreams down as well, and I'm happy to share them with you. I'm curious as to whether they're similar."

One of her eyebrows lifted. "They're similar. But okay."

I went to the desk for my notebook. Then I crouched down, opening it on the floor in front of her, slowly flipping the pages.

"Wait," she said suddenly. "Go back a few pages, to the drawing."

I flipped back until I came to a rough sketch I'd made of a man and a woman. The pair stood close, holding a single bow with a knocked arrow. It was a mental image that had visited me several times in recent weeks.

She studied the drawing only a moment before opening her own book. When she found the page she was looking for, she took a piece of paper out of a pocket and showed it to me—my breath stopped. With the exception of hers being more skillfully executed, the sketches were identical.

Frowning like she'd remembered something, she set the paper down and turned another page, retrieving a second sheet. Her eyes moved over it, and then she held it out to me—a portrait of a man.

"Who is this?" I asked.

"It's *you*, isn't it?"

Glancing back at the portrait, I felt a chill. It was so unexpected that I hadn't seen it at first. "When was the sketch made?"

"*Before* you came to my apartment the first time."

I sank back on my heels, letting out a breath. "Clearly we *are* connected in some way."

I caught her look of dismay.

I thought about all I had done and seen—there was very little that surprised me anymore. But *this* . . . I knew nothing about the life of the woman in my study. We came from far-flung generations—and likely, *realities*. With our vastly different perspectives, was it even possible for us to relate to each other, let alone examine this mystery together?

I heard the distant chiming of the kitchen clock—five in the morning. It forced my mind to practicalities . . . I imagined the look on Mrs. Marsh's face were she to enter my study right now.

"Miss Kelly, I should tell you that I'm a bachelor living alone. I have two household servants—a cook and a housekeeper—who live nearby. They arrive quite early, I'm not even sure at what hour. Your presence here . . ." It was a delicate matter and I wasn't sure how to continue. "Your presence here will be difficult to explain. If we agree that it's not safe for you to return to Portland, we must make a decision about what *is* to be done."

She looked puzzled, or possibly annoyed. It was I, after all, who had brought her here. As I studied her face, I noticed she had a rounded nose and a very slight chin cleft. *What a helpful observation.*

"I've offended you," I said.

"No, it's not that. I just . . ." She hesitated. "Does it matter?"

Now I was puzzled.

"I mean considering what's happening to us," she continued, "what people will think about an unexpected visitor doesn't seem like a big thing to me."

"Ah." She was obviously an independent young woman, and perhaps society had changed much in the years that stretched between us. "I don't disagree with you, it's only that . . ." I gnawed my lip. "It's only that we are very rural here and it is certain to create a scandal, which I don't mind for myself—I'm already eyed askance by my neighbors—but . . ."

I was not equal to it. I had been in battle, traveled through time, and persuaded a tree to slay an elf king, but I could not bring myself to speak more explicitly to a virtual stranger about the impropriety of her presence in my home.

Her eyes suddenly brightened. "You're worried about *me*. You're trying to be a gentleman."

"I am," I replied, the tightness in my chest easing. "Rather gracelessly."

She laughed. "Okay, that's adorable."

My face grew hot, and I cleared my throat. Even in the lamplight, I could see her own color rising. I didn't care that it was *me* she was laughing at—I wanted to hear the sound again.

"So what do we do?" she asked.

I walked to the fireplace, considering our options. After stoking the coals, I tossed on more turf bricks. I was chilled myself, and fatigued. So much so that I almost failed to notice the ticking in my head had gone soft again, fading to the background of my thoughts.

Thank heaven for that, at least.

"The cottage has two bedrooms," I said. "Let us both retire, and we can decide on a course of action in the clear light of day."

I turned, and she said, "What about your housekeeper?"

"I'll think of something."

She nodded and then attempted to rise. She wobbled, and I moved to steady her.

"Thanks," she murmured, grasping the arm I'd offered. "The room spins every time I move. I feel like I had one too many at the pub."

I swallowed a chuckle that was sure to sound insensitive. Clearly, some experiences were universal. "It's the traveling. It happens to me too."

What I didn't know was whether she would adjust or continue

to experience the vertigo for as long as she was here. She had already been out of her own time for longer than I ever had.

I led her to the spare bedroom, and I couldn't help noticing the way she smelled—it was a sweet, nutty aroma that was also slightly floral. The scent was familiar, and I bent a little closer.

Coconut. I'd tasted the milk once at Queen Isolde's court.

When we reached the bedroom, she sank onto the mattress while I turned down the bedclothes and set about raising a fire in the cold hearth.

"I'm afraid I have no women's things here," I said, keeping my gaze on the turf bricks I'd arranged in the fireplace. "I hope you will be comfortable."

"It's fine," she replied. "This is what I sleep in at home."

She had an odd, short way of speaking that could easily be interpreted as rudeness. But I didn't sense that it was intentional. She was American, after all.

I was surprised to hear the bed creaking behind me, followed by the rustling of the bedcover. No woman from my time would be comfortable retiring while there was a man in her bedchamber. *Unless that man was her husband.* The thought of it caused a warm tugging sensation low in my belly.

I supposed that my guest was unmarried, since she had said she wouldn't immediately be missed. I was glad no one in Portland was frantic with worry. It struck me that I was also glad there was no husband.

I blew on the flames that flickered in the kindling, and then I turned to inform her that I intended to retire for an hour or so. Her head rested on the pillow and her eyes were closed. Light from the oil lamp I'd carried in gleamed on her bare shoulder. The rise and fall of her breathing was soft.

I watched for a moment, feeling an unaccountable tightness in my chest.

Winter stalks thee, summer flower,
Yet bide a while in autumn's bower

Finally I gave myself a shake and quietly left the room.

I couldn't sleep. I kept revisiting the events of the last hour in my mind, and not only because of the strange circumstances. I was looking forward to further conversation with Miss Kelly. I empathized with her situation and worried for her safety.

Come on, man. The truth was that she was intriguing and lovely. It piqued me that I was forced to put her out of my mind so I could grapple with how to manage my domestic situation.

She was right that it hardly seemed important. Yet I didn't like the idea of my neighbors judging her. Too, some of my mother's people were still in the area, and she had endured enough gossip on my account already.

I will simply have to lie. Simply? I was a horrible liar.

But I was a fair enough storyteller.

I heard the click of a door opening, followed by quiet, feminine murmurs. I had run out of time. The women had come in the side entrance, which led into the kitchen, and I hurried to meet them there.

"Good morning, ladies."

They both started, clearly surprised to find me here, and blurted in unison, "Good morning, sir."

"I wanted to inform you that we have a guest." Had the lightness of my tone sounded forced?

Mrs. Marsh's brows lifted. "So early!"

"An American woman, Miss Kelly," I continued. "A cousin of mine, in fact. She has wound up here by mistake, I'm afraid."

"Oh?" said Mrs. Marsh, exchanging a puzzled glance with Mrs. Tobin.

"She was to visit Lolly and Lily, you see, but somehow it was not communicated to her that my sisters had relocated to Dublin."

"Heavens!" replied Mrs. Marsh, looking alarmed. "The poor thing."

"Indeed," I replied, nodding gravely. "And that's not the worst of it. Her trunk was mislaid in the journey and she has arrived here with nothing but a few borrowed things. I was hoping that you ladies might be able to help me procure clothing and other necessaries for her."

Again the women eyed each other, clucking. "Well, it's a disgrace, isn't it?" said Mrs. Tobin.

"To be sure, it is," agreed Mrs. Marsh, smoothing her apron. "Shall I go and speak to her, Mr. Yeats?"

"Oh, I'd advise against it just now," I replied, rather too quickly. "The crossing was rough and she was very ill aboard ship—has been ill here too, I'm afraid. She will want to lie in, I'm sure of it."

Mrs. Marsh shook her head. "It's a great deal of ill luck for one lady, isn't it? No matter, Mr. Marsh can drive me to Sligo, he's going anyway. How shall I know about fit and such, Mr. Yeats?"

"Ah. I believe she's close to Lily's size—perhaps you might visit her dressmaker? One moment, Mrs. Marsh."

I had some ready cash in my study and went to retrieve it. I fervently hoped that the errand and the excitement would stave off questions that I would find difficult to answer. The story was thin.

When I returned to the kitchen, Mrs. Marsh said, "Tobin will stay here and make breakfast for you both. I'm afraid it's likely to be after midday before I can get back, Mr. Yeats."

"I understand, Mrs. Marsh, and I'm so sorry for the bother."

I had hoped she and Mrs. Tobin would go together so I might make Miss Kelly aware of the titanic falsehood I had been forced to employ, but I imagined my guest would sleep for some time yet.

"Will Miss Kelly go to town right away?" asked Mrs. Tobin.

"To Dublin?" *Quickly now, Will.* "I think not. At least not until she's recovered a little from her journey. When she wakes, I'll ride to Sligo myself and send a telegram to Lolly. We'll decide what's to be done."

I felt the weight of Mrs. Marsh's gaze on me as Mrs. Tobin replied, "Very good, sir."

My cook was a placid and trusting soul, but Mrs. Marsh was sharp as a tack and had no doubt smelled something off in my story. Nevertheless, she wrapped her scarf about her neck and stepped back out into the chilly October morning.

Leaving Mrs. Tobin to her work, I went to my desk and composed a note for my guest that I hoped would keep us out of trouble.

MORNING LIGHT

NEVE

I woke disoriented, and confused about the light—or more like the lack of it. My third-floor bedroom faced east, and at some point almost every morning I ended up stuffing my head under a pillow. I often got up promising myself that this would be the day I took down the sheer curtains and replaced them with something light-blocking.

But I had not woken up in *my* bedroom. Instead of looking out the window onto the neighbor's swing set, I had a view of a steep, flat-topped hill. Closer to the cottage there was a small orchard, the trees gnarled and squat. Yellow and orange leaves decorated the spindly gray branches and littered the ground. A few fallen apples gleamed red in the sunlight. Half a dozen fat sheep were grazing between the orchard and the hill.

This is Ireland. It wasn't hard to believe. It looked like every idyllic photo I'd ever seen of the place.

I sat up slowly in case the vertigo returned. While I did feel hungover, it was an improvement from the night before. I had some stiffness and a few bruises, probably from dropping onto a hardwood floor while tangled up with another person.

A hot Victorian poet person.

The guy was, by twenty-first century (and probably any other) standards, easy on the eyes. And ears, because *that accent*, obviously. But was he *the* W. B. Yeats? It must be a common enough name—though I'd never known or heard of another person called Yeats.

My eyes drifted from the window to the fireplace, where the embers had died. I wondered what time it was. I wondered whether I was late for work yet, but then remembered I had the next two days off. No one would notice I was missing right away. I wondered how long it would take someone to figure it out. Maybe I'd be home in time to make my next shift.

Then I remembered my disappearance was in the future so technically it hadn't actually happened yet, and I started to feel dizzy again.

A floorboard creaked on the other side of the door—I held my breath. Was it Will, or one of his servants? As I listened, I noticed a piece of paper lying on the floor in front of the door.

Slowly I got out of bed, trying not to make noise. The floorboards creaked anyway. One of the hazards of an old house.

The paper was folded, with "Miss Kelly" written on the outside in elegant cursive. I opened and read it once quickly—it had been typed, thankfully—and a second time more carefully. So he'd come up with a story. It wasn't half bad, but I worried about my ability to carry it off. Maybe the fact I was American would help explain my strangeness.

Will had suggested in the note that I pretend to sleep until his housekeeper got back from town with clothes for me. She was expected "after midday." Assessing the angle of the light outside the window, I thought it was possible that no pretending would be necessary. My stomach lodged a loud complaint.

Then I heard a woman's voice somewhere in the house. Two women, actually, chatting energetically—in a language I didn't recognize—while attempting to keep their voices low.

Will's voice came then, not far from the door. I hurried back to the bed, stuffed the note under the pillow—*housekeeper!*—then under the mattress, and jumped back under the covers. Didn't Victorians sleep fully dressed? Would they think I was a prostitute or something? Did *Will* think I was a prostitute? Anxiety made a fist in my gut.

Footsteps approached, and I gripped the quilt so hard my fingers cramped. There was a soft knock.

"Yes?" I called in what I hoped would pass for a just-woke-up voice.

"It's Mrs. Marsh, Mr. Yeats's housekeeper." The voice was friendly and carried a note of concern. She spoke English but her accent was thick. "I've some things for you, Miss Kelly. May I come in?"

"Sure." I winced and added, "All right." I wished I'd spent less time on genre fiction and more on old English novels.

The door opened slowly, and a middle-aged woman with an armload of boxes entered the room. She was smiling, and there were bright pink splotches on her cheeks, like she'd come in from outdoors. Her salt-and-pepper hair was coiled on the back of her head. She looked like a kindly nanny and I instantly loved her.

"Good afternoon, my dear," she said, setting the boxes on top of the chest at the foot of the bed. "One moment . . ."

She stepped back out and then reappeared carrying a basin with a pitcher inside. These she set on top of a dresser next to the door, and I began to worry that this meant indoor plumbing wasn't a thing here.

Mrs. Marsh clasped her hands together, against her spotless apron. "Are you well, Miss Kelly?"

"Yes, thank you," I replied, keeping my death grip on the quilt.

"Do you have an appetite? Lunch is almost ready, and I can set a placc for you. Or we can bring a tray to your room if you prefer it."

"Um—maybe I'll eat in here?" I replied. "I don't want to be any trouble."

Mrs. Marsh brightened, and I knew I had said the wrong thing if I wanted to be left alone. "Oh, it's no trouble, Miss Kelly, none at all. Now then . . ." her gaze shifted to the boxes. "I have purchased a day dress and nightdress for you. Mr. Yeats suggested you might be close to his youngest sister's size, so I bought the gown from her seamstress. It is a sample, and the only one she had that she thought might do. If small alterations are required, I can make them for you. I assume you have at least one pair of shoes, but you'll want something sturdy for the country."

Her gaze moved around the room, and I hoped she wasn't about to ask where my shoes were. Thankfully she continued: "I've found a pair of mud boots left behind by one of Mr. Yeats's sisters, and as long as you don't have a particularly long foot, they should do for the time being. I've cleaned them and left them by the front door." Her eyes settled on me again, and before I could thank her she added, "There are also soap, teeth powder, and other items you might require, but if there's anything wanting you must tell me."

How kind she was. *Motherly*, I thought.

Don't be daft, this is her job.

"Thank you so much, Mrs. Marsh," I said. "I'm sorry about all this."

She raised her eyebrows. "And why should you be sorry?" Her tone was suddenly annoyed. "It is I who am sorry for all you've been through."

Though she'd been lied to about what exactly I'd "been through," the sentiment still applied, and I kind of choked up.

"Shall I stay to help you dress?" she asked.

"It's all right. I think I can manage." This was a stretch, but I could not get out of the bed until she was gone.

She too looked skeptical. "Should you change your mind, just call me."

She closed the door, and I got up and started opening boxes. I thought the dress might have cost more than my rent. There was a bunch of stuff that looked like it was supposed to go underneath, including a corset. I tossed everything onto the bed with a sigh of defeat.

If I'd still been holding onto a subconscious worry that my being here was an elaborate delusion, it had fallen away now. There was no way I could have hallucinated such detail.

I went to the dresser and poured some water into the basin. Then I took off my T-shirt and boxers and used a cloth next to the bowl to give myself a sponge bath. I found a wooden tooth brush—*hallelujah*—as well as a brown paper packet of powder that smelled faintly herbal. Hoping it was "teeth powder," I wet the bristles in the pitcher and dipped it in the powder. When I finished brushing, I looked around for somewhere to spit. Did it go in the basin? I went to the window, pushed the casement open, and spit into a rose bush, scaring off some small birds.

There was a hairbrush as well, and I worked through the tangles at the nape of my neck until there was nothing left to do but face the task of dressing.

The "day dress" was fancier than anything I'd ever worn. It was made of a soft, sage-colored fabric embroidered with pink flowers, and had a creamy lace overskirt.

There was a pair of lightweight shorts that weren't much different from my boxers, and I pulled those on first. Drawstring tie, no problem. There was also a petticoat—I decided that went next. So far so good. That left the corset, and a belt with wire half hoops on one side that looked like some kind of kinky sex device. *More likely a bustle.* I put the latter on with the wire frame at the back.

Finally I picked up the corset, and it flapped awkwardly open. Thin strips of something hard had been sewn into the front to keep the thing stiff.

This is not clothing, it's armor.

Panels of a stretchy fabric had been sewn under the arms—there was hope. Sucking in a breath, I pulled it around my ribs and fastened the front hooks. I wouldn't call it comfortable, but I could still breathe. That probably meant it was too big, but I wasn't about to tell Mrs. Marsh. I tugged at the front until it felt like it was in the right place, and then I turned to the full-length mirror next to the dresser. My boobs were small, my butt was not—you'd never guess either of these facts from this costume, which made the most of the former and completely hid the latter.

Next, I spread out the dress and unfastened the two million fabric-covered buttons that ran down the back. Then I picked it up and let it pool on the floor. I stepped carefully into the opening and began pulling it up over my legs, but it wouldn't go over the bustle frame. Maybe I should have put the bustle on afterward? Or maybe the dress needed to go over my head? With all those yards of fabric involved, I didn't think I could do either by myself.

I laid the dress back down. Picking up my T-shirt and boxers, I tossed them under the bed.

What I did next—well I had read enough romance novels to know better. I went to the door, listening a second before pushing it halfway open and calling, "Mrs. Marsh?"

"Oh!" Will was just passing the door. He froze, and his eyes dropped for a fraction of a second to my propped-up boobs. Then he turned and walked the other way, murmuring, "I beg your pardon, Miss Kelly. I'll fetch her for you."

Despite the fact I was far more covered by the clothing I wore now than the clothing I'd worn last night, heat flashed over my face and chest. I wasn't sure whether I was embarrassed for him or for me, but I ducked back inside and pulled the door almost closed, watching the pink fade from my new cleavage.

There came another soft knock, and I stepped back and opened the door again.

"Well you're nearly there, dear," said Mrs. Marsh encouragingly. "I *thought* you might need another set of hands."

She came in, and together we hoisted the dress. She dropped it down over my head and shoulders and buttoned me in. It fit well enough, though a little roomy in the bodice. She offered to take it home with her that evening and take in the side seams. Then she made me sit at the vanity while she pinned up my hair.

"I've never worked as a lady's maid," she said, "but I used to do for Lolly and Lily. Nothing fancy, mind you, but I don't think they were ever ashamed."

"Thanks so much," I said, smiling at her in the mirror. Her brow creased as she returned my smile, and I guessed that I wasn't doing a great job of adjusting my speech to the time period.

I watched the deft workings of her fingers until finally she stood up and laid her hands on my shoulders. "There now, fresh as a daisy. Come and join Mr. Yeats. It's a fine autumn day and he thought you might enjoy lunch in the garden."

I followed her, catching a glimpse of myself again in the long mirror on the way out. The clothes were not comfortable, but I had to admit I felt elegant and pretty. I never wore my hair up in anything except a messy ponytail—I had always been self-conscious about my long neck and sharp cheekbones. In these clothes, I almost felt statuesque.

By this time the state of my bladder had become pretty desperate. I'd been trying to figure out what the appropriate word might be, and some inoffensive way to ask, but I didn't have time for that anymore.

"Mrs. Marsh, could you show me the way to the . . . um . . . ?"

She turned, eyebrows raised in expectation.

Ugh.

"Ah yes," she said, suddenly translating my expression of misery. "It's just outside, dear."

We stopped by the front door of the cottage so I could put on Lolly's mud boots, and then she pointed me to the outhouse, or rather "the privy." It was less unpleasant than I expected, but I would have gotten excited about a portable toilet at an outdoor concert at that point. Luckily, the lady boxers were split between the legs.

Afterward, Mrs. Marsh led me through a murder-in-an-English-village-worthy garden to the orchard behind the cottage. Will was sitting at a table there, writing. When he noticed us approaching, he set his notebook aside and stood up.

"Miss Kelly," he said, smiling and pulling a chair out for me, "you look very well."

I got a warm, frothy feeling in my chest—I was childishly glad to see him.

"Thank you." I sank into the chair and automatically reached to the sides to pull it closer to the table—then stopped as Will began scooting it in for me.

He went back to his seat, and Mrs. Marsh returned to the cottage.

There were a few moments of *very* awkward silence until, finally, we both spoke at the same time:

"It's so beautiful here," and, "You found my note?"

We both answered "yes," and then we were laughing.

"You first," I said.

He lifted a bottle from the table and offered to fill my glass.

"Brandy?" I asked. *Breakfast of champions.* Then I recalled it wasn't breakfast time for anyone but me.

"Sherry. Would you prefer—"

"No—no thanks." Again I laughed. "Everything here is more complicated than I'm used to."

He gave me another one of those adorable, half-squinting smiles that made me feel like he was laughing at me—in the best way possible.

"Speaking of which," I continued, "The 'Miss Kelly' thing—is that required here?"

"Is it considered impolite?"

"Not exactly . . . where I come from it's very formal. No one has called me that since this old professor I had in college." I shrugged. "I think mainly it feels odd for someone my own age to call me 'Miss.'"

There was a playful glint in his brown eyes. "Am I your own age?"

My heart did a fluttery thing and my cleavage was hot again. Innocent as he seemed, it was a distinctly flirty question.

"Okay, obviously I don't know." My butt squirmed in the chair. "That'd be my guess."

He nodded, the smile still on his lips. "To answer your question, since I've convinced the ladies you're a member of my family, I think I could use your Christian name without alarming anyone."

"That's great."

"Neve, then? We have a name in Ireland that is very similar—*Nee-av.*"

My eyes popped open. "That's how my mother pronounced my name."

"Well, it's an important name in Ireland, and maybe why your mother chose it. *Nee-av* was an immortal in—"

He broke off suddenly and went blank, as if something had interrupted his thought. When he focused again, there was something new in his expression. An increased . . . intensity?

"Here we are." Mrs. Marsh appeared with a food tray and I jumped. Apparently, the world had closed in so tightly around the two of us that I forgot anyone else was in it. She set a plate containing a small roasted bird and potatoes in front of each of us. "Now what else do we need?"

"Wow," I said, my mouth watering, "this smells amazing."

She gave me another of the puzzled smiles that warned me I was talking weird, and Will said, "Thank you, Mrs. Marsh. I believe we have everything we need."

She dipped her head and left us.

"So *Nee-av* was an immortal?" I prompted, picking up my fork.

"That's right," he said, curling his fingers around the base of his water glass. Something had dampened his mood—his smile was a ghost of its former self. *And no squinty right eye.*

"Do you know the story of *Awsheen*?" he asked.

I shook my head and forked loose a bite of mystery bird.

"He was a poet and member of the Fianna, the warrior band of the Tuatha De Danaan."

Fianna. That word rang a bell. I knew a little about the Tuatha De Danaan from mythology class. I'd enjoyed studying ancient gods—they were like people, tangible and fallible.

"They were mythological beings like fairies, right?"

He frowned. "Yes and no. It's true that they were an ancient people of Ireland, like the fairies. Most of them faded away to Faery or the Land of Promise long ago."

He talked about them like they were real, but then he *was* a poet. "*Nee-av* was one of them too?"

"She was Faery royalty. The two met and fell in love. They married and lived a life of adventure. The details of the tale after they wed depend on which account you read. They spent their lives on the run from her father, or they traveled for many years through Faery. I'm writing a poem about an account that ends with them fighting and dying in the Tuatha De Danaan's final war with their ancient foes, the Fomorians."

Parts of this story were sounding familiar, and I realized that the name I had heard as "Awsheen" must be *Oisin.* His lover's name was *Niamh,* and I had never connected it with my own. They were probably Gaelic spellings.

"When you said they were only *sort of* mythological beings, did you mean their stories are based on real people and events?"

He hesitated a beat and said, "That's accurate."

Then he became interested in his lunch, and it was obvious he'd thought of something he didn't want to share.

I focused on my meal too, and soon noticed I was feeling much better. The headache I'd had since arriving in his time was now barely noticeable. I took advantage of the lull in conversation to appreciate the ridiculously storybook setting. The cottage was charming, with its whitewashed stone walls, thatched roof, and brightly painted door and window frames. Out beyond the orchard were waves of grass, moving in the breeze like a golden sea. Beyond *that* was the big hill, which looked like a ship sailing across the plain toward the distant whitecaps. If he'd grown up here, it was no wonder he was a poet.

"I've brought your book." *He speaks at last.* He reached into the empty chair opposite me and set my book on the table. "You left it in my study. Would you be willing to continue our discussion from last night?"

"Sure."

He pushed his dishes off to one side and touched the book's cover. "Do you mind if I look?"

I nodded, though I still felt uneasy. It wasn't that I didn't trust him—considering I'd known him less than a day, I probably trusted him more than I should. But the things I'd written in that book felt personal. Which was silly, because none of it had anything to do with me.

"The last dream I wrote down had the most detail," I said.

He flipped through to the last of the used pages and took the folded sheet out of its pocket. It was the dream from the bus.

By the light of the triumphal fire, I can see myself reflected in my enemy's dead-dark eyes. Hair the color of summer wheat fans out in a corona around my face. Blood streams from a gash across my forehead, stinging my eyes and marring my vision.

My love lies dead beside me. The beasts have clasped our hands together in mockery of our union, yet I am grateful for this gift.

I watched his face as he read. His eyes moved slowly over each line. Occasionally he touched a word he couldn't make out. He'd lift his gaze and ask me in the gentle-strong voice that did funny things to my insides. I'd answer, and his attention would go back to the page.

When he finished, he looked up. His eyes shone with something I'd almost call *awe*.

"Do you think they're the same man and woman?" he asked.

"The same as . . . ?"

He flipped backward through the book. "These." He held it up, showing my sketch of the couple with the bow and arrow. "Them."

"Huh. I'd assumed the imagery was symbolic rather than literal, but yeah, it would make sense."

He cleared his throat and glanced again at the drawing.

"What is it?"

The gears behind his eyes continued to spin.

"Will," I said, the edge in my tone bringing his eyes to my face. "We're helping each other, right? Sharing information to figure this out? We're not going to get very far if you keep stuff from me."

"Right." He blinked a few times. "I don't know. It's beautiful. It's terrible. It . . ." He gave a self-conscious laugh. "It breaks my heart."

I felt moisture under my eyelids. I realized I had been burying my feelings about all of this. The tragedy and heaviness of the story, whatever it was, along with the mystery of why it was telling itself to *me*—it had all been too much to think about. I hadn't allowed myself to feel what he was feeling, and now it ambushed me.

"Yeah," I said feebly, looking down at my empty plate, trying to swallow this grief that didn't really belong to me.

"But it's more than that," he continued, his voice gaining strength. "I begin to understand it."

That got my attention. "You do?"

"I think we may be *part of* these dream events."

BEHIND THE VEIL

NEVE

"What? How?"

He replaced the paper and closed the book. "You're right that I owe it to you not to hold back," he said. "I confess I've been trying to avoid delivering too much of a shock all at once. Yet it's very difficult to explain myself without giving you what I believe will be shocking information."

My stomach soured, and I gripped the edge of the table. "If you think you've figured something out, I need to hear it."

He sat a little longer thinking—planning his words, I guessed—and looking generally miserable. I began to shiver, but not from the crisp air.

"In my world," he began, "mythical beings are real. I've surmised from some of the things you've said that it's not the case in yours."

"Do you mean in your *time?*" He must. I knew that plenty of people in earlier times believed in things like fairies and dragons.

I watched the muscles of his throat move as he swallowed. "I mean beings that are mythical in *your* version of reality are living, breathing beings in mine."

"*Version of reality?*" My heart raced. What the hell did *that* mean? "Are you telling me this is like Wonderland?" Would he even get that reference?

"I can understand why it would seem like that, but it's not the same as what happens when you pass through a door to Faery. I'm talking about a world similar to yours, but with a different sequence of events."

I stared. "It sounds like you're talking about parallel worlds."

His features softened with relief, while I tried to control my rising panic. "Precisely. You know this already, then."

It was so *not* what I wanted him to say. I knew that parallel worlds weren't just science fiction—that they were theoretically possible. They were no less likely than the throat-tunnel in my ceiling. Or the fact time traveling was real. And yet . . . It was *one more thing* making me feel untethered from reality. *He tried to warn you.*

"Will, are you saying that not only did I time travel, I traveled between worlds?"

He sobered. "I can't be sure, but I do believe that to be true."

The stiff spine I'd maintained since putting on the dress came unglued, and I slumped uncomfortably against the back of my chair. I sat for what felt like a *long* time studying a grease spot on the tablecloth next to my plate. It was a thing of mine. When faced with a crisis, my mind would fixate on some small problem. After I got the call about my mom, I suddenly couldn't stop looking at a new chip in the coffee mug I was holding. I'd felt incredible guilt about it later.

Will was watching me, probably wondering whether ladies in my *version of reality* fainted.

"Okay," I said, trying to regain my equilibrium.

I supposed there was some comfort in the fact I couldn't mess up my own timeline in Will's reality. I was more like Doctor Who than Claire Fraser.

"When you say 'mythical beings,'" I continued, "do you mean like the story you told me—Oisin and Niamh? Or do you mean like unicorns?"

"Both, actually."

I caught myself glancing around the garden, as if a unicorn might jump out of a rosebush.

"I've never seen a unicorn," he clarified. "I *have* been in a battle between the Tuatha De Danaan and the Fomorians—on the plain beyond the orchard—and one between the Irish fairy court and the Icelandic shadow elves."

"So fairies and elves are real."

"Very much so."

"Okay," I repeated. Apparently, it was all I had. "What does all of this have to do with my book and our dreams and the throat-tunnel?"

He tapped his fingertips on the cover of my book. I watched the movement—his fingers were slender and tapered, with a tracing of dark hair between the joints.

"In this reality," he said, "mythic heroes have at times traveled from the past to inhabit the bodies of their mortal descendants. I have seen it firsthand. My friends Lord and Lady Meath each shared their minds with an ancestor for a short time—the Fianna warrior Diarmuid, and Cliona, the lady he loved and crossed centuries to find."

I began to see where he was headed with this. "But you said I'm not from your world," I pointed out.

"That's true, and I can't yet explain that. But in other ways it makes sense." He drank from his water glass. "What first made me think of this was your Irish ancestry, and your name. The fact that we're having the same dreams, and that I happen to be writing an epic poem about Oisin, who was also a poet. I know their story well. We dream of war and death and loss. They lived it. Our dreams may be their memories."

Oisin and Niamh.

There was something else too. When earlier he'd been reading the write-up of my last dream, I was reminded that I'd included the word "Fianna." It wasn't a word that I would have consciously used or even really recognized before my conversations with Will.

God help me. I'm in way over my head.

"What ended up happening to your lord and lady friends?" I asked quietly.

He let out a breath, and he rested his head in his hands. "They too were drawn into a bloody conflict."

WILL

Among other things. I thought about Diarmuid and Cliona, who had been lovers in ancient times, and again in modern day as Lord Meath and Miss Ada Quicksilver. If my theory was correct, did it mean that the woman sitting across from me was fated to become . . .

Our eyes met, and the ground beneath my chair seemed to shift. I had a fleeting vision—a woman dressed in gold and green, walking away from me into the mist of a lush forest, her wheat-colored hair swinging at her waist. At the last moment she turned, and I saw the same gray-green eyes.

"Do you think that's what's going to happen to us?"

The blood rushed into my face and my breath stopped—then I realized that, of course, my companion was referring to what I'd actually said aloud: *They too were drawn into a bloody conflict.*

"It's a possibility we should consider."

Was it all happening again? I thought back on the people I had known who had connected with their mythic ancestors. Lord Meath and his wife. Ireland's Queen Isolde with the ancient Queen Maeve. The queen's cousin, Duncan O'Malley, with King Finvara of Faery.

There was something they all had in common. "Have you been hearing voices in your head?" I asked her.

The color drained from her face, and I was afraid the vertigo had returned. Before I could ask, she replied, "I—*no*." There was a tremor in her voice. "Have you?"

I shook my head.

"Then what made you ask?"

"It's how it began with the others—the immortals spoke in their thoughts. It might mean I'm mistaken about this."

The truth was, evidence notwithstanding, I could hardly get my head around the possibility that I might be descended from Oisin. I *had* been interested in him for most of my life, and I recalled that Queen Koli, the wife of King Finvara, had once suggested a vague connection between myself and the ancient warrior poet.

Oisin sounds much like yourself.

To which I had answered, *I am no warrior, lady*. Only now I was. Or had been, in a way, in the Battle of Knock Ma—with my army of trees.

Noting my guest's silence, I glanced at her and saw she was still very pale. "Are you well? I know all of this is—"

"A *lot*." She lifted her napkin from her lap and dropped it on the table. "Could we—I mean, do you think it would create any drama with your household staff if we went for a walk? I'm feeling sort of ungrounded."

I imagined that was an understatement. I stood up. "Certainly." I couldn't help smiling as the meaning of her odd phrasing sank in. "I think my household staff secretly enjoys a little drama."

She laughed. "If *Masterpiece Theatre* is any authority, I'd say you can count on it."

My confusion must have been visible, because she replied, "Sorry. Anachronism."

I offered her my arm, which seemed to take her by surprise. "Is it considered improper?" I asked.

"More like unnecessary. But that doesn't mean it isn't sweet."

"Another anachronism," I suggested.

"Exactly," she said, laughing again. Her cheeks had recovered their color.

Before we could get underway, Mrs. Marsh joined us.

"Miss Kelly," she said, breathless from her brisk approach, "I've brought you a wrap and pair of gloves. You've been unwell, and you can't be too careful."

Neve offered Mrs. Marsh an earnest smile that momentarily altered the rhythm of my heart. *And* made me fail to take proper notice of the fact Mrs. Marsh was watching us closely enough that she'd anticipated our walk.

"I hope you won't tire her, Mr. Yeats," she admonished. Mrs. Marsh met my gaze only briefly, but in that moment I saw that the jig was up. She had seen through my deception, at least to some degree. She hadn't confronted me, though that didn't mean she *wouldn't*.

"We'll be gone only as long as Miss Kelly likes," I assured her.

This time she took the offered arm, gloved fingers pressing lightly inside my elbow.

We followed the gravel path into the apple orchard, where the brilliantly hued fallen leaves made way with a swishing sound. The fruit on the ground had begun to turn, releasing a sweet, yeasty aroma and reminding me of the cider that Mrs. Tobin made every autumn.

My companion was quiet, and I thought about the vision

from a moment ago. It reminded me of the dreams I'd been having—I was always searching for a woman. Until now I'd never actually seen her face. Yet I couldn't help wondering if my mind had merely filled in Neve's likeness because of our conversation.

At the back of the orchard, we passed through a stile and stepped onto the path that led through the tall grass. The breeze that reached us here had traveled from the Atlantic—salty, clean, and sharp. *A banshee's kiss.* But the afternoon sunlight softened its edge.

"You were serious about the fairies?" asked Neve.

"I was," I replied.

"Are there any here?"

My gaze drifted to the face of Ben Bulben, and I pointed to the westernmost edge. "There's a fairy door on that rock formation. When I was a child, I would climb up and watch it for hours. And I would see them occasionally. The fairies had been exiled to their own world for many centuries, but they would slip through in some places. The seal between worlds was broken just six years ago."

"You climbed *that* when you were a kid?"

I smiled at her expression of alarm, and I pointed to the inland approach, to the east. "From there it's a safe enough ascent."

"Does the seal being broken mean you see them all the time now?"

"It would stand to reason, but no. They stay close to the fairy king's court, or to Dublin Castle and the court of Queen Isolde. Some choose never to leave Faery." I shrugged. "But Faery overlaps our world and absinthe can be used to see behind the veil. Though there are people who will never see a fairy, not even one standing right in front of them, and no one really knows why. There's a pastor not far from here who asserts that the fairies are a form of madness inflicted by the devil on the weak-minded."

She was studying me with a puzzled frown, and I laughed. "I wish I had a less complicated answer for you, but nothing about fairies is simple."

"You seem to know a lot about them."

"I was born a fairy seer. I've watched them all my life."

Her eyes moved over the tall grass, and out beyond, toward Ben Bulben. "You mentioned this was a battlefield?"

"It was. I can give you a tour if you like."

A path had been worn between the monuments, and the ground was dry for this time of year, so we had no trouble making our way. Most of the fallen had not been buried here—they had been honored in the old way. A memorial stone dedicated to their service was all that was left of them, their ashes having been scattered to the four winds. Some creatures viewed a body left in the ground as an opportunity for mischief, and the queen had been unwilling to take the risk.

I led Neve to the memorial stone first, and then to the other points of interest—the ground where Lord Meath, who was also Diarmuid at that time, was saved by his lady; the hill where the queen had directed her army; the small crater where Diarmuid's sword, Great Fury, had fallen and struck the earth. As we walked, I outlined for her the causes of the conflict, and the key figures.

"Where I came from, there wasn't ever an Irish queen," she said as we continued toward the small graveyard at the foot of Ben Bulben, where the bog men had been buried. "Unless maybe in ancient times. In the late nineteenth century the country was ruled by Queen Victoria of England. Do you have one of those here?"

I smiled again at her odd phrasing. "Indeed, England's queen is Victoria. There is a library in Faery where you can read other versions of Irish history. Some list no modern kings or queens because our country was overtaken by Northmen, Fomorians, the French, or the English."

We'd stopped on a patch of coarse vegetation. The breeze had stiffened, whipping loose strands of hair against the high lines of her cheekbones. Her cheeks were pink from the exercise and exposure. I noticed Mrs. Marsh had coincidentally purchased a dress nearly the same shade as her eyes—the green of the sea washing over the strand.

If she was lovely before, she was luminous in this natural setting.

She could easily be a princess of Faery.

Though we had stopped, she still held my arm, and I found myself hoping she wouldn't notice and let go.

She looked away then, and I realized I'd been staring at her.

"You look cold," I said, attempting to cover my awkwardness. "If we don't return soon, I'll have to answer to Mrs. Marsh."

Neve shivered visibly, but she hesitated, studying the handful of small headstones in the graveyard. "Whose are these?"

Her hand was cold enough that I could feel it through the glove, and I covered it with my own without thinking. Her eyes followed the motion—she didn't pull away. Her fingers tightened on my arm, and I felt a tug deep in my chest.

"Bog men," I said. "Ancient warriors who were naturally preserved inside the wet turf for a millennium or more, until they were raised to fight for Ireland."

"How did they—" Her eyes were still fixed on the graves, and suddenly they went wide. "What is *that*?"

Following her gaze, I glimpsed a disturbance on top of one of the small mounds—likely a bird or rat. Then I saw something poke up through the soil, and the hair on the back of my neck lifted. Instinctively I drew her closer.

"Will?" she said in a voice low with fear.

"Let us go," I said. Yet I stood watching as the soil crumbled away from the stick-like protrusion—*a leg bone*. There was some enchantment at work here.

"Start back to the cottage," I said. "I'll follow shortly."

NEVE

"Like *hell*."

I shuddered and gripped Will's arm as the leather-and-bone things finished digging themselves out of their *graves* and began creepy-crawling—thankfully—in the opposite direction from *us*. A steep, rocky slope jutted over the cemetery. The creatures headed right for it, managing to latch on with what limbs and digits they had left, sometimes spiking the jagged ends of broken bones directly into the soil. They moved like giant bats climbing on the roof of a cave. As they pulled themselves higher, they were well camouflaged against the hillside, but they dislodged pebbles and small plants, making it easier for our eyes to follow them. I dragged Will a few steps back so they wouldn't land on us if they fell.

"Where are they going?" I asked.

He pointed. "To the fairy door, I think."

"I don't see . . ." Did he mean the white spot near the top of the rock face? "Are *they* fairies?"

"They're men, or they were. Bog men's souls are trapped in their preserved bodies, but if they leave the bog they disintegrate and die. The Morrigan enchanted them so they could fight at Ben Bulben."

What. I stared at him. "Did you say the *Morrigan*? Like the Celtic goddess of war?"

"That's right," he said, like I'd asked him if it was true that it rained a lot in Ireland. "After the battle, the bog king asked that the remains of his fallen warriors be laid to rest in the earth."

I tucked away the factoid he had so casually dropped—that there was a literal goddess of war—because right now, I just couldn't. "So these are dead," I said.

He nodded.

"They're not acting dead."

"No."

We watched the creatures as they reached the white spot—where, one by one, they vanished.

A gust of wind blasted against us, and he said, "Let's go back."

"No argument from me."

We found the path again, and ducking our heads against the wind, we were soon out of the shadow created by the jutting rock face. The air warmed, the wind slackened to a breeze, and I began to breathe easier.

"I take it that even with all the stuff you've told me, this isn't something you see every day."

"It isn't."

"And you're worried about it? I mean for reasons other than the obvious."

I had to shuffle my feet in the clunky boots, and at that moment I kicked a big rock and tripped. My other foot instinctively shot out to stop the fall, but it hung up in the heavy layers of dress fabric.

Will caught my arm and helped to right me. Then he reached for my hand and placed it on his arm again. I could get used to this.

Neve. Just no.

"We're almost there," he said.

I side-eyed him. "You're not gonna answer my question."

"Sorry, I've been thinking. You're right, I *am* worried." He helped me through the stile and into the orchard again before meeting my gaze. "Mostly I'm worried about you."

My heart spasmed. "Me! Why?"

"Because of the dreams, because of the threat in your home, because I don't understand what's happening, or why." He shook his head. "In my experience, disturbances like what we've been witnessing—they have preceded . . ."

"Bloody conflict. Yeah, you said."

He stared at me, thoughts flitting like ghosts behind his brown eyes. Finally he said, "There's no point in us racing to meet it. We have time to sort it out." He glanced back at Ben Bulben. "Though maybe not much."

RUSTIC COMFORT

WILL

By the time we reached the cottage, clouds had sidled in and stolen the warmth of the sun. Mrs. Marsh met us inside. She bade my guest sit in the chair by the front door and helped to remove her boots. Then she settled her by the fire with a promise of returning shortly with tea.

I joined Neve by the fire, grateful we were both indoors again, and when Mrs. Marsh arrived with the tray, we drank our tea. I sat thinking over our situation and realized the story I had concocted might have solved the problem at hand, but it had created a whole host of others. Mrs. Marsh would expect me to send a telegram to my sisters, as I had said that I would. We could not openly discuss any of the things that were happening while the servants remained, unless we closed ourselves in my study, which would raise even more questions. And my young, unmarried "cousin" most definitely could not pass another night here alone with me.

I was still trying to work out a solution when Mrs. Marsh came for the tea things.

"Mr. Yeats," she said before going back to the kitchen, "if you have a moment, I was wondering whether you might go out and answer a question for Mr. Evans."

Mr. Evans was my gardener. I didn't think it was his normal work day, but I didn't know the household routine as well as my staff.

I glanced at Neve, who raised her eyebrows and offered a minuscule shrug.

"Of course," I replied, rising to follow Mrs. Marsh through the kitchen.

When I reached the garden, I searched in vain for Mr. Evans. Instead, Mrs. Marsh reappeared.

"I beg your pardon for the deception, sir," she began, "but I was hoping I might have a word with you in private."

Here it comes. "What can I do for you, Mrs. Marsh?"

She wrung her hands, and I felt a pang for my part in her discomfort.

"Mr. Yeats, I know it's not my place to question, but Miss Kelly . . ."

"Miss Kelly . . . ?" Though I knew where this was going, I needed to know how much she'd guessed.

"Well, sir . . . she's no relation of yours, is she?" Despite her discomfort, she still managed to fix a shrewdly appraising eye on me.

I shook my head. "No. She is not."

"Forgive me, sir, but is she—have you . . ."

She trailed off. Asking the true nature of my relationship with my guest was too much for the poor woman.

"I assure you, Mrs. Marsh, there is nothing improper between the lady and myself. What has brought her here—well, I'm afraid that explanation is rather complicated, and of a nature that—"

To my surprise, she raised a hand and waved me silent like she might an unruly child.

"I felt that I must ask—as an employee in your household—you understand. But I am well aware of your previous . . ." She glanced about, like she might find the word she was looking for in the shrubbery, and settled on ". . . adventures. You were always a fey child. I know that you were favored by the good folk and born with the sight."

She unfolded and refolded her hands. I wanted to do or say something to let us both out of this difficulty, but it would have to play out.

"What I mean to say is that I believe you must have a good reason for passing off this guest as your relation. I do not ask you who she is, or what she may be doing here. I simply wish to know whether she will be staying on, and if so would propose that I might stay here with her until such a time as she might return to . . . to wherever she's come from . . . and that you might take a room in the village."

Relief flooded through me. I had never valued my housekeeper's good sense and down-to-earth nature more than in this moment.

"That is an excellent suggestion, Mrs. Marsh, and I thank you for proposing it. I assure you this has taken me quite by surprise, or I would never impose on you in this way."

She nodded brusquely. "I flatter myself I have the measure of your character, Mr. Yeats, and I believe you would do all you could to avoid harming the young lady. But there's no reason to carry on with a charade staged only for the benefit of myself and Mrs. Tobin—though I think we best let it lie as it is with her. She'll not question you too closely."

"I dare say you're right."

"Very well, then." She smoothed her apron. "I'll fetch some

things from home, and I can inquire about a room at Drumcliff House while I'm out. If there's anything you need before I return, Mrs. Tobin will see to it."

"I will, and thank you again, Mrs. Marsh."

I watched her as far as the lane, and I murmured an earnest prayer of gratitude to my grandmother for finding Rosemary Marsh.

NEVE

When Will left with Mrs. Marsh, I got up to take a closer look at the room and its furnishings. It was decorated much like his library, with cozy furniture and rugs. An unusual amount of artwork lined the lumpy whitewashed walls, like at a gallery exhibition. I noticed the signature on an ocean landscape: Lily Yeats. The artist was one of Will's sisters.

When I moved to a painting of Ben Bulben, I saw my book lying on an end table. Mrs. Marsh must have picked it up when she cleared the lunch dishes. I grabbed it and returned to my chair—and tried to wait patiently for Will to come back. Even ensconced in rustic comfort, I still managed to feel anxious. Partly because of bog people and all of Will's outlandish reveals, partly because of feeling out of place and not wanting to be a problem for Will, and *a lot* because I was stuck sitting on the edge of a chair thanks to the metal contraption hanging over my backside.

First chance I got, I was taking the damn thing off. If the skirt dragged the ground in the back, so be it.

Will returned then, and I stood up. "Is everything okay?"

He nodded. "Mrs. Marsh is in on our secret. We can breathe a little easier."

Easy for you to say, you're not wearing a corset.

"You told her the truth?"

"She guessed that you aren't my cousin, and she proposed that I take a room at an inn for the duration of your visit. I think that's wise."

He was *leaving*? "Oh."

He took a step closer. "I'm not abandoning you. It's less than a mile south of here, and I'll only be away in the evenings. There's a small servant's room off the kitchen—Mrs. Marsh will stay here with you."

"I get it. Nosy neighbors."

He smiled, and I allowed myself two seconds to appreciate the contrast of soft lips and rough beard.

"We have a while yet before supper," he said. "Shall we make the most of it?"

I could think of about a million ways I'd like to make the most of it with Will.

"Sure," I said, trying to sound casual.

I picked up my book and we went to his study, settling into the high-backed chairs in front of the hearth. Fires seemed to crackle away day and night here.

"You must be eager to go home," he said, angling his chair toward mine.

It wasn't really the opener I'd expected, and with him watching me so intently I got flustered.

"I am and I'm not," I said finally.

He rested his elbows on his knees and leaned in.

Heaven help me. Death by brown eyes—it wasn't the worst thing that could happen.

"At home, I was starting to kind of fall apart."

He looked at the book in my lap. "You mean because of the dreams?"

I debated with myself about how much to tell him. "Yes" would have probably been the right way to answer. So of course I said, "My mother had a mental disorder called schizophrenia. I'm not sure if doctors know about it in your time."

His brow furrowed. "I'm not familiar with the term, though I am familiar with mental illnesses generally."

"Well, it's a disorder that can be inherited, and I've always worried it might happen to me too."

"What are the symptoms of her condition?"

I closed my eyes and took a deep breath. "She heard voices in her head, and saw things that weren't real. She said a lot of things that were scary, or made no sense at all."

"Voices," he said, like something registered. "Yesterday, when I asked if you had been hearing voices . . ."

"Right. I panicked a little. But I think you meant something different. With schizophrenia, the voices are . . ." *Horrible.* "They're usually angry, or scared. It's a constant stream of abusive or paranoid nonsense. At least that's what her doctor told me. And from the stuff she would say, I could imagine."

It had been agony seeing her like that. There was *nothing* worse.

"What do you mean by 'paranoid'?" Will asked gently.

"Oh." I thought for a second. "She felt like people were secretly trying to hurt her, or were laughing at her. To the person with the disorder it's very real. In my time, there are medications that can help, though it can be hard to get the person to agree or remember to take them."

"You said your mother *had* the disorder. Did the medication cure her?"

My throat tightened. "There's no cure. When she would take the medication, it helped. When I went away for college, they put her in the hospital and they forced her to take it. So she got better, and they let her out. Then she stopped taking it again, and she—she didn't make it."

He frowned, confused. “It’s a fatal disorder?”

“It can be. She killed herself.”

His face fell. “Neve, I’m so sorry. Please forgive me for reopening that wound.”

I shook my head. “I’m the one who brought it up.”

I remembered how Noah used to look at me when I talked about what happened to my mom—like I might break. He’d go to the kitchen for bowls of ice cream or suggest we binge-watch *The Lord of the Rings*, which he hated.

But Will just let me be. We watched the fire. Listened to the pop and crackle, which had a soothing rhythm to it. It was nice. Until my anxiety joined the party. Had I scared him? The weird stranger, spontaneously opening up with her darkest secrets.

“Your dreams,” he said finally, “they made you think you might have your mother’s illness?”

“Exactly.”

“You implied that you feel safer from that here. Why is that?”

“I think it’s because of you.” His cheeks went slightly pink and I added, “Because it’s happening to you too. It means, most likely, there must be some other explanation.”

“I agree,” he said with a nod.

He didn’t need to know the whole truth. Which was that for some reason *he* made me feel safer.

He leaned toward the fireplace and picked up a poker, using it to make space for another brick of whatever fuel was stacked in the bin on the hearth. He tossed one in, and a shower of orange sparks flew up the chimney.

“I understand your ambivalent feelings about going home,” he said. “And I’m glad our shared experience has given you some relief. Shall we continue our discussion about that?”

Opening my book in my lap, I said, “Yep, let’s do it.” I checked the table between our two chairs for a pen before it occurred to me I wasn't going to find one casually lying around. Pens in this time probably involved ink pots, fuss, and mess.

"Do you have something I could write with?" I asked.

He went to his desk, then returned with a pencil that looked like a modern one, minus the eraser.

"Thanks." I flipped to the first blank spread. "I wanted to do a quick sketch of the throat-tunnel while it's fresh in my memory."

Actually "want" had nothing to do with it. Documenting this stuff had become nothing short of compulsion, and the fact I hadn't done it yet had started to eat at me.

"Of course," he said, standing with his back to the fire. "There's something I've been thinking about since our walk. Maybe I could talk to you about it while you work?"

You can read me the dictionary if you want.

"Go ahead." I outlined the tunnel across the spread, utilizing the gutter in the middle for the hole.

"It's the bog men. Because it was the Morrigan's enchantment that allowed them to leave the bog in the first place, I can't help wondering if she had something do with what happened today."

"You mean . . . maybe she brought them back to life?"

"I do."

The idea of a living goddess in his world—it was somehow more alarming than all the other "imaginary" things that existed. I couldn't really see the harm in fairies, and to be honest I think that subconsciously I'd never completely ruled them out. Though I did get the sense my idea of fairies didn't quite mesh with Will's reality. But I had studied the Morrigan in mythology. While I could appreciate her on an intellectual level—agent of change, cycle of birth and death and all that—I'd never want to meet her.

"I can tell you're not thrilled by the idea she's involved," I said.

"If she *has* done it, she has her reasons. In my experience, we mortals don't always like her reasons." He turned and leaned his arms against the mantle, staring into the fire. He'd folded up his sleeves, and I found myself studying the bones of his wrists, and the smooth dark hairs over his forearms. "She sees the larger patterns of things," he continued. "Most of *us* . . . we're no more than ants on her path."

Well, this was comforting. "What would she want with a handful of broken bog men?"

"Nothing that I can imagine. What worries me is that it might have something to do with the two of us."

A chill ran through me. I dropped the pencil in the book's gutter. "Why would it?"

"If there's one thing I've *stopped* believing in, it's coincidences."

We had that in common. Only I'd never really believed in them. I was about to say something to that effect when my vision went fuzzy and I felt like I was floating out of the chair.

The fool is sleeping in the grass. Fingers threaded together, hands resting at the center of his chest, peaceful expression—he looks like he's dead. Like his people composed his body this way and left him.

A wolf will eat him. It will serve them right.

I step into the clearing. He's one of the Tuatha De Danaan. A warrior, by his armor.

Fianna.

I too am Danaan, on my father's side—we are the children of the goddess. But I know by the runes on his breastplate that this warrior is descended from those who left Faery to conquer Ireland, dividing our people in two. Something has called me to this place where the border between our worlds is thin. Not a voice, not a vision, but a tugging at my being. I was powerless against it, but I wasn't fool enough to come unprepared.

I step closer, tightening my grip on my weapon—a shieldmaiden's sword, made by dwarves in the north for my mother, who was descended from the light elves.

The man has dark hair and a bearded jaw. His lips are full and round, and I find myself wondering about their texture. And about the color of his eyes.

I begin to suspect there's some enchantment at work—that I'm being drawn into a trap. Suddenly his eyes snap open.

The sword that I didn't glimpse lying by his side in the grass is now pointed at my chest. Having been quick to raise my own sword, its tip has jabbed his cheek and drawn a single drop of bright-red blood.

A slow, untroubled, and even mischievous smile spreads over his face, releasing a thousand butterflies in my belly.

"It seems a pity, does it not, my lady?"

His voice brought me back. "Neve?"

Where am I?

"It's all right," he said gently. He'd crouched in front of my chair, hands on the arms. "You're here with me."

Our eyes met and he smiled. *You're here with me.* He was trying to ground me in reality, but a whole different kind of ungrounding was happening.

Easy, Neve. I took a deep breath and said, "It happened again."

"I suspected. You seemed to drift away for a few minutes. Then you started writing. Can you tell me about it?"

Writing? I looked down at the book in my lap. As usual, I'd written the dream down before snapping out of it. The difference was that this time I actually *remembered* the dream.

I handed him the book and watched the creases form across his forehead while he read. When he glanced up, I said, "He looked like you. *Just* like you."

He hesitated a beat and said, "I had a vision when we were out in the garden. It was fleeting, and I thought my mind might be making connections that weren't there, but I saw you too—walking away from me into the mist."

Yeah, so this is happening.

WILL

The pattern felt so familiar. Ancient heroes speaking to us from the grave. The Morrigan interfering in the world of mortals. What were our ancestors trying to tell us, if in fact they *were* our ancestors? I had read everything I could find on Oisin in the Faery library, stories of all the great events of his life, a good number of them written *by him*. They mostly told of battles he'd fought alongside his father, Finn, chief of the Fianna, and how he'd met Niamh and journeyed across Faery with her. The poem I was writing about his life would conclude with the final ancient battle between the Fianna and the Fomorians, the Battle of Connacht. The one that he and Niamh returned from Faery to fight. The one where they met their deaths.

Six years ago the Fomorians had returned to Ireland, only to be defeated decisively at Ben Bulben. Could they be planning another attack?

Neve had gone back to her book. She seemed to be reading her dream description—or maybe only staring at the page. I could see her fingers trembling.

I'd be lying to myself if I said that I regretted her being here, but I did regret her involvement in this. I felt somehow responsible, and I felt an obligation—rather, a compulsion—to protect her if I could.

She hasn't asked for your protection.

Sighing, she closed the book and set it on the table. Then she looked at me. "What now?"

I glanced at the window, out to the garden and orchard—the

light was low. "I think we'll have to go to Dublin. If the Morrigan is plotting, the queen will want to know."

"We're going to see the *queen*?"

"I imagine it's more than you bargained for. The journey there and back will take several days, and I don't feel comfortable leaving you here alone."

"That makes two of us," she replied.

Someone tapped lightly on the open door. "Mr. Yeats?" Mrs. Tobin stood in the hallway. "Supper's ready, sir."

Over supper we agreed that the two of us would set out for Dublin the following day. As Mrs. Marsh had suggested, I'd spend this evening at the guest house in Drumcliff. After our meal I packed a bag, and I stood shuffling through the papers and books on my desk, trying to decide which to take with me. No one liked riding out after a hot meal and glass of brandy into the cold night, but my stalling had more to do with my guest. I was uneasy about leaving her. It felt like the wrong thing to be doing, though I couldn't see what choice we had.

Finally, I stuffed a few notebooks into my bag and left my study.

"I'm going, Miss Kelly," I called through the door to the second bedroom.

The door opened and she appeared, one eyebrow raised high. "I thought we were done with the 'Miss Kelly' business."

I smiled. "So we were."

Her expression grew more serious and she said, "I want to thank you, Will."

"What for?"

She had a hand on the doorknob, and it made quiet squeaking noises as she twisted it slightly back and forth. "For everything. This is all hard, and strange. I've invaded your home, and now you have to spend the night at a hotel. You're . . ." She met my gaze. "You're a really great guy."

The vulnerability and openness in her expression stirred more protective impulses. "That's kind of you. Recall, however, that I'm the one who brought you here."

She smiled. "Sorry, but that actually proves my point." She let go of the knob and folded her arms. "I hope the inn's not too terrible."

"Not at all. It's clean and comfortable. I hope you will rest easy here with Mrs. Marsh."

"I adore Mrs. Marsh. We'll be fine."

"I'm glad."

"Will . . ." She glanced toward the kitchen. Then she took a quick step toward me, put her arms around my neck, and briefly pulled me close.

My heart galloped away into the night.

Her cheeks were flushed when she stepped back into the doorway. "Have a good night."

"And you," I managed, still recovering. "I'll see you very soon."

HUMAN CHILD

NEVE

From the look on Will's face, I was pretty sure hugs hadn't been invented here yet.

I can't believe I did that.

But he hadn't run screaming, and for a second I had felt his hand at my back.

Sighing, I went to his study for my book. I intended to take it back to my room, but I lingered. I loved the big leather chairs, and the smell of . . . I wasn't sure what. It was a blend of smells—old books, typewriter ink, the pungent earthiness of whatever was burning in the fireplace, and a nutty, sweet top note that I suspected had to do with old whiskey stains on the rugs.

It smells like Will.

Since when do I know what Will smells like?

Since I tackled him in the hallway.

I stood near the fire, thinking over the day's events. So much new information, yet still no real answers. I had managed to erect a flimsy barrier between me and the knowledge of just how badly my life had been upended. Each time I went there, I drew back like I'd touched a hot pan. It was the real reason I'd come to this room, I realized—I felt closest to Will here, and he was the one tether to reality I didn't feel like might snap at any moment.

Was I *falling* for him?

Mrs. Marsh came in then, asking if I wanted help undressing before she went to bed. I almost said no, then realized I could end up sleeping in the dress I was wearing.

We returned to my room, and while she was helping me with the buttons I asked, "Do you know what time it is, Mrs. Marsh?"

"I can check for you in a moment, dear."

When the dress was off, she reached into a pocket of her apron and pulled out a watch. "I'm afraid Mr. Yeats won't allow a clock in any part of the house except the kitchen. The ticking aggravates his condition." She peered at the little clock face. "Half past nine."

"Condition?"

I realized too late it probably wasn't polite to ask, but she replied, "He often has headaches."

I couldn't help wondering whether it had something to do with his time traveling.

"Why don't you take this," she said, holding out the watch.

"Oh no," I protested, "it's okay."

"I insist. With one in the kitchen, I don't really need it. You can give it back to me when you no longer have need of it."

She was still holding it out. I had a thing for clocks, and this one—from a kind woman I was growing fonder of by the second—took on a significance that was probably all in my head.

Fairies are real. Why not talismans? I thought of the locket my mother had given me.

"Thank you, Mrs. Marsh." I could see she was pleased as I took it from her.

She left me then, and I managed the nightdress on my own. It was a crisp white garment as voluminous as a sheet—I looked like the ghost of Christmas past.

Then I returned to the study and my book. Mrs. Marsh had built up the fire once more before retiring, and I curled up like a cat in one of the leather chairs to flesh out the sketch I'd started earlier. Pretty quickly, though, I discovered that with Will gone the memory of the throat-tunnel was a little bit too *real.* Closing the book, I noticed a piece of the binding cord had come loose, and on a whim, I grasped it and ran it through the metal loop at the top of the watch. I knotted the bottom end to another section of cord, securing the watch below the knight figure in the book's spine. Hopefully, now I wouldn't lose it.

Then I got up and stretched, strolling around the room, feeling the plushness of the rug through my thin stockings. I peered at sepia-toned photos of people that I assumed were Will's family—certainly the two sisters at least, as they were posed beside easels and wielding paintbrushes. I ran my fingertips over the cold, hard keys of the typewriter. The "a" was almost rubbed away—I pressed its key hard enough to raise the typebar but not to strike the sheet of paper in the platen. Then I noticed there were words on the sheet.

Come away, O human child!
To the waters and the wild
With a faery, hand in hand,
For the world's more full of weeping than you can
understand.

I was no Yeats scholar, but I recognized this poem. A sudden wave of dizziness caused me to stumble—I caught hold of the corner of the desk.

I squeezed my eyes shut, clenching my jaw until the room stopped moving. Then I walked slowly to the drink caddy where Will kept his booze. I examined labels until I found something familiar, and then I poured half an inch into a glass and went back to my chair.

Taking a mouthful of the faintly green liquid, I let it slide down my throat.

All. Of. This. Is. Real.

I continued to sip, breathed in and out, and willed my heartbeat to slow the hell down.

Nothing changed in the last five minutes.

And yet somehow everything had.

I finished the absinthe and set the glass on the table—only I did it without looking and must have left it hanging off the edge, because it dropped. In my clumsy scramble to save it, I knocked my book down too. The glass shattered on the hearth, and the book splayed open to the throat-tunnel.

Groaning, I knelt and picked up the glass, cursing as one of the fragments sliced my thumb. A droplet of blood welled and fell onto the open book. I stuck my thumb in my mouth to stop the bleeding. Then a gust of hot air whooshed against my face—hot, *fetid* air.

Heart racing, I glanced around—looking for what, I don't exactly know. Had the gust of air come out of the book? Out of the *drawing?* I reached out a finger to touch the page—then yelped as the book flew up and plastered itself against the ceiling.

I jumped up, watching in horror as my drawing of the throat-tunnel *stretched and contorted.* The pencil outlines filled in with real color—gray stone, living tissue in shades of red and pink. The rest of the book—cover, binding, pages—absorbed into the ceiling.

I dashed for the door—but had made it only a few steps when

the tunnel started *sucking*. The powerful upward draft whipped my nightdress like the sail of a ship and my feet left the ground.

I screamed and folded my arms over my head as I was yanked toward the hole.

"Mrs. Marsh!"

No one can save me this time.

Inside the fleshy cave it was hot, damp, and foul, like a monster was swallowing me—I had no reason to think that wasn't exactly what was happening. The low, red-tinged light was fading fast. Before it went out, I got a glimpse of the tunnel walls *contracting*, the raw, moist tissue *grazing my skin*. I screamed again.

I covered my face with my hands, expecting any moment to splash into a pool of hot stomach acid. I thought about Will and Noah and my mother. A vision flashed in my mind—the warrior from my earlier dream raised his sword in one hand, that same arrogant glint in his eyes, and he reached for my hand.

The tunnel vanished. Starlight brightened the darkness. No longer hurtling toward an unknown destination, I floated. Flailing my arms and legs, I tried to connect with something solid in the void.

It was only a respite—a heartbeat later I was back in the tunnel. Falling this time, the wind pushing instead of pulling. This journey was brief. I tumbled down onto a hard surface.

The gusting breath continued to tear at my clothes and hair, and I curled myself into a ball. My body shook and tears streamed down my cheeks.

I thought the wind might be subsiding, and when I couldn't feel it anymore I opened my eyes. All had gone quiet.

Where am I?

The floor was stone, and the room was cold and dimly lit. I took a ragged breath and sat up, both old and new bruises protesting.

I was circled by green light disks embedded in the floor. A few sheets of clean typewriter paper and small desk items were strewn around me—stuff from Will's study. I felt something bulky under one shin—my book. I was shifting it aside when I heard a metallic creaking noise and froze.

Something flickered in the deep shadows beyond the light circle.

"Who's there?" I called.

Then came an awful scraping sound—metal on rock. My eyes were adjusting and I could barely make out a figure rising.

"Well, well." The voice made me flinch. There was a hissing sound. "And how, may I ask, did you do *that*?"

All I could tell was he was *big*. His voice was a breathy, crackling bass that would have scared Darth Vader.

"Where am I?" I asked, my own voice shaky. "Who are *you*?"

There was a pause and another hiss. "You answer my question, I'll answer yours."

I kept moving my head around trying to see him better, but the light was watery and weird. The floor disks reminded me of the circles of glass you looked through at aquariums.

"I came here through a tunnel in the ceiling. I don't know why." I kept still, so my book would stay hidden under me. I was ready to light the thing on fire, but my gut said to give away as little as I could until I figured out who he was.

"And where did you come from?"

"America," I said. *By way of Ireland.*

The creature's exhale was an odd shudder. "Please be more specific."

"I live in Portland. On the Pacific coast. That's three questions now, so *who are you*?"

I heard more scraping noises and movement—then a heavy clamping, like you might hear in a factory that stamped out metal parts. *He's coming this way.*

My heart pounded and my fists clenched, fingernails digging into my palms.

The light disks around me brightened.

My first glimpse of the monster stopped my breath. He was like a man only in that he stood upright and had the correct number of limbs. He wore a kind of helmet that looked like it was made out of riveted metal. Yet unlike a helmet, it was flat on top, and asymmetrical, covering one ear while the other protruded from a hole. There were eyeholes too, though one eye was obscured by some kind of eyepiece. The thing took another step, and its one visible, milky eye fixed on me. The hissing sound came again, and I realized *he* was making it—just by breathing. He took another step, and I saw that much of the flesh on the lower half of his face was held together with thin pieces of wire, like stitches through vellum. I saw similarly sewn-together skin on one of his arms—but the skin on either side of the stitches was not the same color, like the lower part had come from *someone else.*

My throat and tongue refused to form words. He saved me the trouble.

"My name is Far Dorocha, and I serve the Morrigan. We expected you earlier—I thought my attempt to collect you had failed."

"That was *you*?" I finally managed. The Morrigan's servant made a throat-tunnel in my ceiling? *Will was right about her.*

"I've never used the Gap for such complicated travel before. I feared you'd been lost." His blackened lips curved in a smile that revealed broken and missing teeth. "We're glad you're here now. The time has come to fetch the poet."

WILL

It was late by the time I started for Drumcliff House, so I was glad the clouds had moved on, leaving the moon and stars to light my way. My thoughts were so preoccupied with Neve—and the unexpected embrace—that I might have easily ridden my horse into the bog.

The cottage was less than a mile from the inn, but I had only covered half the distance when I began to feel strong misgivings. Was it wise to leave her after everything that had happened? After the things we'd seen and had yet to understand? Mrs. Marsh might safeguard her reputation, but what about her *person*? In the light of day we'd felt safe enough, but now . . .

Enough. I had not survived this long by ignoring my instincts.

I turned my horse around. Neighbors be damned—they'd whispered about me for years anyway.

There was no one on hand at the stable where I boarded my mare—the groom had likely gone to his rest. I untacked and gave her some hay before walking back to the cottage. The breeze had a wintery bite, and I was happy to be going inside to the fire. Maybe Neve would still be awake and we could discuss our upcoming trip.

I dreaded the coming interview with Mrs. Marsh. It might very well be the end of our association. I hoped not. She had served my family well for some years now.

A lamp burned in the front window—at least one of the ladies was awake. As soon as I opened the door, my housekeeper came at me in a rush. I was surprised to find her dressed for bed—or rather surprised to find her dressed for bed and outside of the bedroom.

"Mr. Yeats! Thank heaven!"

My stomach dropped. "What is it?"

"Miss Kelly is gone!"

"*Gone!*" I walked across to my guest's room, Mrs. Marsh following close behind me. The room was empty. The fire had burned down to coals.

"Such strange things I heard, Mr. Yeats, I—"

"Was she taken from the house forcibly?"

Mrs. Marsh shook her head. "I don't know, sir, I only heard her scream."

Heart racing, I placed a hand on each of the matron's shoulders to steady her. "Where did you last see her?"

"She was in your study, sir."

I went to the open door of that room. My eyes moved over furnishings, walls, ceiling, rugs—shards of broken glass caught my eye near the fireplace. Hurrying over, I squatted and carefully picked up the largest fragment. There were also a few drops of wine on the hearth tiles—yet I was sure I smelled absinthe on the glass. I touched one of the drops and rubbed my fingers together.

Not wine, blood.

Neve might have cut herself on the broken glass, but what had caused the glass to break? Had there been some kind of attack?

"Do you know what's happened to her, sir?" asked Mrs. Marsh in a quiet, desperate voice.

I looked at her. "Did you hear anything else?"

"I heard something break—the glass, I imagine—that's what first woke me. Then a great *heaving* noise." Shuddering visibly, she closed her eyes. "She screamed like the devil himself was after her."

Might it have been the tunnel again? Had it come for her *here?* "You checked on her then?"

"I did, sir. I looked all over the house. I was on my way to check the garden when you returned."

What could I do? All I could think was to return to her home, on the possibility the tunnel somehow connected *here* to *there.* Yet I had never time traveled voluntarily.

"I'm so sorry, Mr. Yeats." My housekeeper's expression was pure anguish. "I never should have sent you away. Why did I interfere?"

"It's hardly your fault," I assured her. "You were trying to help, and you couldn't have known. But I think that you should go, for your own safety."

"What will *you* do?" she asked.

I pressed a thumb and forefinger to my temples. "Look for her." But how?

"Sir," she said in a more determined voice, "I'll not go until—"

Mrs. Marsh was cut off by the roaring of wind. I looked up, knowing what I would find: Neve's throat-tunnel had opened in the ceiling of my study.

"Run!" I shouted.

Thank heaven she obeyed me and stumbled out the door as another hot blast came through the opening. Instinct was propelling me in the same direction when I came to my senses.

The wind shifted direction, and I stepped back into the middle of the room.

Take me to her.

SPELLWORK

NEVE

The monster's mouth opened, and the howl that came out was all too familiar. I crammed my hands against my ears. Then his jaws began *peeling apart,* like some grimdark comic book character. His features continued to gruesomely contort until he'd been transformed into the gaping maw I'd just flown through in Will's study.

I cowered against the floor as the wind blasted down.

He's the throat-tunnel. He's going after Will.

I lay there, shaking, trying to think what to do. What *could* I do, other than hope Will made it here alive?

A minute or two passed before a figure was spit out onto the floor beside me.

"Will?" I cried.

"Neve!" Gasping for breath, he mopped his hair out of his face. "Are you all right?"

I don't think I'd ever been so glad to see anyone. "Yeah, but we've got a—"

The wind dropped suddenly and cut off the noise, causing my voice to ring out loudly.

Then I noticed my book lying on the floor between Will and me—I must have shifted off of it while cringing away from the throat-tunnel. I scooted toward him until I could subtly flip the corner of my nightdress over it.

"What have you got there?"

My heart slammed into my sternum and I looked up. Far Dorocha had reverted to his semihuman form and was walking—more like lumbering—toward us. Will gave a startled grunt and sat up.

Far Dorocha came close, and I wanted to crawl right out of my skin as he reached out his meaty hand and struck like a rattlesnake, grabbing the lower half of Will's face as I gave a yelp.

I held my breath while the monster studied Will. "Success," he said finally and let go.

He hasn't seen the book. I wasn't even sure why I was protecting the thing so hard. But my instincts were screaming at me to keep it hidden. It had somehow brought me here; maybe it would get us out.

"Who are you?" demanded Will, not sounding nearly as worried as I felt he should. I was coming to realize that he had mad skills when it came to holding his shit together.

"He says he's the Morrigan's servant," I told him.

Alarm flashed over Will's face as looked back to me. "What?"

"Far Dorocha," the monster said, another hiss sounding. "I believe we missed meeting at Knock Ma a few years ago."

Will stared, his fear level finally catching up to the situation. "That's not possible," he said. "Far Dorocha was killed in that battle."

That explains a lot. Except for the part where he's still walking and talking.

"Indeed," said the monster. "It seems that even death cannot keep a goddess from her vengeance."

"Vengeance?" said Will.

Yet another sickening smile twisted the monster's lips. "Justice was never so poetic. Limbs from nameless corpses made me whole, and human enough to become part of my own experiment." His eyes continued to bore into Will a few seconds. "There are preparations to be made now."

"What does the goddess want with us?"

Ignoring Will, Far Dorocha headed for the door to the cell, one foot scraping the floor as he walked. More light came through when he opened the door, and I could see that leg was more metal than flesh, with gears at the ankle and knee joints. What skin was exposed was sickly purple and yellow. The other leg was fully concealed beneath dark leather.

The door closed behind him, and the green lights again dimmed. I couldn't help feeling like we'd been locked in a tomb. "This is an awful thing to say, but I am *so* glad you're here."

Will gave a weary laugh and rubbed one elbow. "I'm relieved to have found you. When Mrs. Marsh told me you'd vanished, I feared the worst."

"Are you sure this *isn't* the worst?"

He laughed again, resting his arms on his bent knees. "I imagine we'll find out soon enough. I wish I'd been able to keep him talking longer. It would be helpful to understand how and why we're here."

"I can tell you *how*. Far Dorocha is the throat-tunnel."

Will looked at me, and something seemed to click behind his eyes. "That's what he meant by poetic justice. He's actually *become* a Gap gate. A living one."

"You lost me."

He pushed back his hair. It was starting to be my favorite thing he did.

"I think I told you about Gap gates when we walked over the battlefield—how they had once been used to pass through the thousand-year-old seal between Ireland and Faery?"

I nodded. "I remember."

"The Gap gates were created by Far Dorocha—he's a fairy druid. Also a sorcerer and an alchemist."

"And, apparently, the walking dead."

"So it would seem. All gates except the first one he created were destroyed when Faery and Ireland merged after the Battle of Ben Bulben. But the original was damaged, and anyone who passed through it was transformed in some way. Far Dorocha couldn't resist experimenting with it. He put fairies and animals through. He even passed Fomorian remains through and created a revenant king—a barrow-wight."

"Okay, that connects quite a few dots."

Will stood up, and he held out a hand. I grabbed the book and let him haul me to my feet. All my joints creaked and protested.

"Before the second battle," he said, "the one for Knock Ma, I passed through the gate myself as part of a strategy to flank the elven warriors. That's how I became a time traveler."

This single, supporting fact spoke volumes about my new friend. He presented as this kind of nerdy country gentleman, when actually he was unbelievably brave.

"So the Morrigan put Far Dorocha through this broken gate for some reason—for revenge, I think he said—and that's what turned him into a throat-tunnel?"

"That's how I've interpreted it. He had betrayed her—tricked *her* into passing through the gate, a story for another time—and allied with the shadow elves to take over the fairy court at Knock Ma."

"In other words, he's an even bigger asshole than I thought he was." I looked down at the book in my hands. "I have something to tell you too. Far Dorocha said he came for me back in Portland. Obviously, that failed, but he doesn't know it was because of you—he seems to think my arrival here was just delayed by time travel weirdness. It actually had something to do with *this*."

Will's eyes flickered to the book. "What makes you think so?"

"Mainly because it flew up to the ceiling, and then sucked me up through my *drawing* of the throat-tunnel."

Will chewed on this for a minute. "May I see the book?"

I handed it to him, and he flipped pages until he got to the tunnel drawing.

"I'd, um, be *careful*."

Examining the drawing, he said, "I think this is a spell, Neve." He looked up. "You used a spell to come here."

"*I* did? I wouldn't have any idea how to do something like that."

He pointed to a small, dark circle on the page. "Is this your blood?"

I gave him a sheepish look. "Yeah, I broke a glass."

Next, he pointed to a puckered spot on the page. "What's this?"

Er. "Absinthe?" I'd forgotten he told me people used it to see fairies—which sure sounded like a kind of magic.

"I'm no wielder of magic," he said, "but I've known and read about many people who are. This looks very much like spellwork to me."

"You're saying that because I'm clumsy and like to draw things, I accidentally summoned a Far Dorocha throat-tunnel to your house."

A corner of his lips lifted. "Well, it was your theory originally."

I sighed dramatically. What else could I say?

"If you *are* connected to Niamh, she was from Faery. Most

fairies have at least some magic. Blood magic is almost as old as the world. Absinthe—it has long been associated with fairies, and has unusual properties that are not fully understood." He rubbed his beard and added, "Magic is not an exact science. It's personal, affected by your roots, your history, your experience, your education." He gave me a pointed look. "You hid the book from Far Dorocha. Some part of you knew it was better to conceal the way you got here."

I cast a spell. I still couldn't get my head around it.

"Well, regardless of how we got here," I said, "I think we better figure out how we're going to get out."

WILL

I was preoccupied with Far Dorocha's transformation. I kept thinking about the barrow-wight he created using his malfunctioning Gap gate—the Alchemy Gate. Now the Morrigan had done something very similar to *him*. I recalled the bog men Neve and I had seen climbing up to the fairy door. It all began to feel connected.

"Will?" Neve was eyeing me expectantly.

"Agreed, we need to escape if we can."

She took her book from my hands and stared at the plain wood cover. "I have an idea. It's probably silly."

"Tell me."

"I don't suppose you have a pencil."

I patted the breast pocket of my jacket and drew out a two-inch stub.

She took the pencil, and let out an audible breath. "God bless geeks in every century." I had no idea what this meant, but I waited to see what she would do next.

She moved closer to one of the light disks, and she opened

the book to a blank page and began to sketch. After a few moments, I recognized my home—the cottage, as seen from the apple orchard.

"I don't really know what I'm doing," she said. "I thought if—"

We heard noises outside the room, like someone descending stairs. The rhythmic squeak and metal-on-stone scraping suggested Far Dorocha was returning.

Neve was closing the book but stopped, taking the top corner of the page, along with several pages behind it, and folding them down. Then she shoved the book inside my jacket. As the door opened, I clamped my arm down, pinning it against my ribs.

The revenant stepped into the room, the apparatuses that kept him alive emitting quiet clicks and hisses. Outside the door was a mossy stone stairway leading steeply up. The natural light coming through was low, like twilight, yet bright enough for me to see the enclosure that imprisoned us—it was a cave. Farther back there were a few furnishings—a high drafting table, a bookshelf, and a cabinet with glass doors whose objects were too far away to make out. There was also a long, narrow table—it might have been a trick of the shadows, but I thought I could make out a *person* lying on top of it. The cave appeared to be a kind of study or laboratory, yet there were no lamps, candles, or other sources of light beyond the green disks embedded in the floor. Did the natural light hurt his eyes?

"Come," ordered Far Dorocha.

Neve stood behind me, and I felt her trembling fingers come to rest, like butterfly wings, on my arm.

"Where are we going?" I asked him.

His head swiveled slightly—it was an odd motion, unnatural on a man. More birdlike.

"My lady wishes to speak with you."

The Morrigan.

I turned to Neve, whose eyes were wide. "Let us go," I said, hoping I sounded more confident than I felt. "We'll try to find out what all this is about."

She nodded, and I gestured for her to precede me. I didn't know what was waiting for us outside the cave, but I didn't like the idea of not being able to see her.

We climbed the stairs and emerged in a bleak forest. Many of the trees around Drumcliff still wore some of their leaves in mid-October—these branches were bare and black. I wasn't even sure they were alive.

There was a stone pathway before us, and Neve hesitated, turning to look at me.

"Walk on," said Far Dorocha, uncomfortably close behind me. I squeezed my arm against the book, reassuring myself it was secure.

Neve stepped onto the path.

In some ways, the forest reminded me of the one surrounding Knock Ma—massive oaks, centuries old. I had last visited that forest in very early spring, the day before the battle, and at that time the trees there had also been bare. That was where the likeness ended. There was water here, on either side of the path—not trickles of it, but puddles and pools in every low spot. Mist floated above, preventing them from reflecting light. There were no sounds of birds or other animals, only a deathly stillness.

There's something wrong about this forest.

I had managed to speak with the trees at Knock Ma, so I tried reaching out to these with my thoughts—I began by offering lines from one of my poems, as I had done then.

Roots half hidden under snows,
Broken boughs and blackened leaves . . .

I felt a coldness creeping from my feet into my legs. I hesitated in my recitation, and then came a piercing reply—

There, through the broken branches, go
The ravens of unresting thought;
Flying, crying, to and fro,
Cruel claw and hungry throat

These other lines from my poem were hurled back at me—*loudly*—and I stumbled. The voices of the trees here were nothing like the others. They were like snapping limbs, cracking ice, and cutting wind.

Angry ghosts.

Neve cast a worried glance back at me. I shook my head, and she walked on. I wished that I had gone ahead of her after all. There might be more threatening creatures here than Far Dorocha.

I looked up through the stark tracery of branches, hoping to orient myself and get some sense of where we might be. The sky was a tea-stained blue-green, the color of a muddy duck egg. There were no clouds, also no sun—just a strange, directionless light.

Faery.

After Ben Bulben, Ireland and Faery had merged in some areas. But Faery was vast—far larger than Ireland. There were places in Faery that had never seen—probably never *would* see—an Irishman. Places where an Irishman wouldn't be safe. This felt like one of those places.

Ahead of me, Neve seemed to float through this boggy wood, her white nightdress billowy and bright against the dark landscape. The plaits that crowned the top of her head still held, though strands had fallen around her shoulders.

As I watched her, I experienced a sense of foreboding. A

notion crept over me that she wasn't real at all, merely part of the melancholy vision that was this place.

It's the trees. When I had spoken with the trees at Knock Ma, a mournful sense of futility had overtaken me. A sense of my own insignificance among beings too expansive and ancient for my mind to grasp.

I was abruptly reassured that Neve was *quite* real when she gave a panicked cry and fell. As I rushed toward her, I saw a hand—bony, with filthy, ragged nails—had reached out of a pool next to the path to grasp her ankle. I worked to pry the hand loose—the fingers were slicked with mud and slid out of my grip. It didn't help that I was still pinning Neve's spellbook under one arm.

A voice suddenly boomed—Far Dorocha, speaking words I couldn't understand. They had the ring of command, though, and the claw released its victim, slipping back into the water.

"All right?" I asked, helping Neve to her feet.

She nodded, but she was pale and trembling.

Far Dorocha called out for us to continue. "Let me go ahead this time," I said.

We walked only a little farther before we came to a large opening—a kind of natural hall, its vaulted ceiling formed by bare branches. On the far end of the enclosure was a high, jagged rock formation. A throne had been carved into its base, and on it sat a woman. Her head was bent forward, and her long black hair hung over her face like a curtain. She held a staff in one hand—the leg bone of some enormous creature—its tip stuck against the mossy flagstones in front of the throne. Thick tendrils of mist rose like columns on either side of her.

Far Dorocha ushered us forward as he approached the throne, his heavy footfalls echoing in the eerie stillness. When he reached the woman, he stopped and bent, murmuring something in her ear.

Her head slowly lifted, hair parting so we could see her face. Neve stepped closer to me, and I held my breath.

The Morrigan had been present at both Ben Bulben and Knock Ma, but this was the first time I'd seen her in human form. She was a shapeshifter, and in war she appeared as a large crow. At Knock Ma she had loomed above the siege as the great airship *Corvus.*

Now she appeared as a tall woman of indeterminant age, with sharp features and chalky white skin. A black stripe had been charcoaled across her eyes and the bridge of her nose, in the style of the Icelandic shadow elves, and her forehead was painted red. There was no distinguishing between her pupil and iris, but the white of her eye was vivid against the charcoal.

"The lovers have found each other, in the end."

Her very speech raised goosebumps, voice alternating between that of a crone, a younger woman, and a child, so that each word had a different pitch and tone.

"And found their benefactress as well, it would seem," replied her servant. While Far Dorocha was speaking, I noticed a subtle change to the goddess's eyes—her irises and pupils lightened to gray before darkening again when he finished. It was eerier than anything else about her.

I took a step toward the throne, drawing her attention to myself and away from my companion. "Lady," I said, "so there's no confusion, my name is—"

She raised the staff and knocked it against the ground—the earth beneath my feet rumbled in response, and I fell silent.

"Do you think there is anything about you that I do not know?" Her tone was mocking and her charcoaled lips curved in a terrifying smile. "Better to *ask*, poet."

I swallowed. "Who am I, my lady?"

The goddess straightened, her smile fading as her eyes

brightened. "The most beloved of the Fianna. The warrior poet, slain by ancient enemies in the final battle before Faery and Ireland were divided—the Battle of Connacht."

I bowed my head respectfully. "Forgive me, but I don't understand how this is possible."

She raised her staff, drawing my eye again, and pointed it at Neve. "On the battlefield stained with your blood, the Faery woman begged me to grant you rebirth. Offered me *anything* in return. The time has come to collect payment."

Neve and I exchanged a wary glance. "What payment, lady?"

The butt of the goddess's staff came to rest again on the flagstones. "Your lives."

Time stopped. My mind grappled with all I had been told. Niamh and Oisin had been killed in battle, and Niamh had beseeched the goddess for another life? If this was true, I'd gotten it wrong—we weren't descended from Oisin and Niamh, we *were* Oisin and Niamh. The Morrigan's servant had come looking for us to exact her price.

"Excuse me."

I looked at Neve, surprised at the control—as well as the edge of annoyance—in her voice. She took a step to stand alongside me. The goddess's eyes followed her.

"Did you just say that you granted a wish for rebirth, and the payment is *death?* You let the two of them be born in different worlds, more than a hundred years apart, not even remembering who they were. Now that they—we—are together again, we have to die? That seems like a really crappy bargain."

If she was trying to say that the goddess's way of wish-granting seemed perverse and even cruel, she was right. Unfortunately, it was hardly out of character.

"Death can be a temporary condition," replied Far Dorocha. His mockery of a smile made it clear he was referencing his own ghastly resurrection. Was the Morrigan planning something similar for *us*?

I had managed to remain calm and respectful thus far, but I was growing alarmed. "Lady," I said, "your servant seems to be connecting our fate with his. I don't understand what purpose that would serve."

The goddess frowned. "The Fianna have gone to ground. No one has seen them since Ben Bulben. I need the son of Finn and daughter of Faery to call them to war. The Tuatha De Danaan will secure Ireland's future in the last great battle. I can't imagine a greater honor."

"War? Forgive me, but we have recently fought *two* battles to secure the future of Ireland. The peoples of Ireland have come together, and our enemies have been chased from our shores. Does some new enemy threaten?"

"Ireland is yet weak," she said dismissively. "The enemy is within."

Before I could ask her to expand on this cryptic reply, Neve said, "I still don't get why we have to be undead to do what you want."

"The raised dead are loyal," replied Far Dorocha.

"Loyal to *whom*?" I asked.

"Loyal to their maker."

I shuddered. When the goddess had asked Lord Meath to lead Faery and the Tuatha De Danaan against the Fomorians, no coercion had been required. When the fairy king and queen needed my assistance in the battle to repel the shadow elves, I had readily agreed. Lord Meath was an Irishman through and through, as was I. The Morrigan would know that. Which suggested she had some reason for thinking we might not agree to help her. Might she be contemplating a course of action that could *harm* Ireland?

I had watched the Morrigan and her servant carefully during this whole exchange. Each time Far Dorocha had spoken, she had stilled, and her eyes had changed color. Also their interaction felt off to me, in that it should have felt *more* off. Would she trust Far Dorocha after he had tricked and almost destroyed her? He himself had opened the door to the shadow elves' invasion.

"What happens if we refuse?" asked Neve.

The goddess glowered and leaned on her staff. "I granted your request. Your lives belong to me."

"Lady," I said, "having no memories of our former lives, I think you can imagine how it might be a strain to feel like this bargain has anything to do with us. *We* have never asked you for anything. Is there not some way we can serve you while *living*?"

Her gaze moved from me to my companion and back again, and I felt a glimmer of hope that my words might penetrate her resolve.

Far Dorocha bent again to her ear, murmuring something.

Blast. I watched the goddess closely, noting when her eyes shifted color. Lifting her staff, she laid it across her lap. She gave a brusque nod. "Don't damage them more than necessary."

Far Dorocha inclined his head in obedience. "When it is done, I will enhance them. Their value is too great for us to allow history to repeat itself."

His words sent a chill down my spine. I recalled the cave, and what I thought I'd seen in the shadows. *Not a person, a corpse.*

Far Dorocha issued another order I couldn't understand—I suspected he was speaking a very ancient form of Irish. Soon I heard someone approaching from one end of the craggy structure, where the blackened trees were obscured by thick fog.

Two creatures marched into view. They were asymmetric amalgamations of metal, leathery hide, and bone. Their joints were constructed of gears, but in each of them different parts had been replaced by metal rods or plates. They wore helms and breastplates and carried pikes. Their eye sockets were deep and empty.

"The bog men," whispered Neve.

She was right. The Morrigan *had* reanimated them, and her servant had made them whole.

We had to leave here. We'd time travel if necessary. Where was the clock in my head when I needed it?

"At least let us say goodbye," Neve said.

I looked from her to the Morrigan—the goddess's head drooped forward, and her hair fell back over her face.

It wasn't exactly a blessing, but Neve didn't wait—she turned to me and slipped her hands inside my jacket. Before I'd recovered from the surprise of *that*, she rose on her toes and kissed me. The sudden warm press of her jolted me out of time and place. Behind my closed eyes I saw Niamh again. The wind whipped her hair like a banner; the frothy waters of the Faery sea paid tribute to the mischief in her eyes. She reached up and sprinkled sugary sand down my chest—then followed the trail of it with her fingers.

I thought I would go up in flames. I moved to take Neve in my arms—and my stomach lurched as the book fell from its hiding place.

But her hand was there to catch it.

Seconds later, the ground went out from under us.

FAERY

NEVE

I held onto the book, and he held onto me. There was no throat-tunnel this time—no wind or stench, and no sense of falling forever. We landed together, in a heap, but the ground was softer here. Wherever *here* was.

I wondered why I could hear a heartbeat, then realized I was splayed across Will's chest—and had been for probably a minute or two. Slowly, reluctantly, I sat up.

"You okay?"

His hand fell away from my waist, but he was smiling, and a warm wave rolled through me. "Thanks to you, I think. The drawing of the cottage worked?"

I nodded and laughed. "I can't believe it."

The cottage was there, maybe twenty yards away from us, and behind it Ben Bulben. But the place was strangely still. No other houses or farms, and no road. The sky was the same greenish-blue color as before, though without the oily veil.

"This doesn't quite look right," I said. My thumb was throbbing where I'd deliberately stabbed it with Will's pencil nub—which had been like cutting into a pineapple with a butter knife—and I stuck it in my mouth.

He got to his feet and looked around. "You've found my cottage, but I believe we're still in Faery."

I frowned. "I don't understand."

"There is some overlap between Faery and Ireland. Some things exist in both places. It looks like my cottage is one of them."

It made about as much sense as everything else. "Where we were with Far Dorocha and the Morrigan—that was Faery too?"

"That's right."

I looked around again. "This place makes me kinda nervous. Where I grew up, on a warm day when the sky went greenish and everything got quiet, it generally meant all hell was about to break loose."

"In Portland?"

"Oklahoma, where I was born—and where the weather tries to kill you on a regular basis."

He laughed, and my eyes moved to his lips as I recalled what I'd had to do to distract from my spell-making. Sadly, I had no real sense of what it had been like, as I was juggling the book, the pencil, and minor surgery under the less than optimal cover of his jacket.

I bet he was a great kisser.

It wasn't a real kiss.

Ignoring the sinking feeling that created in my chest, I asked, "Do you think we're safe from the Sith twins here?"

"Probably not for long."

We seemed to have reached a point in our relationship where

he could interpret the pop culture references that I was apparently incapable of filtering out.

"So how do we get out of here?"

He blew at the hair that had flopped down over his face. "If we really are Oisin and Niamh, we *should* have the ability to pass between Faery and Ireland."

Having just used *magic* to save our lives, it didn't seem outside the realm of possibility. But I was out of tricks. "I'm inferring from your reply that you don't actually know."

"I've never crossed the border without a guide."

We continued helplessly surveying our surroundings, until finally Will said, "I don't think we can afford to tarry here long enough to figure it out."

"We're walking out of here like mere mortals, then?"

"We are." He looked at me. "Is that all right?"

I shrugged. "Preferable to ritual sacrifice." Tucking the book under my arm I got up. "What I wouldn't give for Lolly's mud boots right now."

Will made a kind of startled noise, and he said, "Wait a moment."

He jogged toward the cottage and went inside. A moment later he came out carrying—Lolly's mud boots. He set them down in front of me. I brushed off the bottoms of my stockings and then stepped into them with a sigh of relief.

"Was Mrs. Tobin in there too? A ham sandwich sounds pretty good right now."

"There's no one inside," he replied, taking me seriously. "We shouldn't risk eating or drinking anything while we're here. Plenty of mortals have been trapped in Faery that way."

"That bit of folksy wisdom actually rings a bell," I admitted. It occurred to me that he might be able to get clothes for me as well, but on second thought, the nightdress was plenty modest and had the additional benefit of having no corset and no bustle contraption.

Will searched and discovered a path, several feet wide and composed of dark, rich earth. It looked dry enough, but I was glad to be wearing shoes again.

"Where will this take us?" I asked.

"It's headed roughly in the direction of Knock Ma, and the boundary between worlds is all but nonexistent there. On Irish soil, it would be a very long walk—close to eighty miles. In Faery . . ."

"You don't know."

"Right."

We walked briskly and without talking. I started to adjust to the odd light and intense stillness. It was hard to imagine living in a place like this, though apparently some earlier version of me had. Maybe it hadn't always felt so lost and lonely.

The silence and listless atmosphere left plenty of space for my brain to obsess over what had happened with the Morrigan. The part where we almost died, obviously, but also the fact that Will and I had been lovers in our previous lives. So much so that Original Me came up with a harebrained scheme to bring us back. I couldn't say I hated the idea of Will and me—and *that* scared the crap out of me. Maybe we were inseparable a thousand years ago, but really all we had now was circumstance and some chemistry. As soon as we sorted all this out, I'd hopefully be headed back to my real life.

Glancing at him, I asked, "Are we going to be okay?"

He smiled. "I like to think we will be. And I'll do everything in my power to ensure it. That probably doesn't help much."

"It does, actually." Will's calm, competent presence was reassuring. I liked how he took things in stride, and how he didn't fuss. "I feel bad I even asked you. I don't want to be a burden. I just know you're more used to all this."

The path had led us onto a low ridge, and the hill below was blanketed in blooming heather. There was a richness—a saturation—to the colors here that I couldn't help appreciating. Like we were inside a Pre-Raphaelite painting. I felt the same deep stirring in my chest and abdomen that I often felt when I got lost in one of my projects.

The place was growing on me. *Or maybe it's just Will.*

"I'm used to it . . . to a degree," he said. "The battles, the old heroes come to life—for much of it I was little more than an observer. A witness and recorder of extraordinary events."

We reached the bottom of the hill, and he offered his hand as we navigated a few smooth stepping stones over a stream lined with vividly green plants. I noticed tiny fish sparkling like diamonds beneath the surface of the water, despite the absence of any direct light. I stopped for a closer look and discovered that although they did have scaly silver tales, they weren't actually fish.

"They have faces!"

Will came closer, and we both crouched down. The silvery things played in the gentle current, oblivious to our staring at them. Besides faces, they had long flowing hair. They were no more than an inch and a half long.

"Some type of merrow, I think," said Will, clearly as charmed by them as I was. My heart convulsed, and I wanted to kiss him—for real this time. We were close enough that I'd only have to lean in a little. Would he kiss me back? Take me in his arms again?

I shivered and looked down. "I'm glad *some* fairies are cute."

"I probably shouldn't tell you there are merrows with wickedly long teeth and claws."

I reached upstream and flicked water at him and he laughed, wiping the drops from his forehead. He stood up and offered his hand again.

When we made it to the other bank, we started up a second rise—another hill blanketed with purple and pink flowers. We'd been on solid ground again for several moments before he let my fingers slip from his.

Glancing at me, he said, "I know that our lives have been very different. And I can barely imagine what this must be like for you. But I assure you that none of this feels ordinary to me. I've been shaken by today's revelations too, and I'm frightened. Not only of the danger, but also of the fact that if we do manage to survive, this may never be over. If I'm a notorious Fianna warrior, what possibility is there I will ever live simply?"

"Is that what you want?" I asked him. "Because from my perspective your life has kind of been one big, scary adventure."

He shrugged. "I grew up simply, and when I was a young man, adventure appealed to me. Some choices, I made to protect my family and my countrymen. But after the battles, I chose a different path. I attended university in Dublin, and I retired to my grandparents' cottage to write. That's what I was doing until I suddenly found myself in Portland."

All of this helped to ease some of the tightness in my chest. Maybe it had to do with his gentle voice. Listening to him talk was like listening to waves moving back and forth over sand. But it was also grounding to hear about his regular hopes and fears.

"Thanks for sharing that with me," I said. "It makes me feel less adrift in all this."

He grinned. "It's the least I can do after you saved my life."

I shook my head. "*That* was luck."

"The only *luck* involved was your book not falling to the ground when you kissed me. I had no idea what you were planning to do."

I laughed, hot with embarrassment. "I didn't either until right before I did it."

"Well it rendered me fairly useless, so it was also lucky that you didn't really *need* me."

Heat danced in my belly at this confession. How many times had he been kissed, I wondered? Based on what I knew about Victorians in general, and about Will specifically, I guessed it was probably a lot fewer times than any other guy I knew.

"I was right then," he continued, "it *is* spellwork?"

I looked at the tip of my finger, which was red and swollen and probably on its way to being infected. *But I'm not dead.*

"That looks painful," he said, reaching for my hand. My heart gave a mushy throb as his warm fingers closed over mine so he could examine the puncture. "How did you do it?"

"Your pencil, sorry. I think the lead broke off immediately. It was probably the rough edge of the wood that opened the skin."

"It was some quick thinking." He reached into a pocket of his jacket, pulling out a handkerchief.

"You're kind of a walking Swiss Army knife," I observed, watching him wrap the soft cloth around my finger.

His brow furrowed, but he was smiling. "You'll have to tell me if I should be offended by that."

"Nah," I said. "I make bad jokes when I'm nervous."

WILL

Was *I* making her nervous? The fact that we'd been lovers in a previous life was certainly an awkward piece of information to assimilate, especially considering we'd only met the day before.

Or maybe it's the kiss.

The kiss that for a moment or two I had believed was real. The kiss that had made me forget everything but her.

Thank goodness for her clear head.

I watched her out of the corner of my eye. Her gaze was on the path, and she seemed lost in thought. Suddenly I was overtaken by a strong feeling I'd been here before—with her. And in this very spot. It was possible that I *had*. I thought about the woman in the mist and how she was always moving away from me. I had feared that I'd never catch up to her. Without time traveling, I never *would* have. Yet even now, I couldn't help feeling like she might always be out of reach.

We were approaching another wood, but unlike the Morrigan's forest, this one had a healthy canopy of green leaves, which was typical of Faery. There were no seasons here—or rather there was only one. I began to worry about where Neve's thoughts were drifting. The connection I'd felt between us at the stream seemed to have ebbed.

"I'm curious about how you cast your spell," I said.

She laughed, and it released some of the tension. "Yeah, me too," she said. "I guess you were right about the book. The bloodletting seems to be what triggered it."

"Blood magic."

She looked at me. "Do you know much about it?"

"I know more about elemental magic. Spells that draw on earth, air, fire, and water. Blood is used in more powerful spellwork. And for darker forms of magic, where the blood does not necessarily come from a willing participant."

"Yikes!"

I smiled at the strange exclamation. "Blood magic does have an evil reputation, but I think that's only due to the more extreme forms of it."

"Have you ever heard of drawings used in magic?"

"Symbols and runes are very common in spellwork. Faery magic often uses ogham—an ancient Irish alphabet. But I think your drawings are working more like incantations, in place of spoken—" Suddenly I recalled something from my research in the Faery library.

"Will?"

"Sorry. I've remembered a line in a poem Oisin wrote about

Niamh—I had always read it as metaphor, but now I wonder whether it might have been literal. 'The strokes of her brush waken magic.' Lines in other poems of his make similar references."

"So Niamh may have used art to do spellwork too?"

"She might have."

A smile spread slowly over Neve's features.

"What is it?"

"Nothing, I just . . ." She cleared her throat. "What kind of metaphor did you think it *was*, Will?"

The strokes of her brush waken magic. Heat flooded my cheeks. Of course she was right; it was the main reason I'd remembered the line.

She laughed. "I think maybe you're not quite as innocent as you seem."

I grinned at her. "Perhaps you'd best not make assumptions based on my gentlemanly demeanor."

"I promise you I never will again!"

It felt good to laugh with her and lighten the weight of recent revelations and events. Also, I'd suspected before this that I might seem overly proper compared to the men she was used to, and I didn't regret dispelling that notion.

We reached the entrance to the forest, and Neve stopped to stare up at an oak tree with branches that arced over the path.

"These are not like the others," I assured her.

"Not dead, you mean?"

"Not dead, but more than that. The ones in the Morrigan's lair—they were agitated and angry. I wish I'd had more time to understand why."

I was anxious to get under cover. I felt too exposed on the open hills. When the Morrigan came looking for us, it wouldn't be on foot. Thanks to Neve's quick thinking, we'd done something unexpected and escaped—I doubted we'd escape her that way a second time.

I held out my arm to her. "Shall we?"

She took hold with both hands, the gentle but eager pressure of her fingers interfering with the rhythm of my heart. As we stepped under the branches, the color palette changed—dark, leathery green leaves over our heads, and gray stones covered with bright moss and silver lichen at our feet.

"How do you know so much about magic?" she asked as we crossed a thick root reaching over the path.

"Mostly from knowing a number of practitioners. Also from reading books in the Faery library."

"Well, I think you're wrong about something."

"I don't doubt it. Please correct my error."

"Earlier you said that you don't do magic."

Nodding, I replied, "I believe that to be true."

She gave me a pointed look. "You just basically told me that you talk to trees."

"Sometimes," I acknowledged.

"And it sounds like they talk back."

I raised an eyebrow, repeating, "Sometimes."

"Does *everyone* here talk to trees?"

I laughed. "Not as far as I know."

"Ha! Now, should we talk about time travel?"

"You'll recall that my time traveling ability is not innate. But I admit you may have a point."

"*May?* You said yourself that magic is personal. I'd say a poet who can talk to trees is pretty good evidence."

"What purpose have you in Connacht, strangers?"

Neve jumped. A group of woodland fairies—*firglas*—had slipped silently out of the trees and now blocked the path in front of us. There were many firglas who chose to remain in Faery after the seal between worlds was broken, but they were fierce fighters and King Finvara also relied on them for protection of his family at Knock Ma. Based on the armor and weaponry these carried, I guessed they were a patrol, despite the fact they were far from the castle.

Tall and reedy, their flesh was the color of tree bark and the tips of pointed ears protruded from their dark hair. They were armed with pikes and severe expressions.

"Our purpose is our own, friend." I spoke Irish, as they had. "I too am of Connacht, and I am no stranger to the king and queen of fairies."

The leader stepped toward me. "Then name yourself, friend."

"Will Yeats, of Sligo."

The fairy turned his head to one side as the other three behind him began to murmur. I caught the word *scéalaí*—storyteller.

"Will?" Neve whispered nervously.

"It's all right," I told her. Then continued in Irish, "We're no threat to you, or to the noble family you serve. In fact, I'm pleased to see you. We find ourselves trapped in Faery."

A couple of them exchanged puzzled glances, and their leader said, "You are known to us, but *she* . . ." His gaze flickered to Neve. "She's an outlander."

"Yet she travels under my protection," I said, "and that would be good enough for King Finvara." The firglas could be haughty, but they respected authority.

I'd stepped ahead of Neve, partly shielding her from view—I pulled her forward now. The leader's gaze fell on her, and his demeanor changed.

"Forgive me, my lady." He bowed his head. "We believed the descendants of Niamh had all faded to Tír na nÓg."

He'd recognized her! The resemblance between Niamh and Neve wasn't only in my dreams. The firglas could live centuries—it was possible he had *known* Niamh.

Though Neve wasn't in fact a descendant, it was a mere

technicality and I wasn't about to complicate matters. "The lady and I have urgent business at Knock Ma. Can you escort us there?"

There was another consultation, and the leader raised his fingers to his lips, letting out a soft but high-pitched whistle.

"Safe journey, lady," he said, bowing his head again.

The patrolmen regrouped and strode toward us, and we moved aside to let them pass. Neve and I exchanged a puzzled look as they receded into the forest. Then I noticed the ground was quaking slightly. The quaking intensified to a thumping, and then a pounding that shook twigs from the trees.

NEVE

"It's all right," Will said, his hand lightly pressing the small of my back.

"You keep saying that," I replied, laughing nervously.

Something was coming—something big.

Will peered back along the path, where the annoyed-looking fairies had marched off. I followed his gaze, and soon caught glimpses of movement. Then we heard a sound like a cross between neighing and screaming.

"I think they've summoned Aughisky," said Will. "She's a water horse, a type of fairy."

"Hopefully not the kind with fangs and claws."

He laughed. I wasn't joking.

Aughisky was, in fact, a *huge* black horse—and she was running right at us. I couldn't help taking a few steps back. She came to a terrifyingly sudden halt in front of Will, snorting and panting. He murmured soothingly and held out a hand toward her muzzle. She tossed her big head a couple of times and did not let him touch her. Her eyes were *orange*.

"Please be careful."

Her black coat gleamed, wet and flecked with foam. Seaweed clung to her legs and tail, and the pungent smell of low tide wafted in our direction. The shells threaded into her mane rattled and clinked each time she tossed her head. Lifting a giant, barnacle-crusted hoof, she began pawing and rutting the ground.

"Come," said Will, "I'll help you up."

My head swiveled. "What?"

"She'll greatly abbreviate our journey."

Growing up in small-town Oklahoma, I had friends with horses. They were all *much* closer to the ground than the fairy horse, and I had never done more than sit on the back of one while being led around.

"We don't get around on horses where I come from," I informed him. *Especially not demonic ones.*

He held out his hand. "Leave it to me, then."

Hesitantly, I took his hand and let him lead me to the mare's side. Twisting her neck, she sniffed at the top of my head once, then blew a warm, fishy breath over my face. *Ugh.*

Will made a stirrup with his hands. I secured my spellbook under my arm and stepped into his hands, and he boosted me up. I fell across the mare's broad back and scrambled against the slick coat until I was sitting. Then I threw a leg over, heedless of the fact it hiked my nightdress above my knees. No way I was riding sidesaddle on this thing.

Will looked around until he found a tree with a lowish horizontal branch, and he climbed up. He clucked a couple times and the mare started toward him—her first step tossed me backward, and I grabbed a fistful of mane. Once she was positioned beside the branch, Will climbed onto her back, settling behind me. He had just reached around and taken hold of strands of mane when she took off like a shot.

I squealed and hunched forward on her neck, gripping

slime-coated horse hair and shells in both fists now. Will's arms tightened, his body snugging against mine, supporting me so I could sit up straight again.

"I've got you."

Wind whipped my face, the speed made me dizzy, and the passing landscape became a blur of changing colors. I experienced a few minutes of sheer terror, imagining Will losing his grip and both of us flying off and breaking our necks. But the pressure of Will's arms and legs was steady, and I could feel the sure-footedness of the powerful animal. Gradually I began to trust that we might survive.

I sank back against Will and closed my eyes. I felt his chin graze the top of my head and shivered. Entanglement with a time traveling, tree-talking warrior poet—especially one I'd eventually have to say goodbye to—was the last thing I needed. But there were worse ways to travel, and if this was going to save us from the Morrigan it was definitely worth it.

It didn't take long for me to reconsider. The lovely heat kindled by our close contact was harder to enjoy as my legs went tingly in some places and numb in others. The damp horse hair chafed the skin on the insides of my legs, and my butt was so sore I wondered whether I'd be able to walk when we got to wherever we were going.

It felt like we'd been riding for days when the beast finally began to slow. As the world came back into focus, I saw that we were walking along another forest path. The terrain was more hilly than before, and between the branches I caught glimpses of a castle above us.

"We're almost there," Will said, straightening and adjusting his legs.

I glanced up and saw that the blue-green sky had been replaced by boring rainclouds, just like the ones back in Portland.

My breath drifted out in a fog. I turned my head to ask a question, and a fat raindrop splattered on the tip of my nose.

Will laughed and wiped it off with his thumb.

Again I felt heat in all the places our bodies were touching. I swallowed, but my voice still sounded thin as I asked, "We're not in Faery anymore?"

"We are and we aren't. Knock Ma is one of the places where Faery and Ireland merged after the seal was broken."

"And the king and queen . . . they're going to be fine with us showing up on their doorstep?"

A whoosh of air brushed my face—I gasped and shrunk back against Will. With a loud *thunk*, an arrow lodged in a tree on the other side of the path.

KNOCK MA

NEVE

The fairy horse danced away from the arrow, and I would have fallen had it not been for Will. A woman—or so I thought—stepped out from behind a tree next to the path. She held up a hand and blew across her open palm.

I felt Aughisky relax, and she nickered a greeting.

The woman had an impressive set of glossy black wings, and a pair of very pointy ears. She wore a burgundy gown and an intricate crown of braids. She held a bow in one hand, and its position drew my attention to the rounded shape of her belly.

"Will?" she said, and then spoke a few more words in a different language.

"Your Majesty," he replied in English, bowing his head. "I'm pleased to see you too."

Her glittering eyes lowered to my face, and I squirmed.

"Koli Alfdóttir," said Will, "Raven Queen of Knock Ma, this is my friend, Neve Kelly, a visitor from America."

The queen smiled and let the bow hang at her side. "Welcome, Miss Kelly," she replied in English, "friend of Will Yeats."

She had a slight accent, but it didn't sound Irish. I noticed movement beside her and glanced down—a child peeped out from behind her skirt. He had dark curly hair, and his big round eyes were a steely shade of blue.

"Your Highness," said Will to the boy, bowing his head again, "I'm pleased to finally make your acquaintance."

The imp giggled and disappeared again. The queen made a hissing noise and muttered, "Don't be rude to our guests, Loki." She glanced up. "I apologize to the both of you. I fear we are raising a changeling."

Will laughed. "I think you need not worry on that count, Your Majesty. He looks just like his father."

"And shares his disposition," she said, and Will laughed again. "Come." She gestured with her bow. "I'll walk with you back to the castle and save you from being scowled at by the firglas. Finvara's noble cousins have come to stay through Samhain, so the patrols are more vigilant than usual."

"Lord and Lady Meath are here?" asked Will, brightening.

The winged queen stepped onto the path, dragging the boy, who clung to her skirts. After a moment he let go and ran ahead.

"Yes, along with their silver-haired sprite. Lady Alva is five, nearly a year older than Loki—a far more impressive accomplishment than her being named heir to the Irish throne—so of course he is fascinated by her. I had to take him hunting to give her a chance to recover from his overattentiveness. Queen Isolde is also with us."

Another queen?

"A family reunion, then," said Will. "I'm very pleased for this opportunity to see them all again."

Will's tone had gone serious, and the lady stopped, eyeing him keenly. "But you've brought some troubling news."

He nodded. "I'm afraid so, Your Majesty."

She returned the nod and continued walking. "Let us go inside."

The path wound around the side of the hill and then up a series of switchbacks to the castle. It was my first time seeing a real one up close, and I was thoroughly impressed. It rested on top of the highest peak around, towering over the surrounding forest, which pressed in close. There was a moat and a drawbridge, multiple towers, a defensive wall, and an arched gate—all the things I associated with castles. Two standards flapped in the breeze above the keep, bright against the leaden sky—one was green with a gold harp, and the other had a red boar on it and looked like a family crest. We followed the queen across the drawbridge, stopping inside an open area where there was a stable and some other outbuildings.

The men working here cast wary glances at our horse, all of them keeping their distance. Needless to say, I felt validated.

Will jumped down first and waited to help me. Terrified the mare would run away with me, I wasted no time. I handed my spellbook down to him, and then I swung my leg around behind me and eased myself toward the distant ground. I slid faster than expected and gasped, but Will caught me around the waist and lowered me gently.

As soon as I'd dismounted, the mare tossed her head, snorted, and took off. Every person in the stable yard stood watching until she was gone—except for the little prince, who tried to run after her, but stopped suddenly when a group of ravens materialized in the air right front of him. He squealed—looking more amused than frightened by their beating wings and scolding cries—and ran back to his mother. Then the birds vanished.

I thought of the Cheshire cat—*We're all mad here.*

"There is much we need to tell you and the others," Will said to the queen, whose eyes grazed my soiled nightgown. "Would it be possible for us to wash first, and perhaps a change of clothes for Miss Kelly?"

"Of course," she replied. "Follow me."

We climbed a dozen rough stone steps to the entrance gate, and then passed through a large hall with a banquet table nearly as long as the room. Servants were busy sweeping and polishing things. Others were arranging apples, pears, and bright autumn leaves into centerpieces. There were odder elements—animal bones and antlers, hollowed-out vegetables with faces carved into them. I remembered the queen had mentioned Samhain, which I thought was an ancestor of Halloween. Maybe there was going to be a party.

We exited the hall through another set of doors and walked down a torch-lit corridor to a flight of stairs, then up to another corridor. I noticed the torch flames were brighter and lighter in color than regular fire, and I wondered whether they were kept lit by magic.

There were four doors along the right side of the upper corridor, and the queen pushed one open. "You can use these two bedchambers," she said, opening another. The prince tried to dash through, but his mom grabbed him and dragged him back. He squirmed free and took off at a run toward the stairs.

The queen laughed and rolled her eyes. "I'll have water brought up, and I'll see what clothing I can find." Her eyes moved over me again, sizing me up, and she said, "If you'll excuse me."

"Thank you, Your Majesty," said Will.

She called after the prince and then followed him. I stood mesmerized by her wings and the swirl of her voluminous skirts until she disappeared around a corner.

"We've lost time," said Will, leaning against the door frame of the first room.

"We have?"

To my thinking, we'd actually covered eighty miles in *record* time, thanks to the demonic horse.

"Before we were snatched into Faery, Samhain was still a fortnight away. It happens sometimes when you travel in Faery. The boundaries are fluid—geographical as well as chronological. Even more so since the seal was broken."

"Well, that's unsettling."

"I can't help wondering what the Morrigan may have been doing in the meantime," he said.

"Maybe looking for us?"

"I suspect so." He stared at one of the torches on the corridor wall, thinking. "She may have assumed we left Faery when we escaped her—we *would* have if we'd known how. Maybe it's just as well that we were stuck there for a while."

Apparently, even goddesses were at the mercy of the supernatural aspects of his world.

"Do you think she might guess that we're at the castle?"

"I do. I wouldn't be surprised if she's already looked for us here—the grounds are riddled with hidden ways in and out."

"Comforting. But we may have a little time then?"

"Time enough to warn the others about what's coming."

"Time enough for me to change into real clothes before I go meet the queen of Ireland?"

The half-squinting smile returned. "For that too."

I started toward the other room, then decided to finally raise the subject that had been dangling around in the back of my brain since the Morrigan's revelation. "Do you think she could be lying to us, Will?"

He stopped and turned. "I wondered that too at first, but now

I don't think so. Besides the fact it would be an elaborate lie with no clear reason behind it, one of the firglas patrolmen recognized you. It's why they agreed to help us."

Okay, then. I touched one of the rough stone bricks in the wall, gathering my thoughts and my courage.

"What is it, Neve?"

God, the way he said my *name.*

I took a deep breath. "I don't know what this is supposed to mean for us, I mean for Neve and Will. We're working together because we're trying to survive. But beyond that we . . . we live in different worlds, *literally.* I don't think I can . . ."

I risked a glance at him—he got it. Maybe he'd been thinking about it too. He stepped closer and my heart threatened to take off after Loki down the stairs.

"It doesn't have to mean anything," he said evenly. "The people I've known who were bound up with immortals—in the end, they made their own choices. There is no reason to think it can't be the same with us."

Whew. I think. My head was a mess.

Mercifully a parade of servants appeared, bearing basins of steaming water. We made way, and half of them went through one door and half through the other.

Will had been carrying my book under his arm, and he handed it to me. "I'll see you soon," he said, and he walked into the first room.

I let out my tension in a sigh and followed the servants into my room, which looked like a spread in a luxury travel magazine. They moved around with the efficiency of ants—emptying water into a small brass tub, lighting lamps, starting a fire, laying out clothing on the four-poster canopy bed. One of them had also set a board of bread, cheese, and sliced apple on a table next to an ornately carved chair. When they'd finished, they reformed ranks and exited the room, the leader nodding at me as she passed.

"Thank you," I said, unsure whether it was expected.

Hearing a distant rumble of thunder, I went to the window. It offered a view of the courtyard, where there were gardens and even a conservatory. I was no expert on architecture, but I believed the conservatory was more modern than the rest of the castle—lots of glass and wrought iron.

The fragrance of the flowers the servants had tossed into the bathwater lured me to the tub, which had been moved close to the fireplace. Standing on some kind of deep, animal-skin rug, I worked the buttons of the nightdress loose and tossed it over the chair. Then I took off my boots and stockings, and stepped gingerly into the tub. Despite the fact the water had been carried through corridors and up stairways, it was still hot and steamy. I lowered myself slowly, not minding a bit of a scalding because the whole thing was so damn cozy and nice—*I'm soaking in a rose-scented bath in front of a roaring fire on a rainy day in an Irish fairy castle.* More prosaically, I assumed there'd be no warming up the water again once it had gone cold.

And go cold it eventually did, so I got out and grabbed a folded bath sheet from a stand beside the tub and went over to check out the clothing options. I was relieved to find the under layers were straightforward and lightweight, and the dress designs were from an earlier century than the one I had traveled to—long flowing things without the mechanics. I tried an ash-plum dress that looked about the right length and had a simple drawstring closure at the back. It was a little short, but that was fine with me. The fact that purple brightened the green in my eyes was definitely irrelevant.

Next, I picked up a snug leather vest trimmed with silver and white fur, in case the place was drafty. There were a few worn pairs of soft boots, and one set fit me better than the mud boots.

When I was dressed, I went to the vanity to find a brush and look in the mirror.

Ren Faire here I come. Admittedly the getup was flattering, and as a bonus, I would not be meeting another queen while wearing a dirty nightdress.

I pulled the brush through my damp hair a few times. Then a clap of thunder made me jump.

The wind blew the casement open and I looked up—a strange animal sat on the sill *staring at me.*

WILL

I had made myself presentable in perhaps a quarter of an hour, but gave my traveling companion more time. After the topic she'd raised in the corridor, the last thing she needed was me crowding her.

It was understandable she'd wish to establish a boundary between us. I couldn't imagine myself in her place, separated from her country and friends, now feeling threatened from all sides. Caught up in a conflict that had nothing to do with her. Though as the reincarnation of Niamh, it could be argued that in coming here, she had only come home.

By that logic, I too was part of "home" for her. I had a suspicion that my feelings on that matter might end up being quite different from hers. Since hers had been made fairly clear, mine didn't much signify.

I was deliberating about whether enough time had passed to check on her, when she shouted my name.

I darted out into the corridor and tugged open her door.

"What *is* that?" she asked, pointing and backing toward me.

Some creature was pacing on the window sill—goat-like, with horns and beard, but also winged. About the size of a barn cat. Its hide was an interesting color and texture—stone splotched with lichen. I followed its gaze to a table near the fire.

"A gargoyle, I think. There are a few like it stationed at the entrance to the castle."

Her head spun in my direction, and on her face was a look I'd seen on many others' faces—I had not expressed sufficient alarm.

"It's an enchantment," I explained, walking to the table. "Earth magic. Besides this castle being half-in, half-out of Faery, it's Samhain. The boundaries between natural and supernatural are even weaker than usual."

I picked up a piece of apple from a plate on the table, and the beast bleated as I tossed it. Rising on hind legs, it caught the fruit, crunching it as it turned and leapt from the sill, dropping out of view for a moment before we saw it circling the courtyard.

"'Trick or treat,' I guess?" said Neve, aiming a bewildered look at me.

It was another of her puzzling observations, but her altered appearance distracted me from asking. When I'd first seen her in Portland, she'd struck me as waif-like—she didn't look undernourished, but something about her reminded me of a stray cat on the doorstep. Maybe it was her fluid way of moving, combined with the rag-like garments she'd worn. Even the dress Mrs. Marsh had bought for her had not sat comfortably on her frame, and her figure had been swallowed up entirely by the voluminous nightdress. The garments she wore now had wrought a change. She looked composed, not about to flit away from the swat of a broom.

She also looked even more like Niamh.

I smiled at her. "You look ready."

"I am," she said, though her tone was not convincing.

"There's no need to worry. All of them are kind, though Queen Isolde can be unpredictable at times."

She laughed. "Thanks, I feel so much better."

She reached up and tucked her hair behind her ears. Her sleeves were a little short and I noticed a bluish mark on the inside of her right wrist.

"What happened here?" I asked, reaching for her hand and gently turning it out. Her skin felt cool against my fingertips, yet I was suddenly quite warm. Then I saw that the mark on her arm was not a bruise, but a drawing inked under the skin. A clock, of all things.

"Oh my gosh!" she cried suddenly, pulling her arm free and inspecting the mark.

"What's wrong?"

"The time changed!" She turned the mark out to me again—the clock read a quarter past one.

"I don't think I follow."

"It was drawn to show midnight. Or noon . . . It's a *tattoo*—how could the time change?"

I looked at the mark more closely. At a loss for an explanation, I asked the obvious. "It's never happened before?"

"If it has, I've never noticed." She rubbed her thumb over it. "You have a thing about clocks, right? Mrs. Marsh said you didn't like them in the house because you get headaches."

"I don't get headaches, and I don't really have anything against clocks—that was a fiction for Mrs. Marsh's benefit. Before I time travel, I hear ticking in my head. Ever since the first time, at the Battle of Knock Ma, a ticking clock has made it difficult for me to concentrate on my writing."

"I can imagine." She lowered her arm and gave her sleeve a tug. "One more thing, I guess."

"One more thing?"

"Clocks. One more connection."

Between us.

"Ah, indeed." She looked troubled, so I let it go. "Shall we go find the others?"

She walked to the bed and picked up her spellbook. "Should I bring this?"

"Do. We'll ask for their thoughts about it."

The queen had not told us where to find them, but I knew she and Finvara favored the cozy lesser hall and the *grianán* for smaller gatherings. The grianán, in the southwest tower, was very informal, so I made for the lesser hall first.

The firglas stationed outside the door were a good indication my guess was correct.

"Are the king and queen within?" I asked.

The two exchanged glances, and one of them knocked once on the door before pushing it slightly open.

"Your guests have arrived, Your Majesty," said the sentry.

Koli's voice answered from the other side. "Let them in."

The sentry pushed the door open wide. Neve's hand curled around my arm—I put my hand over hers for reassurance and led her inside.

This chamber was among my favorite in the castle, with its comfortable furnishings, intimate dining table, and arched window alcove with a casement that opened onto the conservatory. The hall was filled with the fragrance of roses at all times of the year, and you could often see the lights of the tiny fairy creatures that lived among the greenery.

"Mr. Yeats, it has been years. I'm very pleased to see you."

My eyes moved over the faces of those assembled around the hall's blazing hearth. Finvara and Koli, king and queen of fairies, stood on one side of the mantel, while Lord and Lady Meath stood on the other. Queen Isolde, who'd spoken, sat in an armchair directly in front of the fire, her rose-and-gold gown the brightest thing in the room. A footman moved among them, pouring wine. The two gentlemen and Isolde were all first cousins on their O'Malley side.

"Your Majesty," I said, bowing.

"And Will has brought Miss Kelly," said Koli in English.

Neve moved closer to me and bowed her head respectfully.

"Welcome to Knock Ma, Mr. Yeats and Miss Kelly," said King Finvara warmly. He had let his hair grow again and wore it queued behind his head. As usual, his blue eyes glittered with good humor. "Please join us."

He gestured to the footman, who carried over a tray. We each took a glass of wine and then moved closer to the party. The king introduced himself and the others to my companion.

With that finished, Lady Meath said, "I too am very pleased to see you again, Will."

"As am I," said her husband, Edward. "I've missed our conversations."

I had stayed with Lord and Lady Meath several times at their county seat while I was on holiday from university. They were kind and lively hosts. Both had fought at the Battle of Ben Bulben, and they had married shortly thereafter. Lady Meath was a folklore scholar, originally from London. The discoveries she and Lord Meath made helped Ireland prepare for and win the battle.

"I'm very glad to see you both," I replied. "And I am eager to meet Lady Alva."

"The children are resting," said Lady Meath, and I caught the note of relief in her tone. "But you will see her at the bonfire. You will be attending, won't you?"

"I beg your pardon, Lady Meath, is it Samhain *today*?"

Her penetrating eyes narrowed slightly. "Indeed it is—today and tomorrow."

I recalled that she and her husband had also experienced a loss of time, after a navigation error on Grace O'Malley's Gap galleon. I had been a crew member of Captain O'Malley's at the time.

"William," said Queen Isolde, "I understand that in addition to a mysterious companion you have some kind of worrisome news to share with us."

"I'm afraid so, Your Majesty. In fact, I was relieved to learn that all of you were assembled here. Recent events are too concerning to keep to ourselves any longer, and I believe if anyone will know what's to be done, it will be you in this room."

"Very well," said Isolde with a sigh of resignation. "But first enlighten us as to the origins of Miss Kelly. I have learned well enough by now that when a kinsman brings a woman into my court, it pays to ask for particulars."

Everyone but Neve and I laughed at this, and I took the opportunity to fortify myself with a large gulp of wine. I was not a kinsman of the queen's of course, but I had joined her court after Ben Bulben and we had gotten on well.

"Miss Kelly is from America," I said when their laughter had died down.

Isolde's eyebrows lifted. "That *is* shocking, William, dear."

"She is also from the twenty-first century."

NEVE

It felt like the air had been sucked out of the room. The footman dropped a piece of silverware onto the stone floor.

Queen Isolde, another beautiful and terrifying lady, was staring at me like I was a ghost. I guess I kind of was.

"Another time traveler?" asked Lady Meath, sounding more curious than shocked.

"I was carried forward in time to *her*, lady," he said. "When I got there, I found her in danger of being swallowed up by a Gap gate like none we've ever seen. I brought her back here, and we have worked to piece together many things. Before I go into it, you'll want to know that we've seen Far Dorocha—he is *alive*, though much altered, and is a servant of the Morrigan."

The room erupted—gasps, a whistle, a low cry of dismay.

"Doro!" said Queen Koli, exchanging a panicked look with her husband.

"Cousin," Isolde said to the king, "You saw his body, did you not, at the siege of Knock Ma?"

Finvara gave a world-weary sigh and reached for his wife's hand. "Aye, we did. We saw the Morrigan pull his body from the rubble and fly off with it. We wondered about it at the time, and have wondered about it since."

Queen Isolde rose from her chair. Will had said she was descended from a mythical Irish queen and I could easily believe it. She was probably six feet tall, and that wasn't counting her high pile of dark hair. Her expression was queenly to the power of ten. I would almost rather have Far Dorocha after me than her. *Almost.*

"Let us have the rest of the story, William," she said. "Not in your usual diverting manner, but quickly."

Will looked at me as if to ask my permission.

"*Go,*" I said quietly.

I watched the faces of the others as he explained it all—our first meeting, our connections to old Irish heroes, our trip to Faery and escape from the Morrigan. Their expressions flowed between alarmed, frightened, angry, and dying-to-ask-a-question. But they kept quiet and let him finish. Then their attention shifted to Isolde.

"Good *heavens,*" she said, scowling. "A fortnight since you were with the Morrigan?"

"That's right, Your Majesty."

She gazed into the fire. "Are we never to have peace?"

Everyone looked miserable, and I felt awful for being part of the cause. They seemed like good people.

Finally, the queen's gaze settled on *me*. My heart gave a startled flop.

"Where is your book, Miss Kelly?"

My courage failed me—I handed the book to Will, and he carried it to the queen. She gestured to Lady Meath, and Will offered it to her instead.

"What do you make of that, clever girl?" the queen asked.

Lady Meath, who didn't look much older than me but had a full head of silver hair, turned the book over in her hands. She examined the binding, and she opened it randomly—she studied the sketch of Will.

"I'm afraid I've never seen anything like it, Your Majesty."

"May I?" asked Queen Koli.

The question was directed at me—I nodded. It seemed I was incapable of speech.

Lady Meath carried the book to her. The queen first touched the cords of the binding, and she poked at the watch and the knight figure I'd threaded into it. She stared at the cover, and then she brought the book back to me.

"I believe it is a grimoire," Koli said, fixing her eyes on mine as she placed the book in my hands. "*You* should remain its keeper."

"A spellbook," said Will. "So I thought."

Now everyone stared at me, and I hugged the book to my chest, wondering if it could make me invisible.

"Did the Morrigan mention the Fomorians?" Queen Isolde asked Will, and I started breathing again. "Have our old foes recovered from the blow we dealt them?"

Will shook his head. "She only said that it would be the last great battle."

"*Blast!*" Isolde's composure slipped. "Why does she never speak to *me?* Am I not Ireland's queen? Would I not defend this island with every soul under my command—with my own body, if necessary? Why *on earth* would she call an army of the dead?"

There were a few beats of uneasy silence before Finvara answered, "Maybe it is *because* of who you are, Your Majesty."

Isolde gave him a sharp look. "What do you mean, cousin?"

"It's not exactly in either of your natures to defer to another."

The queen raised an eyebrow. "You suggest she cuts me out purposely."

"Forgive me for interrupting," said Will, "but there's something else. Far Dorocha appeared to have considerable influence over her—more than I would have expected, given their history. I wondered even whether he had gotten the upper hand in their relationship."

"You think the fairy fellow might be controlling the Morrigan?" said Lord Meath, sounding doubtful.

"It would not at all surprise me," said Koli gravely. "He is calculating and subtle. Skilled at getting behind an adversary's defenses. He tricked her once before."

"And only one thing motivates Far Dorocha," said King Finvara. "Power."

"*Blast*," repeated the queen.

Everyone stood frowning, staring at the rug or the fire. Finvara reached one arm around his wife's folded wings and pregnant belly, and she leaned back against him. The servant made the rounds with the wine bottle.

Finally Will said, "If Far Dorocha is unchanged—if he still craves power—and if he is influencing the Morrigan . . . might it be that she's preparing an army for a *civil* war? When I asked her what foe was threatening, she said, 'the new enemy is within.'"

Isolde's frown deepened. "She means to wrest control of Ireland from me."

Will shook his head slowly, but it wasn't a denial. He was still thinking it through. "I don't know, Your Majesty. But in the last two battles, she did not go so far as to forcibly conscript anyone. She uses people's emotions and desires to maneuver them like pieces on a chess board."

"Will is right," said Lady Meath. "And her reference to a last great battle may be even more reason for concern. The Morrigan *craves* conflict, because she abhors stasis. A battle to end all battles is not a thing I would expect her to champion."

"It *is* a thing I would expect a would-be usurper to champion," said her husband.

Isolde's lips had set in a grim line. "We must get to the bottom of this. We must prepare." She looked at King Finvara. "Do we cancel the fete?"

"Nay, nay," replied the king, raising a hand. "Maybe you've forgotten that I learned a very costly lesson about offending the fairies. If there really is to be another battle, we will need them. It's certain to work mischief if we ignore one of the most important fcast days."

"Agreed," Isolde said with a frustrated sigh. "But we will have to muster in the meantime. I'll telegraph my generals."

"I'll send riders to Tuam with your messages," said the king. "We can spread the word among my own people this evening."

Isolde fixed her gaze on Will. "The Fianna . . . That's why she wants Oisin and Niamh, yes? The Morrigan wants the Fianna to fight for *her*."

"She said as much, Your Majesty."

"Well, it is good for us that Miss Kelly was clever and resourceful enough to get you both away from there, *and* to keep the Morrigan and her servant from getting their hands on that book."

I confess I was childishly gratified by the praise.

"Where *are* the Fianna?" asked King Finvara.

"The Morrigan mentioned them having 'gone to ground,'" said Will.

Lord Meath was nodding. "They returned to Faery after the Battle of Ben Bulben. No one has seen or heard of them since."

"They must be called back to fight for *us*," Isolde said to the earl. "Can you do it?"

He frowned. "You know I can't. Not without Diarmuid."

I recalled that Will had said Diarmuid was Lord Meath's ancestor, and that the two of them had inhabited one body during the battle.

The queen's gaze came back to Will. "Then it must be *you*."

He let out a breath, and he shook his head. "I may be Oisin, but I have hardly any memories from his life."

"Are you not writing about him?"

"I am, Your Majesty."

"Then you will have done your research. *Think*, William."

His brow furrowed. The hand holding my spellbook began to tingle.

"There was a horn that he sounded in battle," he said, "but I don't know whether—"

Will looked at me, and I flipped the book open and found the sheet with the description of the dream from the bus.

"Read it to us," he said, eyes bright.

"Um," I began, cursing the tremor in my voice, "'In the moment before our last, I hear the call of Borabu, the horn of the Fianna.'"

"That's it," said Will.

"Do you know where it is?" asked Isolde, eying him sharply. "Borabu?"

His face fell. "I've no idea, Your Majesty."

"The horn of Borabu was a gift to Oisin from Uindos, the Horned God, was it not?" said Lady Meath.

"I've read that in the lore," Will agreed.

"William," said the queen, "I want you and Miss Kelly to put your heads together over this at the earliest opportunity. Maybe there's something more you can remember from your past lives. Maybe there's some way Miss Kelly's spellbook can help you."

A yawn snuck up on me out of nowhere, and I covered my mouth—everyone stared. Admittedly it was odd timing for a yawn—probably rude and improper on top of that—but now that my initial terror over meeting these people had passed, my energy was flagging.

"Yes, Your Majesty," said Will, "Perhaps we might retire for a few hours first? We've missed at least one night's sleep, and I don't think we'll be of much use until we recover some of it."

Thank you, Will.

Isolde nodded and waved at the door. "Very well. We will expect to see you later at the fete, where we'll all talk more of this."

Will and I left the hall as the royals resumed their discussion. "Oof," I grunted as we started up the stairs. My legs were already sore from our ride, and I was bone tired.

"I agree," said Will.

I gave him a sideways look and he grinned. Why did he have to be so adorable?

When, ten years later, we made it to the top of the stairs, I said, "Are you happy with how that went?"

"Relieved. We were fortunate to find them all here. They'll know what to do."

"Seems like they feel the same way about you." He gave me a puzzled look, and I added, "They trust you."

He nodded. "We've seen each other through troubling times."

We stopped in front of our rooms, and I asked, "Are you really going to try to sleep?"

"I think we both should, while we can."

"No argument from me." I took hold of the doorknob, but I was not feeling ecstatic about us separating right now.

"If you have any more visitors, or need anything—"

"You'll hear from me, don't worry."

He smiled. "Sweet dreams, then."

I laughed. "You too."

I went inside, leaving the door open as I scanned the room for errant gargoyles or other unwanted guests. The coast was clear, so I closed the door and walked over to the bed. Flopping down, I let my face fall into the covering. It smelled clean, and a lot like Will's house.

This place made me jumpy and I wasn't sure I'd sleep, but my body felt heavy, and after a minute or two I found myself in the weird space between waking and sleeping, where dreams feel especially real. I was walking the heather-covered hills of Faery, but I'd lost Will and was desperately looking for him.

A sound in the room brought me fully awake again.

THE DEAD

NEVE

A breeze wafted through the open casement, stirring the bed curtains—had it been open when I came in? I shivered and looked at the fireplace. The fire had gone out. So what had made the noise?

Something moved in my periphery, and I looked again at the casement—a person was standing there. "Will?"

It was a woman though, wearing a red-and-white gown. She took a couple of slow steps and my blood went cold.

Scooting toward the far side of the bed, I squeaked out, "What do you want?"

My heart stampeded as she moved closer. Then I discovered that she wasn't wearing a red-and-white gown like I'd thought, but a white gown with *a whole bunch of blood* splashed down the front of it. She had blood on her face too. I could see all this plainly because she was kind of glowing. She held something in her hands—it looked like the horn of an animal, maybe a goat. No way I was staying long enough to find out.

I scrambled over the edge of the bed and ran for the door, flinging it open and running out into the corridor. I knocked twice on Will's door before pulling it open.

"Neve?" He sat up. He'd been stretched out on the bed, his back resting against the headboard.

"There's a dead woman in my room."

He processed this for a second before jumping up and dashing out the door.

"Be careful!" I called after him. I followed as far as the door to my room but couldn't make myself go in.

I am never going to get used to this.

I watched him search the room and find nothing. "Whatever it was is gone now," he said.

I walked to the bed and sank down with a sigh. "Ugh, I'm sorry. Maybe I imagined it."

He came and sat next to me, and I resisted a powerful urge to lean my head on his shoulder. "Tell me what you saw."

After I described the visitor, he said, "I doubt you imagined it. The dead walk at this time of year. It's the main reason for the feast—to honor them and ensure they return to the netherworld by the second of November."

"So it's common to see ghosts?"

"Maybe not common, but at Knock Ma, which is hundreds of years old, and on the border between Faery and Ireland, it's hardly surprising."

Right. "Do you have any idea who she might have been?"

"Maybe one of the wives of the original King Finvara. Or a Connacht noblewoman. Did she try to get your attention?"

I frowned. "Maybe? She was holding something out—it was a curved horn, I think. A pretty big one, like a ram's horn."

His eyes came to my face. "A *horn*?"

"Yeah I think so. Why?"

"Might it have been Borabu?"

I was pretty sure the horn from my journal was the kind you blew into—but now it occurred to me that animal horns were sometimes used that way. Or at least they were in movies. And when I thought more about it, I remembered metal bands around the horn at regular intervals, maybe to reinforce it, or as decoration.

"Wow, it could have been." Then my brain took hold of the next logical conclusion. "Do you think the ghost was . . . ?"

"Niamh."

I had just been haunted by *myself*. Luckily I was sitting, because the room tilted. I must have swayed too, because Will put an arm around my shoulders to support me.

"She might be able to tell us where it is," he said.

I nodded. "I shouldn't have left. It never even occurred to me."

"Maybe she'll come back."

I looked at him and swallowed.

WILL

I almost lifted my thumb to smooth away the lines that had formed on her forehead. Instead I said, "I'll wait with you."

Relief softened the lines. *She trusts me.* A wave of warmth washed over me.

"I'm a coward, I know."

I laughed. "That's the last thing you are. Where were you when you saw the ghost?"

"Right here. I'd almost fallen asleep."

Reluctantly, I lifted my arm from her shoulders and stood up. "Go ahead and lie down. Sleep if you can. I'll take a chair by the hearth and watch."

The blood rose into her cheeks. "Would it be bad if you stayed over here with me?"

My heart took a mad bounce, and my tongue stuck to the roof of my mouth.

"Sorry," she quickly added, "I shouldn't have—"

"Wait a moment." I walked to the door and closed it. Then I moved to the bedside nearest the window and sat down.

She smiled and crawled toward me, propping herself against the headboard. I put my feet up and did the same. She folded her hands in her lap. I realized I was holding my breath.

Her head sank onto my shoulder.

When I woke, the only light in the room came from stars glinting between two silvery clouds. A weight rested on my chest—we'd sunk down into the pillows, and Neve's head had fallen onto me. Her breaths came shallow and quick, and her hand splayed across my breastbone. My heart was beating fast beneath it.

Don't move. Don't break the spell.

Then there came a knock on the chamber door. Sighing, I eased out from under her, letting her head slip to the pillows. The marking on the inside of her wrist faced out, and I saw that it was about half past seven—if in fact it was keeping accurate time. My eyes lingered a moment on the pale, soft skin of her wrist.

Smoothing my hair and clearing my throat, I walked over and opened the door a crack. A maid stood outside with a tray. I hesitated, but quickly realized there was no point—she had been here before and would know very well this was the room my companion had taken. I held my finger to my lips and pushed the door open. She came in and quietly set down the tray, which contained a teapot and cup.

"Will you be wanting a fire, sir?" she asked in a low voice, crossing to the window and closing the casement. The room was cold.

"Please."

She stirred the ashes searching for live coals, and I asked, "Do you know the hour?"

"It's about half past seven, sir." That was settled, then.

"And the festivities below, what time do they begin?"

Having coaxed a few flames from fresh kindling and tossed in a few logs, she straightened and replied, "The feast is at eight, sir."

Only half an hour.

"Shall I bring your tray in here, sir?"

I glanced at the maid, but her countenance registered no judgment. Then I looked at Neve, who appeared to still be sleeping soundly. Remembering the warm press of her body, I experienced a strong urge to return. Could I do it without waking her?

I shook my head at both myself and the maid. "I'm going back to my room."

When the maid was gone, I returned to the bed and sat carefully on the edge. Neve's eyes fluttered open. "I'm awake. I waited, in case it might be awkward."

I smiled. "Was it good to sleep?"

She stretched her arms above her head, reminding me again of a cat, and then she sat up. Suddenly we were inches apart, and before I could overcome the impulse, my eyes moved to her mouth. Her lips parted—and my breath stopped.

"Yes," she answered softly. I could no longer remember the question.

I leaned toward her—I couldn't help it. She leaned too, and then I felt her lips against mine.

It was like falling into the Gap, except I wasn't afraid, or disoriented, or dizzy. The silk of her mouth and the spring-green smell of her overwhelmed my senses. Despite the cool tones of these sensations, my body was *burning*—a tree struck by lightning in the midst of a spring shower.

The kiss was soft and sweet, but at the close of it she began again, her hands coming to the sides of my face, fingers slipping into my beard and hair.

Her lips parted and our tongues met—my blood roared like an ocean in my ears. No one had ever touched me like this.

I reached tentatively for her waist, and then I found myself gripping, pulling her close.

Suddenly she froze.

"Forgive me," I said, letting go of her and straightening.

"Don't you dare apologize," she said, dismayed and a little breathless. "That was all me, and after what I said earlier . . . *I'm* the one who's sorry. It suddenly felt like the right thing to do, and I just . . ."

My senses still reeling, I took her hands in mine. Her fingers were trembling. Our eyes met and I said, "I *know.*"

She managed a thin smile, and looked relieved.

By sheer force of will, I released her and stood up.

"The maid brought you tea," I said. "I'll go next door and fetch my jacket, and I'll give you a few minutes to refresh yourself before we go down to the others."

"Okay." Did she look hurt? Had I done the wrong thing?

But the moment had passed. She rose from the bed, and I started for the door.

"Did you see the ghost?" she called after me.

"If she came, we slept through it. Maybe she'll return before the night is out."

Back in my chamber, I drank two cups of hot, black tea and tried to put out of my head what had happened.

It was hopeless.

It suddenly felt like the right thing to do. I had to agree—except I'd been wanting to do it for some time.

My life thus far had not really left room for romantic

attachments. I had always been traveling, spending much of my time in the company of one powerful patroness or another—Captain Grace O'Malley, Queen Isolde, Queen Koli. When I did finally settle into a life of writing and study, I found it suited me. Despite my many adventures, I was naturally reserved and always felt most comfortable in my own company. Indeed, I had more than once been chided for being "passionless" by women whose attention I might have sought, had I felt more sure of myself.

There had been a woman once, *almost*—an aspiring actress called Maud. A beautiful Englishwoman, somewhat wild and with a violent temper, who had also for a short time studied at Dublin's Metropolitan School of Art. There had certainly been a spark between us, though she longed for someone to plunge into danger with. By that time I'd had my fill of adventures, and my desire to quietly retire in Connacht held no appeal for her. If she could but see me now, she'd no doubt have a good laugh over what had become of my plans.

Once, on the cliffs of Howth above Dublin Bay, I had kissed her. It had been poetic in the extreme, with the murmuring of the waves on the rocks below, and the summer sunlight causing the Irish Sea to sparkle like diamonds. I had thought of it many times in the years since, wondering whether I'd lost my only chance at love through poor timing. I couldn't help comparing it to the kiss of five minutes ago. Maud was the most combustible woman I'd ever known—and that was saying something—yet it had been Neve's kiss that lit a fire in me.

I wet my fingers in the basin and ran them a few times through my hair. Then I put on my waistcoat and jacket, and I went to retrieve my companion.

Her eyes and complexion had been brightened by rest, but she avoided looking at me, and I guessed that she, too, was still thinking about the kiss—though perhaps not in the same way I was.

"What will this be like?" she asked as we started downstairs.

"There'll be a feast in the great hall, attended by the royal family and dignitaries from Faery. A bonfire in the courtyard after that. Everyone will drink too much and the fairies will make mischief."

She laughed, and it cracked the thin sheet of ice that had formed between us. "That doesn't sound too different from Halloween parties back home. Will there be costumes?"

"It's not a masquerade, if that's what you mean, though many will wear masks or paint their faces—it's thought to be protection from the dead. The king and queen will likely wear costumes from an earlier century, as Finvara's ancestor would have. It's not a formal occasion, however."

"So I should be okay in this?"

I glanced at her dress, noting the relative thinness of the fabric, and the way it showed the true shape of her body, unlike current-day women's fashions. The color brought out the green in her eyes. She was lovely.

"You shall."

What she said next came in a more somber tone. "I want to apologize again for what happened earlier. I know I must be really confusing you."

I wasn't confused, but I waited to hear what else she'd say.

"You probably get by now that I'm attracted to you, and part of me thinks we should just sleep together and get it over with—I mean, what with the whole 'fate' thing hanging over us. I don't imagine that's something you do here, and besides that, it wouldn't work—it never does."

This utterance almost caused me to lose my footing on the stairs. Glancing at her, I gathered from her wincing grimace that she'd said more than she intended.

"I'll shut up now."

We reached one of the side entrances to the great hall and could see attendees milling about inside. I stopped and looked at her. "There's no need to apologize—I could have prevented what happened if I'd wanted to, so I have my own share of the blame. And I don't want you to feel you have to always be censoring yourself." I touched her arm. "Don't worry so much about shocking me."

She laughed. "I'm not sure that I *have*. Lucky for me you're amazingly tolerant."

I'd said what I did in hopes of easing her discomfort, though in truth I was still stuck on what she'd suggested. It was clear from context that she didn't mean "sleep together" in the sense of what we had just done—actual sleeping. It was also clear that in her timeline, such behavior was not condoned only within the confines of marriage. If I'd put it all together correctly, she was suggesting that through physical relations we might satisfy our carnal urges and thereby get beyond them—which, inexperienced though I might be, seemed highly unlikely.

Before I could answer her, Queen Koli came to usher us inside.

We followed her into the great hall, which was lit by the fire in the enormous hearth at one end of the room, and a multitude of bobbing, glowing globes. The hall was decorated with tree branches and leaves and looked like a forest indoors. Faces had been carved into the hollowed trunks of dead trees, and from the branches hung lanterns made of carved turnips, many of them quite cleverly executed and a few that were truly frightening. Pale blue lights that I knew were fairies floated and blinked among the branches, and the animal familiars of Knock Ma's queen were also present—ravens perched here and there, vocalizing in low, gurgling tones.

"This is amazing!" said Neve, taking it all in with wide eyes.

"The feast days are important to our subjects," said Queen Koli. "A great deal of planning and effort go into them."

At the long table—which was draped in red and gold cloths and adorned with antlers, animal skulls, and baskets of fall fruit and nuts—guests stood behind their chairs or benches waiting for the royal family to take their places. Koli led us toward her husband, who stood at the table's head. I was surprised to see Isolde standing to his left, but when I looked to the other end, near the entrance to the hall, I saw the proud chief of the firglas. *Diplomacy.* This was a fairy fete. Queen Isolde was only a guest.

Still, no one made a move to sit down until the Irish queen had taken her chair. Then Finvara and Koli sat, and the rest of us followed. We took seats on Koli's right side, and Lord and Lady Meath were across from us. The whole party had changed their dress and looked like medieval lords and ladies.

"Before I forget," said Koli, picking up a leather satchel that was lying on the table in front of her, "this is for your spellbook." She motioned for a servant and asked that the bag be delivered to Neve's room. "I think you should always keep it with you."

"Thank you, Your Majesty," said Neve, "I will."

Footmen began moving around the table, pouring green liquid into small cordial glasses—absinthe. When all of the guests had their drinks, the king stood up and raised his glass.

"To the dead. Those who've gone to rest and those who still wander. Be welcome. Be at peace. Accept our offerings."

He sipped the absinthe and then turned and cast the remainder into the fire. The flames leapt and danced, burning bright green instead of orange. A ship formed of green smoke lurched from the hearth, and the guests gave cries of surprise and delight. I recognized it as the *Sea Queen of Connacht*, Captain O'Malley's Gap galleon. She was an ancestor of Finvara, Lord Meath, and Isolde. The captain herself stood proudly at the prow, and the ship sailed the length of the table before it passed through the closed entrance doors.

"To the dead!" cried guests up and down the table, raising their glasses and drinking.

"To the dead," I said, smiling at my bewildered companion and clinking my glass against hers.

NEVE

"Was it magic, or really a ghost?" I asked him.

"I'm not sure there's much difference. But magic, if I must choose."

I tossed back the green shot.

Thank goodness our earlier awkwardness had ebbed—because it had been awful. Especially in contrast to how easy everything had felt between us before. I hoped I hadn't screwed everything up by kissing him—*right* after letting him know how I felt about us getting involved.

One useful thing had come out of it, I supposed—I now had confirmation that giving in to urges with him was not going to make me want to do it *less*.

Servants were again moving around the table, filling wine glasses and removing the smaller ones we'd used for the toast. Others brought out shallow, steaming bowls. One was placed before me and I breathed in the aroma of mushrooms, cream, and herbs. In the center floated what looked like crushed hazelnuts. There was probably at least one four-star restaurant in Portland serving this very thing right now.

Musicians started playing from a raised area near the main entrance to the hall, and like everything else in the room, the music had a charming creepiness to it. Like something you'd hear at a carnival of the dead.

The room seemed to relax then, spoons clinking bowls and people chatting. I ate my soup, which was rich and delicious, while I tried to subtly check out the party guests. At least half of them were the tall, fierce fairies that were so common around here. Will told me they were closely allied to the fairy king. There were shorter, stouter creatures that made me think of Tolkien's dwarves, but Will said they were leprechauns. They were neither wearing green nor smoking pipes—in fact they looked kind of rough and wild with their battered leather tool aprons and soot-smeared eyes. They were also draining ale tankards at an impressive rate.

Then I noticed some ghoulish fellows with knobby features and eyes so bright and bulbous I couldn't look at them for long.

"What are *they*?" I asked Will. "The guys with the red beanies."

"Redcaps," he said, sipping from his wine glass. "Notorious for serving their own interests. Not to be trusted around corpses."

I stared at him. "Why are they *here*?"

"They're fairies, and subjects of King Finvara. Everyone at this table is. Fairies have a long and complicated history. They're as Irish as any human here, yet relations between fairies and mortals have not always been easy."

This only sort of answered my question, but at that moment a servant bent between us, removing our bowls. My gaze shifted to the decorative forest on the other side of the table, and something caught my eye—a ghostly figure was moving among the trees.

"*Will*," I whispered.

I thought that my ghost might have returned. Then Lady Meath, seated opposite us, also turned to look. "That's a banshee, Miss Kelly," she said. "You'll likely see many of them as the evening progresses."

"There are *banshees*?"

Lady Meath laughed. "I know exactly how you feel. When I first came to Ireland from London, I had studied many fairy creatures. Yet the reality came as quite a shock."

"If you go back more than a decade or so," added Lord Meath, "probably the only one of us who'd ever actually *seen* a fairy was Will here."

"I can't tell you how much better that makes me feel," I said, laughing. "You all seem so unaffected."

I continued to watch the banshee—she was a young woman with trailing, threadbare garments and dark flowing hair. She walked on bare feet from trunk to trunk, keeping an eye on the festivities. She wasn't scary at all.

Or maybe I'm starting to get used to all this.

"William," said Queen Isolde. She was seated across from Koli. "Have you learned anything more of Borabu?"

The queen, on the other hand, was still terrifying—especially in her blood-colored gown and party headdress, which was made of red-orange leaves and bird skulls. The big skull right in the center might have once belonged to an owl. Its hooked beak had a blood-red tip.

"We have," said Will. "This afternoon Miss Kelly was visited by a ghostly lady bearing a horn, which I believe was Borabu."

The queen's gaze brightened and shifted to me. I tried not to stare at the owl's big, hollow eyes.

"And did you speak to this ghost?" asked the queen.

Actually I freaked out and ran. "Not yet, Your Majesty," I replied. "We're hoping she'll come back."

The queen pursed her lips. She looked at Finvara. "When your guests have drunk enough not to notice, let us retire and—"

There was a loud bang, like something heavy had hit the front door. The banshee popped out of the forest and let out an ear-piercing yowl—eyes wild and hair rippling, she was sure as hell scary *now*.

Suddenly both entrance doors flew open, and mist swirled into the room.

I thought this might be part of the scheduled fun, until the king jumped up from the table and shouted a command. Will, Lord Meath, and a number of the other party guests also quickly stood. Half a dozen guards poured through each side entrance, wielding long spears.

Gasps erupted as a figure stepped into the hall.

"*A athair?*" Finvara cried. He looked stricken.

"*A mhac!*" the visitor bellowed back. He wore a ratty military jacket and wielded a wicked-looking sword. He was only semihuman—bearded, tall and burly, with parts of his body replaced by metal bits and machinery.

"The old earl," Will said, alarmed. "The king's father. He died two years ago."

"This is no ghost," Finvara hissed. "What's happened to him?"

"The Morrigan," I said, rising with the others. "That's what Far Dorocha looks like now."

"She's right," agreed Will. "He's a revenant."

Something was shouted in Irish, and we glanced back in time to see the earl swing his sword and strike down two of the guards who'd challenged him at the entrance. There had been an important-looking firglas man seated at the opposite end of the table—he'd stood and drawn a knife when the doors burst open, but the earl now shoved him aside and climbed onto the table. Guests scattered like frightened birds.

The earl shouted something else to his son, and Will translated for me: "My flesh is not mine to command. Send me back to your mother."

"Do it, cousin," Isolde muttered urgently.

"Kill my *father*?" Finvara's eyes were wild and angry.

The earl was striding the length of the table toward the royal family, crushing plates and glasses with every step. The guards clambered after him—they were no match for that massive sword.

The crows had been startled off their perches and were screaming wildly, circling and dive-bombing the earl. Spears flew—one missed its mark, one rebounded off a metal body part, and one lodged in his arm, but he yanked it out and kept going. The wound didn't bleed.

"It will be a mercy, husband," said Koli, gripping the king's arm.

Finvara looked sick—he nodded. A guard with a crossbow had jumped onto the table to protect the king. Finvara pulled him down, grabbing the crossbow and taking his place. He quickly loaded and fired—the arrow struck the breastplate and bounced off. Koli grabbed more arrows from the guard and handed them up.

The king shouted another order as he reloaded, his eyes furious and wet with tears. The revenant was close now and Will scooped an arm around my waist, pulling me back from the table. The next arrow pierced the earl's neck, and another quickly followed. One of the guards managed to hit the revenant's sword hand and his weapon dropped, banging onto the table.

Instead of falling, the undead thing began to *run.* Koli drew her husband out of the earl's path, and he kept on straight ahead, jumping from the table, and charging right into the fireplace. The flames swelled outward, and the king's father shouted something back at us.

Horrified, I looked at Will. He translated: "She is coming."

King Finvara made an anguished noise and moved toward the flames. His queen went with him, holding his arm to steady him.

Queen Isolde turned to address the room—the scattered and shocked guests of all shapes and sizes. "Everyone out to the courtyard." Her tone was more measured than angry. "Give your king time to grieve."

Lord and Lady Meath had come around the head of the table and joined us, their expressions grim.

Will said, "Forgive me for asking, Lord Meath, but do you know what was done with your uncle's remains?"

The gentleman rubbed his brow. "He was buried with our ancestors on Clare Island."

Queen Isolde turned, her expression pure fury. "The Morrigan is defiling the dead."

OTHER PURSUITS

NEVE

Will and I and the royals left the great hall to regroup in the smaller one where we'd met earlier. Servants and soldiers came and went as Queen Isolde and King Finvara issued orders to prepare for a siege—watches were doubled, extra patrols were ordered, and more riders were sent with messages for the queen's generals.

Queen Koli called for wine, whiskey, and plates filled with food from the abandoned feast. She made her husband sit down beside her and eat, but most of the rest of us ate standing up. The mood was heavy.

After the dispirited meal, Will and I stood on the sidelines feeling useless, watching Isolde sip from a goblet and pace. At last, she stopped to address us.

"You are a true patriot, William," she said. Her tone was earnest and softer than usual. It took the edge off the effect of the costume. "You have never shirked from serving the peoples of

Ireland, and you've earned the quiet life you've chosen. But we are going to *need* Oisin and Niamh. We may not be able to defeat the Morrigan, but with the Fianna, we at least stand a chance."

"I understand, Your Majesty," he said.

"Good," she replied with a nod. "Now go and find that ghost."

We said goodnight to the others and started back up to our rooms.

"So they're counting on us," I said as we climbed the stairs.

"It's terrifying, isn't it?"

I gave a thin laugh. "It totally is."

We reached my room, and I folded my arms and turned to Will. "I'm not spending another five minutes alone in this castle. Your place or mine?"

"We should stay here," he said. "The ghost may return."

He followed me inside, and I wondered if he'd close the door behind him.

Click.

Fireworks went off in my abdomen.

I walked to the window and opened the casement, leaning out. Servants were piling up wood for the bonfire in the courtyard below.

Will joined me. He'd taken off his jacket, and our arms rested lightly against each other on the sill. It was hard to pay attention to anything else.

Try harder.

"They're going on with the party?" I asked.

He nodded. "I doubt the king and queen would consider canceling the bonfire, even now. It's the oldest part of the celebration and will appease both the fairies and the dead. All the fires in the castle will be put out tonight, and the servants will use the carved lanterns to carry coals from the bonfire to relight them. It's considered ill luck not to do it."

"God knows we don't need more of that." I stared down at his interwoven fingers, wondering if I'd ever noticed anyone having sexy hands before. "Irish immigrants started all this in America too," I said, forcing my eyes back out to the courtyard. "We carve pumpkins though. Actually pretty much everything but the pumpkins and the parties has been forgotten."

"The old festivals have faded here as well, and Christian holidays have taken their place. The opening of Faery has rolled back the clock in many ways."

This caused me to glance down at my tattoo. A few minutes after eleven.

"Are you keeping good time?" I looked up and caught the glint in his eye.

Laughing, I whacked his shoulder with the back of my hand. "I'm starting to rub off on you, and not in a good way." Touching the clock face, I said, "I feel more like it's keeping *me*."

"*That* I can relate to."

We continued to watch the preparations until I worked up the nerve to ask, "Did you know King Finvara's father?"

He turned so his back was against the sill. Our bodies were still close and he was looking down at me. It sent a current of warmth through my belly.

"Only a little," he said. "Lord Mayo fought at both Ben Bulben and Knock Ma. He was stern, but a good man. What the Morrigan did to him . . ." Will folded his arms, like he'd felt a chill. "It's unspeakable."

"I kinda got the sense he'd gone rogue though, didn't you?"

Will lifted his brows.

"He said the Morrigan was controlling him, but he did warn the king."

Will chewed on this a second and nodded. "He also managed to destroy himself in the end."

He left the window to stand in front of the fire. With him gone it felt like the temperature had dropped five degrees, so I went to join him.

"Most of Ireland's dead are buried," said Will. "In churchyards all over this country. After battles, however, there have always been funeral fires—some fairies are particularly drawn to fields of battle and are not always respectful of the dead."

"Redcaps."

"Yes, among others. But it would never have occurred to anyone that we'd need to protect the dead from the Morrigan. The life cycle is sacred to her, fallen warriors in particular."

I frowned. "Apparently, she's not herself."

"Unless that can somehow be righted, things are going to get much worse."

I walked to the bed and picked up my spellbook, sliding it inside the new bag. It fit pretty well, and there was some extra room for any other small items I might want to carry.

"Why don't you tell me again about the ghostly lady and the horn," said Will. "Maybe there's some detail we've missed."

"I should draw it," I said, pulling the book back out of the bag. "I'm better at that than—" *Of course.* "Find me a pencil, Will."

Noting the change in my tone, he walked to the writing desk next to the window and went through the drawers. When that failed, he said, "Finvara's study is down the corridor. I'll be right back."

I hung the bag on the chair at the writing desk and laid my book down, opening to a blank page. I ran my hand over the paper, though it needed no smoothing. As I pictured the horn in my mind, my fingers fidgeted.

Will came back in and joined me at the desk with a pencil. I started sketching immediately, afraid of losing the image.

Could this work again? *It has to. We'll make it work.*

After completing the basic outline, adding the few details I remembered, and applying some shading, I stopped to evaluate my work.

"I think that's the best I can do from memory."

"I doubt it matters whether it's exact," he said encouragingly. "It's just to fix your intention."

I looked up at him. "Do you have a knife?"

His brow clouded—he knew why I was asking.

"Hey," I said, "I'm not thrilled about it myself."

He rubbed at his jaw, thinking. "Blood is the most powerful substance that can be used in a spell, and both of us are less than novices when it comes to this type of magic. I can't help feeling like we're playing with your life, Neve."

He was probably afraid of some dark-magic disaster, and I was worried about more practical things—like lack of antibiotic ointment and when my last tetanus shot was.

"I get it," I replied. "I don't know that we have a choice though."

Slipping his hands in his pockets, he walked slowly to the bed, then turned and walked back. He did it a couple more times. He was worried about me. Like a *lot.* It wasn't the first time, but that didn't make it any less hot.

Finally he stopped and said, "I've seen dozens of grimoires in the Faery library. They're primarily recipe books for spells." He looked at my spellbook, still open on the desk. "This feels more like a magical object. You've already given it blood. Absinthe. Symbolic charms. Your artistry. Perhaps now you only need *use* it."

I followed his gaze. I had to agree that in a way the book had come to feel like a living thing. I thought about the objects I had incorporated in the binding—the watch Mrs. Marsh had given me, and the knight figure—and how they felt connected to the story that was unfolding.

The story of us. Why did just *thinking* these words make my insides feel like gelatin?

Especially when there can be no story of us.

Sighing, I replied, "You could be right. It would be great if you are. But I don't know what else to do, and they're all waiting on us to figure this out."

He nodded, but he stood looking out the window. "There *was* something else you did in the Morrigan's lair that may have affected your spell."

His eyes came back to me and suddenly I knew exactly what he was talking about—the fake kiss. Or the kiss that was supposed to be fake and instead made everything messy.

"At its simplest," he continued, "magic is about imagining what you want and performing a ritual to help things along—something that causes the unseen forces of nature to sense a change and pay attention. It might be chanting or singing. It might be burning something, washing it, or burying it in the ground. Walking backward for a mile."

"Or kissing someone," I finally managed to say. Sex magic? Wasn't that a thing? *Oh my god, stop.*

Will's gaze had gone a little smoky, and a silken ribbon of lust tickled its way down my belly.

"I think it's possible," he said. "It doesn't mean it's the only way. But maybe we need to look at our other options before we continue deliberately causing you injury."

He'd said this last part for my benefit, out of respect for my reservations about anything beyond friendly partnership between us. The problem was that the kissing thing kind of made sense.

He was watching me intently, and I reached for a release valve. Gazing down at my fresh drawing, I ran a finger lightly over its lines. *Breathe in, breathe out.*

"I don't know for sure what will happen if this works," I said, looking up. "Hopefully the horn will just appear, but it's a total crapshoot."

"I know."

Of course he did. I was stalling.

I closed the book and stuck it back in the bag along with the pencil. Rising from the desk, I settled its strap across my chest. My spell might end up flinging us out of the castle, and I couldn't risk leaving the book behind.

I took a couple of steps toward him.

His brow furrowed. "You're sure about this?"

I couldn't help laughing. "It's not like torture, Will. That's why we picked it, remember?"

He smiled. "Right you are."

I reached up and rested my hands on his biceps, curling a thumb around the hard edge of the muscle. I remembered what he'd felt like next to me in the bed—warm through his shirt, and strong in a long-limbed, wiry way.

"So." I took a deep breath and raised an eyebrow. "I'm guessing this won't work if it's like kissing your sister."

There was that smoky look again. "I don't think it's going to be."

My knees suddenly forgot what they were supposed to be doing. I think he noticed, because his hands came to my waist.

He bent his head and caught my lips with his. There was no longer any tentativeness—our mouths had done this before. His body knew how to fit against mine. His lips parted, and when his tongue touched mine I heard a soft whimpering sound—then realized it had come out of *me*. I was losing myself to sensation—to the chemical reaction that sparked when we touched, and clearly wouldn't be finished until my whole body was on fire.

WILL

Maybe I should have been focusing on the spell, but I wasn't equal to it. I smoothed my hands over her back, pulling her close, feeling her body against mine. The small sound she made sent waves of heat rolling through me. Images crowded together in my thoughts—bare limbs and bellies, flesh against luminous flesh, like a memory of something I'd never actually experienced.

I felt a light motion at the base of my throat and opened my eyes. She had unfastened the top button of my shirt. My breath stopped. I took her face between my hands, searching her eyes.

"Talk to me."

With an embarrassed smile, she said, "Obviously the kissing is not doing what we hoped, and we can go back to the blood thing, but I thought first . . . maybe wizarding school can wait a few minutes."

"I . . . what?" Likely I'd misunderstood her. "Have you changed your mind about . . . ?"

"About the whole 'just sleep together and get it over with,' thing? Yeah. Because I want to do so much more than kiss you, and it's starting to be all I can think about."

I swallowed thickly. My heart was making a thunderous racket.

"But only if you want to," she added.

"You've seemed reluctant to—"

"I still am. But what if we end up dead, like *they* did? Am I going to be proud of myself for doing the sensible thing instead of the thing I really want? I mean I don't want to fall in love with you, and I don't want you to fall in love with me." She groaned. "I know I'm being impossible, and I hate myself for—"

"*Neve.*" I laid my palm against her cheek. "Yes. Whatever you want."

She rolled her eyes. "I'm not asking for gentlemanly pity. If you don't—"

"I assure you I *do*. I'm trying to respect your wishes, but—"

She laughed. "They're a moving target."

"Indeed. Though that's not all."

She waited.

Just tell her.

"I've never done this before. It might not be all you're expecting."

Her eyes went wide. "*What?*"

Heat crept down my face and neck. "Please don't make me say that again."

She shook her head. "No, I heard you. That was totally none of my business—I'm sorry I made you feel like you had to say it. It never occurred to me . . ." Again she shook her head. "I know most women in your time don't just go out and have sex—physical intimacy—with whoever, but I thought men pretty much always did what they wanted."

"You're not wrong . . . I wouldn't say *all* men though." I looked over her shoulder, as if I might find a hole to crawl in on the other side of the room. "I have often been preoccupied with other pursuits."

Her gaze felt heavy, and it drew my eyes back to her face.

"Will, you can say if you don't like women. Or sex. Or blondes. It won't hurt my feelings."

Laughing, I said, "I like women. I simply haven't had many opportunities."

She eyed me skeptically. "I don't believe that. You're sweet, and smart, and, you know, easy on the eyes."

She was still standing close, and I placed my hands on her waist. She rested her hands lightly against my chest.

"There must have been at least one you liked."

"One, yes."

"I knew it." Her hand came to my face, thumb lightly tracing along my chin. Her caresses seemed to have a direct connection to the lower region of my belly. "What was she like?"

"Beautiful. Rather a handful."

"Ah-ha, you have a type!"

I laughed again. "Perhaps I do."

"What happened?"

"We had seemed to have many things in common, but over time I worried she was more drawn to my experiences than myself. She was strangely preoccupied with violent conflict, whereas I held out hope Ireland had seen the last of that."

"Well, I approve of you rejecting her. A war fetish seems like a total red flag."

"We rejected each other," I corrected.

Her smile faded, and she rested her cheek against my chest. So many feelings and instincts flooded me in that moment—they were too complicated for even a poet to untangle. At the same time, nothing else in my life had ever made so much sense.

I lifted my hands from her waist and wrapped my arms around her. I resisted an urge to press my lips to the top of her head. Her words came back to me: *I don't want you to fall in love with me.*

"Your story made me realize something about someone back home," she said.

I felt a prick of envy. "Tell me."

"I had a roommate for a few years—a man, I know you don't do that in your time. We were close friends, and he was always taking care of me. So much that it became very one-sided. Recently he decided he wanted to be more than friends."

"And you rejected him?"

"I did. And it hurt him a lot."

I let one of my hands rub her back lightly. "I can imagine."

"I've been beating myself up about it since it happened. Superficially, it was a relationship that made sense, like yours with—what's her name?"

"Maud."

"Maud. On a certain level I love Noah, and I love being around him. But I realize now that my rejection of him was for a real reason. I didn't want to fall into a honeytrap of never having to deal with my own shit."

This last declaration should probably have been baffling, but I understood her despite the odd metaphors. She didn't want to be with someone who would make it unnecessary for her to find her own strength.

She lifted her head from my chest. "Do me a favor, Will."

"Anything."

"Forget that stuff I said earlier. Let's get back to work."

My heart, which had bubbled up to a dizzying height over the last quarter hour, now sank like a stone. "May I ask why?"

"I can't be your first. Your first is special."

To me this sounded more like an argument *in favor.*

"And I still feel like it's best if we don't," she continued. "We could get really hurt. I just had a moment of weakness."

Her reservations were valid. We didn't know how much time we would have together. We were from different worlds, and we were plunging into danger. In spite of all that—or maybe because of it—something shifted in me then. It struck me that I strongly disagreed with her reasoning, though the fact that I was a gentleman had caused me to go along with her as she rode the waves of uncertainty. If I wasn't careful, I'd end up exactly like her friend. Someone who believed it was his responsibility to take care of her—to make her feel better, while never expressing his own needs or desires. At some point we'd both end up resenting it.

I reached up and held her face in my hands. "You are a beautiful, unusual woman, and I respect any decision you make on your own behalf. But I'll thank you to let *me* be the one to decide what's best for me."

The sudden change in her face was gratifying. Her mouth fell slightly open and she nodded.

Her eyes flickered down to my lips, and I took that as

permission to tilt her head back and kiss her. I let it be slow at first—tender and tentative—ready to let go if she stiffened or tried to pull away. She didn't. Her arms slipped around my waist, and she pulled me close. I let go of my restraint, parting her lips with my tongue.

Then the floor beneath us literally dropped away.

BELOW

NEVE

As my feet met the ground, I stumbled to my hands and knees onto flagstones. There had been no throat-tunnel, but wherever this was, it felt uncomfortably like the *last* place. *Damp. Dark. Stones.*

Will rose to his feet beside me and then reached out to help me up. His arm came around me as we caught our breath and reoriented.

"Was that you or me?" I asked.

"We haven't time traveled, if that's what you're asking. At least I don't think so."

"No ticking?"

"Right."

Just kissing.

I dragged my eyes away from his lips and looked around. We were definitely in a cavern—on closer inspection, it was very different from before. Tendrils of wood wound down from the ceiling like stalactites—*tree roots,* I realized. The flagstones beneath us were old—vivid moss covered many of them and some were crumbling—like they belonged to a ruin. I could hear the cheerful tones of running water, maybe a nearby spring or fountain. Globes of silvery light, like the ones in the banquet hall at Knock Ma, floated in the air around us.

The place had a strange, caffeine-buzz kind of energy.

It feels extra alive.

"Do you think we're back in Faery?" I asked.

"It feels different, but I'm not sure." He stared up the length of a twisting root that reached all the way from ceiling to floor. "The trees here are . . . noisy."

I supposed he meant in his head, because I couldn't hear anything except the water. "What are they saying?"

He closed his eyes. "There's so much it's hard to make out, but I'm fairly sure they're talking about *us.*"

I stared up into the root canopy. There were things moving around up there—I glimpsed a four-inch centipede and couple of big blue moths. The tongue of some animal I couldn't quite see flicked out and caught one of the moths in midflight.

"Well," I said, "if you didn't bring us here, *I* must have, right? Maybe the horn is here."

"Agreed. I'm going to try to ask them."

So the spell had eventually worked. I considered it a miracle, since all I'd been able to think about once our lips touched again was getting his clothes off. That great idea I'd had about using sex to exorcise what I was starting to feel for him? Pretty close to my most deluded ever.

Will looked at me. "You've done it. The trees say it's here."

"Thank god. Did they say where?"

"Something here has it"—he shook his head—"but I can't make out what."

My skin prickled. *Something?*

"Something very old, and possibly dangerous. A guardian of some kind."

I sighed. "I guess we'd better go look for it." *Because that's how we roll.*

"We'll stay close." He held out his hand. I grasped it, and the warmth of his skin revived that fizzy feeling in my stomach. It was nicer to focus on than subterranean monsters.

After a few minutes we reached a stream, shallow and clear and lined with smooth stones. I could see long, dark shadows in the water that I thought might be fish. Cattails and tall grasses grew along the streambank, and hidden frogs made music.

The cavern was no brighter than a night with a full moon, yet so many things were awake and alive—it felt *off.*

We followed the stream until we came to an open area—a meadow of waist-high grass, seed fronds silvery in the magical white light. Across the meadow we could see a knot of larger, thicker tree roots. Water cascaded out of the roots over a big pile of rocks. At the base of the waterfall was a pool, and at its center sat an island housing some kind of gleaming, light-colored structure.

As we moved closer, I saw the island was more like a platform. And it was made entirely of *bones*. There must have been thousands of skulls, both animal and human. It reminded me of photos I'd seen of the famous bone church in the Czech Republic.

"Will?" I whispered.

We exchanged a tense look and he squeezed my hand.

We approached slowly, and soon I saw someone—some creature—standing on the platform. It had an animal skull for a head, as well as a set of enormous antlers. Except they looked more like gnarled tree branches that had been stripped of bark to reveal a deep red color. The creature's torso was broad, hard, and chiseled like a bodybuilder's—the richly brown skin looked very much alive. Below the waist thick tree roots stood in place of legs.

Hopefully, that means it can't run after us.

"Look," whispered Will.

As soon as he spoke, I saw it—the horn from my ghost visitor was hanging from a strap slung over the tree creature's shoulder.

"The trees tell me you have come for Borabu." The voice was half grating, half growling, like a rudely woken grizzly bear.

"We have," said Will, moving closer. "We would not disturb you if we didn't have urgent need of it. Forgive me, but may we know whom we're addressing?"

"You *should* know me, warrior poet. It was I who gave you the horn, before the Battle of Connacht."

Who had Lady Meath said gave the horn to Oisin? Some god?

"It was a very long time ago," replied Will, "and there is much I have forgotten."

The creature made a disapproving noise. "Then I will tell you—I am Uindos. Son of Dana. Lord of forests, and the creatures that fill them."

"Uindos," repeated Will. "The Horned God. And did you reclaim Borabu after the battle?"

"When your brothers and enemies had finished spilling each other's blood, along with the blood of nearly every living creature I sent to aid you, I did reclaim it. You said the battle was necessary to protect Ireland from ruthless enemies, and that it would be the last. But the ancient trees of Knock Ma have told me that your war-making continues. How do you account for yourself, son of Finn?"

Oh boy.

Will hesitated. "In the Battle of Knock Ma, my lord," he began carefully, "Ireland was attacked by foes from across the sea. Had the trees not aided us, we might all now be under the dominion of Iceland's shadow elves."

"Only those who walk on two legs concern themselves with such things. Your greed and hunger for power bring destruction and death to all. I have no dominion over war, but I will never again take part in it. I will not give you Borabu."

The god's head adjusted slightly—he was looking at *me* now.

"You are welcome here, daughter of Faery. The age of immortals passed long ago. I thought you had faded to the Land of Promise."

I swallowed. "I'm told that I've been reborn, my lord. I have few memories of my former life."

"Borabu was created at your request, so that Oisin might call both his army and mine to battle, yet even you will not persuade me to return it."

"Will . . . *Oisin* and I hate war as much as anyone. We wouldn't ask you to get involved, but the Morrigan has been raising warriors from the dead so she can take over Ireland, and—"

"The Morrigan!" The ground shook and I fell back a step. "What you say is not possible."

"I wish it weren't," said Will. "We have *seen* it. The Earl of Mayo was raised from the grave. Last night he attacked King Finvara at Knock Ma—his own son, my lord."

The god made a deep rumbling sound. "We have our differences, my sister and I, but it is not in her nature to do such a thing."

Sister?!

"Death is as sacred to her as life is to *me*."

"Something has changed her," said Will. "We believe she may be under the influence of a powerful druid. A sorcerer."

The god's fists balled, and every muscle in his amazing torso bulged. I braced for impact.

"*Far Dorocha*." I don't think he could have possibly packed any more disgust into those two words.

"Indeed," said Will.

"I warned her of him. He should have been destroyed many centuries ago. There is nothing more dangerous than a creature desperate to become a god."

Apparently, the Horned God's aversion to violence wasn't entirely consistent.

He raised a hand, palm side up, and made gurgling, clicking noise. A bird dropped down from the living rafters to perch in his big hand—a crow, satiny feathers gleaming in the faux moonlight. The two of them seemed to have a conversation, and after a moment the bird flew up into the roots of the waterfall and disappeared.

"How have you learned of this plot, Danaan warrior?"

"From the goddess herself," said Will. "Far Dorocha brought us before her. She intended to make revenants of us. Then we were to enlist the Fianna to fight for her."

"And so you have come to me for Borabu. What proof can you offer that it's not *you* who have corrupt intention?"

Will and I exchanged a look of dismay. Proof? We couldn't prove *anything.*

Then Will said, "Ask the trees."

The god's head pivoted a fraction, and he seemed to eye the ceiling of the cavern. "The trees are always truthful. What will I learn from them?"

"I have no way of proving my own intentions, but if you ask about the wood around the Morrigan's lair, my lord, you will know that we've spoken the truth about *her* corruption."

Uindos folded his beefy arms slowly, and then went still. Will and I shared another anxious glance.

"*It is as you have told me.*" I jumped when the god finally spoke, and again the ground rumbled. "The trees have been destroyed and defiled."

Brilliant, Will.

Then we heard a loud caw, and the crow dropped back down out of the roots. Uindos held out his hand, and the bird landed there again, ruffling droplets out of its feathers before letting out a stream of gurgles and squawks. When it stopped making noise, the god gently tossed it into the air and it flew off into the shadows.

"You're too late, Fianna warrior."

"Too late? How so, my lord?

"Knock Ma has been taken."

I gasped and looked at Will.

"How is that possible?" he asked.

"Will," I said, "is this weird Faery time again?" I looked down at my wrist—the clock hands were *missing*.

"Are we in Faery, my lord?" Will asked.

"The hall of the Horned God is Below. *I* order time here. Crow has been two days in his journey Above."

We lost two days waiting on *proof*.

"Will you please help us?" I said. *Since this is basically your fault.*

For what felt like hours, Uindos did nothing but stare out of those empty, hollowed out eyes. I thought about the people we'd left back at the castle and felt a hard ache in my throat. We'd failed them. We'd *abandoned* them, even if it hadn't been on purpose.

The god then extended an arm to one side. My breath stopped as the strap holding the horn slipped down shoulder, forearm, and finally fingers. Free, the horn began floating through the space between us, until finally Will lifted his hands and caught it.

"Go and stop her if you can."

"Will you come with us?" asked Will. "I fear it will take more than the Fianna now."

Will waited half a minute and said, "My lord?"

The god might as well have turned to stone.

Will looked at me. "Time to work your magic again."

DEFEAT

WILL

Neve sank down in the tall grass, folding her legs and laying the satchel in her lap. She pulled out the book and then fished around inside until she found the pencil.

"Okay, okay," she murmured to herself. Her hands were shaking.

"Neve." She glanced up, eyes bright. "It's all right. Breathe."

She gave a panicky laugh. "Right."

I squatted down beside her. "We have time yet. All will be well."

I don't think she believed me—and I had no reason to believe it myself—but she nodded and bent her head over the book. "Where should we go? I can draw something from my room, or the banquet hall . . . ?"

"Not the castle."

She shook her head. "Sorry, yeah, it's sacked. I'm not sure I remember anything about the forest in enough detail to make a very accurate drawing." She thought for a second. "What if I draw the prince? They may have stashed the kids somewhere safe. And maybe he'll be able to give us an idea what's going on."

Or we might find ourselves in the prison tower. But what were our choices? She could only draw the places or things she had seen, and it was no use going back to Drumcliffe. We had the horn; I had to trust that meant we also had hope.

"Yes, all right," I said.

While she was absorbed in her sketch, I hung the strap to Borabu over my shoulder, tucking the horn itself under my arm for good measure. Then I drew a pen knife out of my pocket and made a small cut on the pad of my thumb. A drop of blood welled. Haste was needed, and I wasn't about to force intimacy on her.

"What do you think?" She held up the drawing so I could see. The light was low, and it was little more than an outline—she had definitely captured the round, mischievous eyes and dark curls. When we met the prince in the forest, he'd been wearing a tunic with a raven sewn on the breast, and she'd sketched that too.

"It's a good likeness. Are you ready?"

I could see in her expression what she believed I meant—I noted perhaps a softening in her features as I bent toward her. Then I reached out and drew my thumb across the page, leaving a blood smear beneath the portrait.

Her eyes jumped to my face as I curled an arm around her. I felt the familiar, momentary vacuum beneath us and pinned the horn tighter against my side.

Cold air replaced the warmth of the Horned God's hall. There was daylight, though also patchy fog that inhibited visibility. We had returned to the forest after all. *Better than the prison tower.*

Neve was still close—I felt her body against mine and her breath on my neck, and I shivered. "Wait a moment," I whispered, and she nodded.

Silence. There was nothing restful or easy about this quiet. I sensed suppressed violence, like a levee before it gives way. The trees' voices had been cut off. Also, the birds, frogs, and insects.

"Your Highness, are you here?" I called quietly.

I waited. No sound but Neve's breathing.

Then a twig snapped and our gazes followed the sound. I thought I glimpsed movement in the drifting fog.

"I am your mother's friend, Your Highness—Will Yeats. And this is my friend Neve. Remember the black horse? Don't be afraid of us. We want to help you."

Neve and I exchanged glances. I was speaking Irish and she wouldn't have understood me. Both of us kept still, listening, beads of moisture collecting on our faces. I let go of her and stood, picking my way over some thick roots along the ground. A loud and sudden squawk knocked me backward, and I batted a crow out of my face. The fog shifted and I saw an oak tree with a hollow base. Inside, a small figure was crouching. If it hadn't been for the frightened, wide-open eyes I might not have noticed him in the shadows.

Neve called softly in English, "It's all right, Your Highness, we won't hurt you."

I knelt in front of the opening, the boy's eyes following me closely. He had a bruise on his forehead and a scratch under one eye. Something glinted on the ground in front of him, and I noticed his small fingers were tightly gripping a sword hilt. The blade was probably as long as he was, and engraved with runes—I immediately recognized it.

"Great Fury!" I said. "That's Lord Meath's sword." More precisely it was the sword of Diarmuid, the Fianna ancestor of Lord Meath. He had used it against the Fomorians in the Battle of Ben Bulben. "How did you come by it?"

Fear flickered in the boy's eyes, and intuiting the situation,

Neve said, "You're not in trouble, Loki." The sound of the prince's given name drew his attention to her—only his mother and father would ever have spoken to him in such a familiar way. "Do you know what happened to your family?"

The boy had likely learned English—along with Irish and Elvish—but I wasn't certain. "*Arrachtaigh*," he replied in his small voice, tightening his grip on the sword.

Monsters. Great Fury was picky about who wielded it. If it was in the boy's possession, might it mean Lord Meath was *dead*?

"Monsters in the castle?" I asked the prince in English.

He eyed me warily—clearly my companion was more trustworthy—and gave a vigorous nod.

"Many monsters?" asked Neve. Another nod. "Do you know where your parents are?"

"Mama!" he squeaked. His eyes filled with tears, and his lower lip pushed out.

The prince crawled out of the hollow, backside first, and pulled out the sword with both hands. He stood up and started walking away from us, dragging the tip along the ground.

"Where are you going?" asked Neve.

He stopped and briskly waved his empty hand. "Show you," he said in English.

We exchanged a glance and followed.

"Can Will carry your sword for you if he promises to give it back?"

The boy stopped again, his eyes moving between us. For some reason, I was still regarded with suspicion. Neve was masking her worry better than I—perhaps he thought I was angry.

"I promise to return the sword," I agreed.

Finally he held up the hilt, blade still in the dirt. I eyed it a moment, wondering what was going to happen if the sword rejected me. I reached out and grasped the hilt, bracing for some reaction.

Nothing happened, however, and I raised it in front of me. It wasn't as heavy as it looked, yet heavy *enough* for a child of five.

"Thank you," I said, to both the boy and the sword. "I'll take good care of it."

The prince turned and ran off, and we hurried to keep up.

I worried about blundering into the Morrigan's monsters, but we appeared to be nowhere near the king's road, nor even any of the footpaths that wended throughout the grounds. We crawled up embankments, scrambled down rocky slopes, and slogged through boggy sections thick with mist. We'd gone perhaps a quarter of a mile when we reached a stretch of burned forest. Larger trees were still standing, their trunks blackened—many others had fallen. Smoke was still rising in places.

Knock Ma's forest had been almost older than time itself.

"I'm so sorry, Will," said Neve, laying a hand on my arm. I realized then that my eyes were wet with tears.

"Show you," the prince repeated, again waving for us to follow.

We continued uphill and eventually came to a small rise. The trees at the top, also burned, had collapsed against each other, forming a natural shelter. The prince led us inside, pointing through an opening among the dead branches. We were actually quite close to the castle here, and could see the prison tower.

"Arrachtaigh," said the boy, his small face pale and frightened.

Following the line of his pointing finger, we could see that the standards flying from the keep had been changed—the Irish flag and O'Malley clan standard had been replaced with a single red banner depicting a diving crow. What next caught my eye—and stopped my breath—was a large iron birdcage hanging from the turret above the prison tower.

Pale fingers curled around the bars. Strands of dark hair and the tip of a wing poked out from between them.

"Mama," the boy choked out.

"Jesus," hissed Neve, and she put her arms around him. He pressed his face against her side and began to quietly sob. "She's *pregnant*, Will," she said angrily.

A feminine voice drifted down to us then, and we all went still—the queen was singing in Elvish. Loki raised his head, listening. We kept quiet until the last strain of the song had ended.

"Like a lullaby," Neve said. "I think she knows he's here."

Borabu had been dangling at my back since our arrival, and I reached for it now. I rubbed my thumb against the slight pitting of the bone, then over one of the gold bands engraved with figures and runes.

"Wait, Will."

I looked at Neve. "We have to help her. The others may have been taken too."

She nodded. "We definitely do. But let's think it through."

"The call of the horn will bring the Fianna. There are no fiercer fighters in the history of Ireland."

"Can the Fianna defeat a goddess?"

I didn't know the answer. Far Dorocha had defeated the goddess, once and possibly twice. He had used trickery and magic though. As far as I knew, no one had ever gone to battle with the Morrigan.

"I get that we have to try," she continued. "I just feel like we need some kind of plan, don't you? Obviously, I'm no warrior, but I've read a lot about war. Okay, mostly fictional war."

She sighed and seemed to give up. She was right. My emotions were affecting my judgment. It was a new development in my character—maybe the resurfacing of Oisin, who was known for his passions. I wasn't sure it was a useful trait.

"I agree," I said finally, letting the horn fall against my hip. "I fear our options are limited, but we need to understand the situation better before we act."

Neve watched the cage as she continued to think. I was grateful for her clear head, and I held my tongue and watched with her. The queen made a slight movement, and the cage swung out slightly.

"She'd want us to get her son to safety," Neve said.

"Without a doubt. But how? The Morrigan's men are probably scouring the grounds for him right now. They'd probably scour all of Ireland."

Loki again buried his face against Neve. No wonder the boy was afraid of me.

"There's a place they may not think to look."

Thinking she meant the place we'd just left, I said, "I'm not sure he'd be safe there. Uindos—"

"God no, not there. He'd probably lose him, or let him play with snakes. I don't think gods make good babysitters. I meant Portland."

Portland. The idea was inspired, and terrifying. Far Dorocha had gone looking for Neve in Portland, but he would have no reason to think *Loki* might be there.

Certainly the prince couldn't stay *here*. Yet could I do it? What if he got lost, or trapped?

"You've done it twice now, right?" said Neve, apparently reading my thoughts. "Three times if we count the battle with the elves. It seems like every time, it was because someone was in danger—we can definitely tick that box. And I have friends in Portland he could stay with . . . it would give us time to figure things out."

I was nodding before she finished, though I still wasn't convinced I could control it. "It's a good plan. Let's see if we can gain a better understanding of the situation first."

The prince was still snuggled into Neve's side. It wasn't hard to understand why he felt better there. "Do you know what happened to your father, Your Highness?" I asked. "And to Lord and Lady Meath? Are they—" I glanced at the cage. "Like this?"

He nodded, and my heart contracted.

"And Lady Alva?"

He chewed his lip, and his eyes moved over the nearby trees like he was looking for something. "*Bean sidhe*," he whispered.

Banshees. Lady Meath's ancestress, Cliona, was known as queen of banshees. The banshees had fought on the side of Ireland in the Battle of Ben Bulben. But they were associated with death, and Cliona was believed to have crossed over to the Land of Promise with Diarmuid, so it was anyone's guess where their current loyalties might lay.

"Are the banshees monsters?" I asked the prince.

He shook his head—it wasn't all that convincing.

"Alva likes them. She's brave."

Neve looked bewildered, and I said, "The banshees have allied with Lady Alva's mother in the past. If they weren't a part of the attack on the castle, I think she is probably in about the safest care she could be."

"You are also very brave," I said to the prince. "And very clever, to have kept away from the monsters. Did you see what happened to Queen Isolde?"

The queen would not have had time to gather her forces before the attack. But if she was free . . . Ireland's military forces joined with the Fianna would be enough for hope.

The boy knotted a hand in the fabric of Neve's gown, pulling himself in tighter. "Auntie is a monster," he hissed.

Neve looked at me, eyes wide.

"You mean Queen Isolde?" I asked. "*She* is a monster?"

He buried his face again.

"This is vitally important," I said to Neve.

She bent over the prince. "Loki, we need you to be brave a

little longer. Can you help us understand what happened to your auntie?"

He studied her a moment, and then he wiped his tears on her skirt and got up. He reached for her hand and said in a voice far too serious for one so small, "Don't be afraid."

She smiled at him, but I could see tears pooling in her eyes. My throat felt raw, and my blood began to slowly simmer.

Neve's voice broke as she replied, "If you go with me, I won't be scared."

The prince led us down the hill, away from the castle. We soon found a faint path winding among the devastated trees, probably a game trail. He moved like a fawn, making hardly any noise. His mother was a huntress, and her elven blood helped her disappear in the shadows. She had not always been comfortable in the company of so many trees, as Iceland had few, yet she had written me that her son was born in this very forest after a sudden onset of labor.

Neve and I, on the other hand, seemed to be disturbing every rock and twig in our path. Against the backdrop of the eerily silent forest, I feared it could be heard for miles. Luckily there were patches of drifting fog to help conceal our movement.

We were gradually circling back around toward the castle gate. When we were far enough south that a course correction to the west would have taken us to the very steps of Knock Ma, the prince stopped. He let go of Neve's hand and scampered over to a giant oak—like some of the others here it was blackened but still standing. He stroked its charred bark for a moment, whispering something against the trunk. Then he began to climb.

When the prince had scaled six or seven feet, he gestured for us to follow.

Neve shot me a wary look. "I've got a heights thing, Will." She fanned out her skirt. "And a wardrobe challenge."

"Leave it to me." I lifted the horn strap over my head and handed it to her, and I set the sword on the ground.

She squeezed my arm. "Be careful."

I grinned and touched my lips to her forehead. "I'm good at this."

She laughed. "I'm astonished."

The branches were thick and fairly evenly spaced—an easy climb. The question was, would the damaged tree hold my weight? Loki was having no trouble, and he had clearly done this before. I started up after him, sticking close to the base of each branch and hoping for the best.

Ravens moved among the limbs as we climbed, the only animals we'd seen since our arrival. Occasionally one would land nearby, cocking its head and studying me with a beady eye before flying up to a higher branch. I thought the boy had perhaps summoned the birds, like his mother.

When I caught up to the prince I had to pause to catch my breath. We had ascended at least a hundred feet. This tree was the tallest in the immediate vicinity—we had a direct line of sight up to Knock Ma's entrance.

The first thing I noticed was the ring of blackened trees—the damage ran all around the castle walls.

"Dead," spat the boy.

I concurred with the sentiment. "Indeed."

Gazing down on the fog around us, I thought it looked almost alive. More solid than gas, it reminded me of the tentacles of an enormous sea creature. Whatever propelled it was not wind, as the air was still as death. *And foul too.* A stench like rotting flesh reached my nostrils.

"Auntie," whispered the boy, and my eyes followed his pointing finger to a figure standing on the roof of the castle gatehouse. I'd missed her at first, the castle looming directly behind her.

Auntie? My first thought was "that can't be."

Her dark hair was loose and flowed around her shoulders, all the way down to her hips. Black paint had been applied to her lips and forehead, stark against her fair skin, and she was wearing a tarnished breastplate. It might have been the Morrigan herself from this distance, but there was no mistaking the lady's jacket—an Irish naval officer's jacket, specially tailored to be worn by a stylish woman. It had been a favorite of Queen Isolde's when I was at court. She held a strange weapon—like a spear or pike that was attached to what appeared to be a double-sided ax head, formed from the two halves of a machine gear, with sharp points along its edge. Even from this distance, I could see that something was wrong with one of her eyes—it had a fiery red glow.

She's a revenant.

The Morrigan had *killed* her.

Swaying from the shock, I tightened my grip on the branches above. The sudden movement caused the top of the tree to sway as well, and the prince, just above me, gasped. The queen's gaze swung toward us.

I quickly ducked behind the trunk and whispered, "We must go!" The prince was already climbing down.

As we descended, balancing between urgency and caution, there came a loud blast like the scream of a locomotive. A shout went up from somewhere close by, and it was answered by another.

The prince skipped the bottom two branches and dropped to the ground. I did the same, wincing at the pain in my ankle as I landed.

"What's happening?" asked Neve, wide-eyed.

"They're coming."

The boy darted past us, heading back the way we'd come, and I called, "Loki, no!"

Neve ran after him, scooping him up and carrying him back while he kicked and grunted. "I'm sorry, kiddo! It's going to be okay!"

How I hoped she was right.

Three firglas guards charged through the trees. Like the queen, their appearance was altered—one of them looked like he'd been broken apart and stitched back together from singed flesh and bits of metal. Iron burned fairies, but maybe once they were dead it no longer mattered.

"Will!" cried Neve.

The clock in my head was marking the passing seconds when the revenants aimed their pikes at us, shouting into the trees behind them for reinforcements. Then they charged.

Though I'd never in my life wielded such a weapon, I raised Diarmuid's sword and ran at the revenants. Fear and anger coursed through me, and I bellowed a curse. The firglas actually faltered backward, raising their shields.

Blue light danced along the blade, and it cut through the leather and wood of two of the shields like they were apples. Then up came the deadly points of the pikes.

I raised Great Fury again—and suddenly found myself surrounded by *a hundred* foes.

If I must fall, let me take as many as I can.

I swung the sword in an arc, and *kept* swinging. Blue flames jumped in all directions and, in my hands, I felt the impact of landed strikes.

"More are coming, Will!"

Neve's voice cut through my battle trance. Blinking, I tried to make sense of what I was seeing. *Three* foes lay violently mangled at my feet.

The horde was only a vision. A memory of another life.

I ran back to Neve and the prince and put my arms around

them. Loki was still struggling to free himself, and in the strongest tone I could muster, I said, "Hold onto Neve!"

He stopped struggling and curled his arms around her neck.

I didn't have to repeat the warning for Neve's benefit—she flung her arms around me, squeezing Loki between us.

"You've got this, Will."

Then she pressed her lips to mine.

THE PAST

NEVE

Who knew I was good with kids? Having no family—literally zero—I'd never hung out with younger cousins, nieces, or nephews. None of my friends had married yet. Most of my exposure came from the bookstore, where I sometimes worked the children's section. And now that I thought back on it, kids liked me. Which was surprising. Or maybe not, since I had perfect recall of how lonely and scary being a kid was sometimes.

Finding myself suddenly back in my apartment felt exactly like waking up from a scary-as-hell dream. For about two seconds, anyway, at which point someone—not Will—shouted my name, and the prince started crying for his mother.

Disentangling myself from Will, I looked up at the wide-eyed speaker.

"Hi, Noah."

He dropped down beside me, eyeing the pile of us. "What the hell happened? Where have you been?"

The prince crawled into my lap and hid against me. I glanced at the ceiling—no throat-tunnel.

I let my eyes return to Noah. I opened my mouth, then closed it again. Finally, I said, "Did you ever read that copy of *Outlander* I gave you?"

Noah had the palest skin of anyone I ever knew, and it turned red for almost any reason. Like not reading a book your best friend had recommended. In fairness, I'm not sure why I thought he'd like it when he gravitated toward depressing literary stuff and poetry. Maybe because the hero had red hair too? "Ugh, that's going to make this so much harder."

"Hello," Will inserted. He let go of the sword hilt and held out a hand to Noah. "I'm Will Yeats."

Noah reached out absently to shake hands while his eyes moved from Will back to me and stuck there. "Is this some kind of joke?"

"Totally," I muttered, "isn't it hilarious?"

His gaze shifted to the child in my lap. I held up a hand. "Not ours. His name is Loki. He's . . . Irish. I'm gonna have to ask you a huge favor having to do with him." I glanced at the kitchen. "Right after I drink all the coffee and eat whatever's in the fridge."

"There's nothing left in the fridge."

I looked at him. "Wait, have you been *staying* here?"

"Neve, *I've been worried sick*. You were gone for more than two weeks. After the police came and went, I offered to stay for a while. You know, in case you came back from being *kidnapped or dead*."

The police. Right.

I noticed then that Loki had fallen asleep in my lap. "Help me up," I said. "We'll put him in my bed. Will can stay with him. You and I can go get food and coffee and I'll explain everything."

I looked at Will. "Okay?"

"Good idea." That's what his mouth said, but he looked worried.

Will took my spellbook bag and Noah helped me get up so I wouldn't wake the prince. I carried him to the bedroom and laid him down as carefully as I could. He immediately gave a little moan and rolled onto his side. *Whew.*

On the edge of the bed was a pink elephant stuffy my mother had won for me at the Arkansas state fair—she'd been taking her meds in those days and it was one of the few bright, golden memories I had of her. I picked up the toy and snuggled it next to the prince, in case he woke up scared. I figured being comforted by soft, squishy things that looked like animals had to be universal.

I walked to the closet and grabbed jeans, a T-shirt, and a hoodie, and then I went into the bathroom and changed my clothes. We'd probably be going back soon, but I couldn't walk to the coffee shop in the Ren Faire outfit. Besides, the idea that the people in Will's time might be worried or confused by my appearance no longer seemed important.

I washed the cuts on my hands, brushed my teeth, and checked myself in the mirror—it wasn't as bad as I thought, except for my hair, which I dampened with my fingers and coiled into a ballerina bun. Then I smoothed on some faintly pink lip goo. Halfway to setting the stick back on the counter, I slipped it into my pocket instead.

When I went back out, Will was waiting inside the door to my room. His eyes moved over me and my scandalous outfit in the same way they might have if we'd met in a bar. That chink in the gentlemanly facade made me want to peel his clothes off. *With my teeth.*

I noticed his white shirt was covered with char from climbing the tree. I went to my dresser and fished around for one of the big T-shirts I slept in. I pulled out a dark gray one with a V-neck that I already knew was going to be dangerously sexy on him.

Carrying it over, I said quietly, "I'll be back quick, I promise. We need Noah's help, and I think it will be easier for me to explain things this way."

"Of course." He held my gaze a moment and said, "You'll be all right?"

The question felt heavy, like there were a bunch of other words that had gotten left out.

"Yeah. Noah and I are good friends."

Will raised an eyebrow. "When you told me about him at Knock Ma, it sounded like that might have changed."

"I know. It's complicated. But it'll be fine."

Will seemed to accept that, or at least accepted that he didn't really have a choice, and he settled into a chair by the window. I felt kind of uneasy about leaving him in my bedroom—there were dirty clothes on the floor, including underwear, and plenty of personal crap like photos and old journals. But what could I do?

"See you soon," I said, turning to go.

Noah and I had made it no further than the street when he said, "Spill."

It was another gorgeous autumn day, with sunshine and crisp blue sky—though there was a distinct bite in the air. The neighbor across the street was cleaning up caved-in jack-o-lanterns from his front steps, and the one next door was raking leaves.

"I guess I missed Halloween." *Sort of.*

"*Neve.*" Noah was glaring at me.

"Okay! It's going to be really hard, so give me a second."

It was four blocks to the bakery, and it took me all of that time to tell him the shortest possible version of the story. Afraid I'd never finish, I kept having to tell him to be quiet as he interjected with questions and exclamations.

When we got to the shop, he plunked down at a table outside, gaze glued to the sidewalk. I decided to leave him there to puzzle it out while I went in for coffee and sandwiches. In my head, it was the most amazing thing ever—ordering coffee like a normal person, from an employee who knew me well enough to thank me by name. In my *gut*, everything felt off. Somehow, *this* part was now starting to feel like a weird dream.

I took the food outside and joined Noah. A man with a little girl wearing a fairy costume strolled by on the sidewalk—there were lots of sparkles and stars and pink and purple fabrics.

Normally on this kind of day, the bakery's patio would be full. Maybe it was too cold, or some off time of day. I looked at my flesh watch. The hands were back to noon—back to working like it was supposed to, which was to say, *not* working.

I drank from my paper cup, closing my eyes to fully appreciate the experience. Though I liked plenty of dairy in my coffee, I rarely ordered it with syrup. But I felt oddly sugar-deficient and had gotten the seasonal special, a pumpkin spice latte. Maybe it was the time travel.

"If I hadn't watched you reappear out of thin air, I would never believe any of this."

"I get it," I said softly. "You'd be as worried about my brain as I was at first."

"I'm still not sure I shouldn't be worried about *mine*." He blinked in an exaggerated way and shook his head. "Maybe I'm imagining this."

I pushed his coffee toward him. "You're not."

He picked up the cup. "And this whole Niamh and Oisin thing—I don't know whether that's the hardest part to swallow, or the part where he's *actually* William Butler Yeats. Are you sure the guy isn't just hitting on you?"

"Noah, what you're saying doesn't even make sense." But this reminded me—*he likes poetry*. "You know much about Yeats?"

He set down his cup and matched my annoyed frown with his own. “Uh, yeah.”

Having finished my coffee, I picked up the BLT and A. Before taking a bite, I casually asked, “Does the name Maud ever come up in connection with him?” Inwardly I shook my head at myself. Of all the damn things I could have asked.

Noah laughed dryly. “You could say that. Yeats was in love with Maud Gonne for most of his life. He proposed to her like half a dozen times.” My heart flopped. “She was a big-time Irish nationalist. Yeats once wrote that she was in love with war, or something like that.”

“Nationalist—you mean she wanted to kick the English out of Northern Ireland?”

“Exactly. Though I think she *was* English.”

“I think in this version of Ireland there is no part controlled by England. I’m not sure there ever was. I mean they have a queen and everything.”

Noah froze. “What do you mean ‘this version of Ireland’?”

Crap. I waved my hand. “There’s also a whole parallel world thing I haven’t even gotten to yet . . . we don’t have time for that. I’m so, *so* sorry to dump all this on you, and I would never ask if I could think of any other way, but the prince is in real and serious danger, and we need someone to hide him while we plot our next move and get back to the castle.”

Noah closed his eyes and shook his head. “I don’t even know where to start with that.”

“Noah! *Please* don’t go all dramatic on me right now. If you don’t want any part of this, I understand, but just say so. I need to figure out a plan B.”

His eyes snapped open. “Dramatic! Are you kidding me?”

I groaned and set down my sandwich. “I’m sorry. You’re right. I know it’s not fair. Somehow it made sense when we were on the run from the undead. Maybe I can figure out a better solution."

Noah's face relaxed. "What is it you're asking me to do with this kid?"

Taking a deep breath in an effort to slow down my words, I said, "We need someone to watch him for a while. There are some really bad people after him in Ireland."

Noah's eyes narrowed. "Let's say for the sake of argument I take him, and you go back there and get yourself killed—which, I have to say, Neve, seems like a distinct possibility. Then what happens?"

It was a fair question that might have *eventually* occurred to me.

"If something happens to me," I replied, thinking out loud, "Will would come for him. If something happens to Will, I think he'd be stuck here. And I'd possibly be stuck in Ireland."

Jesus.

I smoothed the wrinkled paper of my sandwich bag, trying to settle my racing thoughts. "But there are lots of magical people where he lives. Even *I'm* magical there . . . we'd figure something out. I know this probably got lost in the whole time travel, reincarnated-Celtic-hero thing—Will wasn't the only one who came here looking for me and I'm in danger too."

Noah leaned forward. "It was *not* lost. The dark-fae Frankenstein man who tried to suck you through a hole in your ceiling. One with rocks for teeth. Have I got that right?"

"You were really paying attention."

He took a deep, loud breath through his nose, like he wasn't far from losing it.

Tone it down, Neve.

Before I could say anything else, he replied, "I'm not sure why this hasn't occurred to you, but you don't *have* to go back. You're here now. You can stay with me, and he can go back and take out your enemies. You already helped him find the hammer, or helmet, or whatever it was. It's his country. His time. His people. His . . . *dimension*."

He was wrong—it had occurred to me.

"Keep the kid here," he continued. "You can tell people he's a cousin or something. If everything goes swimmingly with this massively bloody-sounding conflict, Yeats can come back and get him. If not, we can figure out what to do from there."

Again I fiddled with my sandwich paper. "I've considered it. Of *course* I've considered it, and honestly I'm still background-processing the idea—shut *up*, I'm not finished." Noah closed his mouth. "Can I just ask, if in theory I do go back with him, is there even the slightest possibility you'd agree?"

He was quiet for a few seconds, and I could hear my heart's impatient thumping.

"I'm not the right person."

"You're an uncle," I pointed out. If memory served, his nephew was actually close to Loki's age. "And you're a *good* uncle."

"What about work?"

"I would hope not to be gone more than a week, but I've got that money set aside from my mom. I'll give you some for child-care and groceries, and I promise Will and I will figure out a plan for if we don't make it back."

"You're going to give me money from your emergency fund."

It was completely out of character. I *never* dipped into it. "Yes. As much as you need. And before you even think it, no I'm not trying to bribe you. I understand that this is a huge ask."

Noah covered his face with his hands. "What kind of hold has this guy got on you? Have you fallen for the whole fate thing? Do you think you're in love with him? Is it just about sex? Because you know you can do that without having to agree to all this."

"Obviously, I know that."

He looked at me. "You didn't answer my question. So let's say for the sake of argument you *are* in love with him, and you *do* win the battle for Middle Earth. What then? Are you going to move to alternate Ireland and make babies? Do they even have espresso machines?"

"Noah!" It was a jerky thing to say, but he wasn't wrong to raise the point. These were the same questions I had asked myself. And this was the reason I hadn't let myself fall for Will. Or that I had tried really hard not to let myself fall for him. Because if I was being honest, some part of me had shipped us by chapter two.

The questions needed answers, but I didn't yet have them.

"I'm sorry," Noah said, "you're scaring the shit out of me. In case you've forgotten, I care about you. I don't want you to disappear from my life, whether it's because Franken-fae kills you or because you run off with a hundred-and-fifty-year-old poet and I have to burn all his books. The latter would be preferable, obviously."

I pressed my lips together, even put a hand over my mouth—it was no use. A second later I was shaking with laughter. Noah's baleful expression cracked open, and then he was laughing too.

When I finally pulled myself together, I had tears running down my face. "I have to admit I've missed you."

"Oh wow, thanks," he replied, wiping a tear from his own eye.

"I mean it, Noah. Whatever happens, I hope we'll always be friends."

He sobered, fixing his gaze on me. "We will always be friends. And I can babysit a half-Irish, half-elf, half-fairy—whatever—princeling for a week if it's important to you."

I reached out and took hold of his hand. "Thank you. And please know that I'm thinking about all of this, even if it may not seem like it. You know how risk-averse I am."

He gave my hand a squeeze and got up. "I know how risk-averse you *used* to be. You look amazing, so I can't say the change doesn't suit you." He picked up his phone and put it in his jeans pocket.

"Where are you going?"

"To my place. My *new* place. I assume you'll want to move the kid from your place—you know, throat-tunnel. I need to tidy up and find some things to put in the fridge, maybe also acquire some kids' books and video games, before you and your new boyfriend jump dimensions."

I groaned. "Please don't be impossible."

"I think I'm earning the right to be impossible."

"Okay, just promise me you won't refer to Will as my boyfriend in front of him."

Noah gave me a wry smile and turned, heading off down the street. "Give me two hours."

I sat, feeling hugely impressed with myself for what I'd accomplished. Then the reality of all those questions I couldn't ignore for much longer came crashing down on my head. *Best to outrun them.* I picked up the sandwiches I'd bought for Will and Loki, and started home.

Will met me at the door, holding a finger to his lips.

I nodded. *Still asleep.* The poor little guy had been through hell. Running from zombies, sleeping inside that tree, and probably getting nothing to eat.

As I closed the door, a vision of Will and me together in that impossibly adorable cottage with a mini-Will toddling around the living room in front of a cozy fire inserted itself into my thoughts. Which got me thinking about how mini-Wills were made, and before I knew it my face was hot and I'd forgotten whatever it was I'd been going to say. *Damn you, Noah.*

"Hungry?" I whispered, holding up the bag.

He nodded, and I motioned him to the bar. I went around

to the other side and got out a plate. He studied the countertop before sitting down. It occurred to me Victorian houses did not have kitchens like this—it probably looked like something from a pub. This house was old too, and retained much of its creaky charm, but modern kitchens and bathrooms had gone in when it was converted to apartments.

"Tea?" I offered.

That got an even more emphatic nod. I put some water in the kettle and fired up the burner.

As I was grabbing a mug from the cabinet, Will said, "You do have some magic here." I saw he was studying the stove.

I grinned. "Not magic. Gas. Someday it's going to make your life a whole lot easier. Or Mrs. Tobin's life, anyway."

As Will started on his sandwich, I noticed he'd changed into the shirt I'd given him, and god knows I had nothing against those white Victorian button-downs, but *I could see arms now.* I watched the small movements of the muscles in his forearms until the almost-whistle of the tea kettle reclaimed my attention. I turned off the burner and filled the mug, dropping in an English Breakfast tea bag.

I set the mug in front of him and said, "So he agreed."

He looked at me blankly for a second, then wiped his mouth with the back of his hand. "That's good news. How did you convince him?"

I grabbed a paper towel and handed it to him. "I don't even know. I think he's only doing it because I asked—and possibly begged a little."

He offered a distinctly bratty grin—I would almost have said a smirk. "Which by the way is what you said made you uncomfortable about him."

I lifted an eyebrow. "And your point?"

His face fell. "I only meant—"

I laughed. "Sorry, I know what you meant. And you're absolutely right. Thankfully, he still considers me a friend."

I watched Will fiddle a minute with the string of the tea bag, raising and lowering it and watching the water change color, before going back to his sandwich. *First tea bag.* It was kind of adorable.

"We're going to have to figure out what to do about Loki if neither of us comes back," I said, sobering. "I promised Noah we would."

Will stopped chewing and swallowed. "Right."

"We can add it to the list of other things we have to figure out, like when to use the horn and whether there's any chance of it saving us."

He set down his sandwich.

"Sorry, I should have waited."

"This is more complicated than it appeared at Knock Ma."

I nodded. "I'm no expert on time travel, obviously, but if we're in the future . . . whatever happens back in your world, it's happened already, right? I don't see why we can't take the time we need to come up with a plan before going back."

He processed for a few seconds. "I should have thought of that."

"Well, in my time there are a lot of . . . *fictional depictions* of time travel, and I watch and read most of them. Though I can't say it ever occurred to me that someday they would have a practical use."

"So you *are* an expert on time travel. Or the closest thing we have to one."

I laughed. "Maybe so."

He lifted his cup and drank his tea all in one go—it must have scorched its way to his stomach. I filled a glass with water and placed it in front of him. "I've got stronger stuff if you need it."

Will reached for the glass, smiling. "How did he take all this? Your friend."

Sighing, I walked around the bar and went to sit on the couch, passing the pile of magical items still lying on the floor. Will followed and sat beside me.

"Like you'd imagine," I replied.

He rolled his eyes toward the ceiling, considering. "He didn't want to believe it, but he saw us time travel so he had to. He's confused and angry and wonders what could possibly make you want to go back with me."

My mouth fell open. "Did you follow us?"

He laughed. "It wasn't hard to guess. And speaking of that . . ." He angled toward me, and it knocked my heart into a funny rhythm. "What *could* possibly make you want to go back with me?"

You can run but you can't hide. I dropped my gaze.

"I'm sure it's occurred to you by now that you could stay behind," he continued. "Even if it hasn't, I would bet that your friend Noah pointed it out. The Morrigan has accomplished what she set out to without us. I don't see her coming for you again."

I glanced up. "I'm not sure I agree. Say you *are* able to raise the Fianna and go after her, what's her next move?"

He thought for a minute, and I saw when he figured it out. But he said, "Why don't you tell me."

My heart pounded. I moistened my lips with my tongue. "I doubt she's really ever needed *both* of us to control the Fianna. Oisin is the warrior and the son of their chief. But if she has us both, she knows she can . . ."

Heat flooded my cheeks and I dropped my gaze again.

Will bent his head to catch my eye. "She knows she can use you for leverage against me, for I am clearly compromised when it comes to you. Is that what you were going to say?"

Appalled, I shook my head. "I, no, I—"

"It's all right, Neve. Will you look at me?"

He reached out and gently lifted my chin—I think I almost died.

"It's what you were going to say because you know it's true." His voice had gone low and soft. "If they took you, I would do whatever was required to get you back. I'm not sure that I've ever felt that way about anyone."

I had a vision then of a warrior with a sword, deadly fierce, defending the people he cared about with everything he had. It wasn't a vision of some dead hero—it was Will at Knock Ma swinging Great Fury.

I reached up and took hold of his shoulders, pulling him toward me until our lips met. He curled over me, deepening the kiss while I sank back into the couch cushions. His hand came to my hip, gripping, and mine slid down his back, pressing him into me. He let out a groan.

We broke apart, breathless, and his eyes locked with mine. *Do you want this?* He didn't have to even say the words, because I had been *such* a Neve about it.

"Life is too short not to do this," I said. "Especially for you, because nobody should die a virgin if they have any choice about it."

He smiled, and I discovered that even when he was about to be bad, he looked like an angel. "I want to do this with you," he said, "I think more than anything. But there's no pressure for it to be anything more than . . ."

"Sex," I said, and grinned, though it was probably a word he'd never heard used that way.

"Sex," he repeated with a laugh.

I shifted him off me and stood, reaching for his hand. The living room was not a good idea with the prince here. That left Noah's old room, and I did feel kind of weird about it—but not weird enough for it to stop me. I led Will inside and closed and locked the door.

"We'll have to listen for him," I said.

Will nodded.

The half-squinty, shy smile increased my need to touch him again. I moved close and his arms came around me. I touched the notch at the base of his throat and let my finger slide down the V opening of his shirt to the top of his pecs. Amazing how that little bit of exposed flesh could be so sexy.

Will reached for the edges of my hoodie and peeled it off my shoulders, letting it drop. I pulled my T-shirt over my head, then took off my bra and jeans. *Slowly.* If what he'd told me about his experience—or lack of it—was true, this was not something to rush through.

When I was naked, his gaze burning a hole through me, I moved close again and put my arms around his neck. The feel of my naked flesh against his clothing lit me on fire. His eyes were a little wild, and I placed a hand on his cheek.

"Have you ever seen a naked woman before?"

He laughed, embarrassed. "Only on accident. I have sisters, remember."

I winced, shaking my head. "Sisters don't count, and we definitely don't talk about them right now."

"The answer is no then."

I raised his shirt over his head and dropped it to the floor. My eyes moved over the lean lines of him. He looked like I'd thought he would—slender and fit, with long, smooth muscles down his arms. A light tracing of dark hair ran down the middle of his chest.

I traced my fingers across his skin and watched it prickle. My thumb lightly brushed a nipple, and he shuddered.

"Is that nice?" I asked.

He gave a choked laugh. "You could say that."

I smiled and took his hand, leading him to the bed. I rose on my toes and whispered in his ear, "I'm going to lie down, and you have my permission to touch anything you want, okay? We'll go slow."

He shuddered again. I heard his throat work as he swallowed, and he nodded.

I crawled onto the bed and lay down on my stomach. He might feel bolder if I wasn't watching him.

"We'll start here, and in a minute I'll turn over. Don't be afraid—you aren't going to hurt me." I had trusted him with my life almost since I met him, but trusting him with my body—it was so much bigger. Yet I had not a single reservation.

The coolness of the dark purple duvet against my belly and breasts spiked the heat between my legs, and I felt moisture seeping onto my thigh.

The pads of his fingers, gentle and warm, landed on one shoulder. They lightly trailed across my shoulder blades before slowly moving down, stopping at my low back. Then they moved to explore the curve of my waist. I watched goosebumps lift on my arm and felt them move across my body.

"You're causing those chills," I told him. "That feels so good."

"I was going to say the same about your skin. I don't think I've ever felt anything so soft."

The need that I felt to take care of him through this had a miraculous effect on *me*. Instead of worrying what would come next, or whether I was doing something wrong, or what he thought about the shape of my body, I focused entirely on him. On the signals his voice, breath, and touch were sending. I wanted it to be good for him. I wanted it to be easy, yet also something he would always remember.

His warm fingers were moving now down my low back and over my ass. I shivered and let out a little moan. He was a quick study, because it prompted him to place the other hand on the other cheek, and I couldn't help pressing up into his hands.

"Ah, *god*," he muttered.

I laughed softly. "Keep going."

Next his fingers trailed down the outsides of my thighs, all the way to my ankles. I spread my legs, because I didn't know how much longer I could stand him not touching me between them. Again he took the hint—fingers glided slowly up the insides of my legs, and my heart pounded from the anticipation of what they would do when they got to the top.

But he stopped short, and I groaned.

Consent, Neve.

I nudged myself out of the trance and choked out, "Yes."

The next light touch came directly to the most sensitive spot on my body, and I let out another groan. "God, Will, I'm going to come if we keep going."

He gave a hoarse chuckle. "Is that a good thing?"

"It's *too* good of a thing."

By sheer force of will, I rolled onto my back, displacing his hand.

I smiled, wiping away the uncertainty on his face.

He scooted up on the bed and lay down alongside me, head propped in one hand. His eyes met mine as he raised his hand over my chest. I nodded, and his fingers traced a line down my sternum, stopping below my breasts. Then he lifted the hand, drawing a slow circle with a finger around one taut nipple.

I wriggled closer to him. "You are *very* good at this, Will."

"Thank you, Miss Kelly."

I laughed, and he lifted his hand and repeated the motion on the other side. I arched my back, pushing into his touch, and he cupped the breast, slightly squeezing.

"That's *really* nice," I said. My voice had dropped a whole octave.

Next he trailed his fingers down the middle of my belly. When my hips gave a jerk toward his hand, he sucked a breath through his teeth.

"Go on," I urged, and as I watched his fingers, I noticed the front of his trousers—he'd gone completely hard. I wanted badly to touch him, but I wanted worse not to interrupt what he was doing.

Slowly his fingers moved into the light curls between my legs, and one finger slipped directly into the warm, moist cleft, rubbing right across the nub there—my whole body went taut and I pressed into his hand.

"Is that all right?" he asked, startled.

I was panting now, and "uh-huh" was all I could manage.

"It—it's really wet," he said, softly stroking between the folds and—oh my *god*.

I placed my hand over his, pressing slightly, and moaned. "That wetness means you're doing everything right."

It means I'm ready for you.

I did reach down then, and brushed my hand lightly down the bulge in his trousers. He gave a jerk, groaned, and pressed himself into my hip.

"If it's okay with you," I whispered, "I really don't think I can wait anymore for you to be inside me."

His eyes met mine as he assured himself he'd heard me right, and he rolled onto his back so he could take off his pants.

My eyes moved over his naked body—and I had a most unwelcome thought.

Condoms.

I had some. They were old. Worse, they were in my bedroom.

Will might as well have been a monk, and I had never had sex without a condom, but I didn't want to get pregnant, recent fantasies notwithstanding.

"Everything all right?" Will asked.

I rolled onto my side now, running my fingers down his chest. "Definitely. I was just thinking about birth control, and how I don't have any. Can I—can we—" I broke off and started again. "I *really* want to feel you inside me. Can we do that for a while, and then I'll use my hand to help you finish?"

He looked bewildered—maybe I hadn't been very nineteenth century in my explanation. "We can do whatever you want, and nothing you don't."

I smiled. "That's a perfect answer."

I sat up and crawled on top of him until I was straddling his thighs. His hands came to my hips, and I watched the muscles in his throat as he swallowed. Rising high enough to accommodate his length, I gently placed him inside me. His head fell back on the bed, and as I slid slowly down, he let out a long shaky groan. When I was flush against his belly, enjoying the sensation of fullness, the fluttering of small muscles as they clenched his heat and hardness, I took one of his hands and tucked his fingers between my legs.

"Small circles," I said, "if you can. If it's too much, let it go. I'll come anyway." I had never come without fingers or a toy before. This was a whole new world.

He nodded, and obediently began tracing slow circles with the tip of his finger. It sent delicious little shocks through my body.

"That's so good, Will." I began rocking against him, and maybe five seconds later I had forgotten everything, including that he was a virgin and wasn't likely to last long. The silky slow circles—the wet friction inside my body—my orgasm erupted, and I locked my lips together so I wouldn't shout. Starbursts filled my body, washing me in heat and exquisite sensation.

As I lusciously wound down, I felt Will's body go stiff and his breathing stopped. Quickly I pulled off of him, wrapping his length in my two hands, easing them back and forth until he released.

"Heaven above," he breathed, shuddering.

I smiled and flopped down over him. His arms came around me, and I burrowed against his chest.

"That was—that was—"

"You're welcome."

He laughed and squeezed his arms tighter around me.

GONNE

WILL

We both slept for a while. I woke first, listening for signs the prince was awake, but all was quiet. Neve was breathing softly against my chest.

I lay marveling over what had just happened. Over the intensity of the experience, and how vividly I recalled every detail. So vividly, in fact, that I felt a stirring at my groin. How kind she had been to me, letting me have this—though she seemed to enjoy it as much as I did, and I'd been given to understand that women usually did not.

Don't let it go to your head.

The truth was it had all been her doing. Her patience and skill had ensured it was pleasurable for us both.

Beyond pleasurable. There ought to be a whole language for describing what we had done. Of course, there *was*—poetry.

I found myself wondering how she had learned so much about

lovemaking, but as the word "experience" came to mind I decided it was a question I might not like to probe too deeply. Suffice it to say I was grateful for her knowledge, and for her decision to give herself to me. I had begun to wonder whether she might consider doing so again, when she stirred and made a noise a cat might make when the sun reached its napping spot.

I stroked my fingers down her back, and she sat up suddenly, staring at me.

My heart sank—regrets?

"Will!"

"What's wrong?"

"I thought of something!"

Relieved that this didn't appear to have anything to do with "sex," I let my gaze slip down to her breasts. They were small and round and perfect.

"Will!" she said again, laughing this time. "Pay attention for a second."

I sat up and redoubled my efforts to focus.

"We don't have to go back to the same day."

My thinking was still disordered, though after a moment I made the connection. "On our return to Ireland?"

"Yes! What if we go back earlier? We could give them more time to get ready."

Of course. As far as I knew there was nothing preventing us from returning to a different point in time. "The queen's army could be waiting."

"Exactly."

Yet might there be unforeseen consequences? "Supposing I was able to make that happen, mightn't there be problems with traveling back to a time where we already exist?"

Her enthusiasm seemed to flatten. "Yeah, there's that. It's always an issue in the stories about time travel, and even just with common sense, it seems like running into yourself can't be a good thing. But then if you go back *too* far, I think you run the risk of changing too many things."

"What do you mean?"

"Well, say you go back before you were born and find the queen. I assume that she'd be pretty young. What if she didn't believe you, or worse, made different decisions based on what you told her about the future?"

"Isn't that what we want her to do?"

"Yes and no. What if she changes other things? It could end up altering your future—or what's now your past—and it might not be for the better. Maybe it would affect her decisions regarding one of the battles you've told me about, and Ireland would end up losing, or someone you love would end up dying."

I frowned. "It's too complicated. Too dangerous."

"*What if*"—she held up a finger—"you *did* go to the more recent past, to a place you know you won't run into yourself? And you don't go to the queen at all. You go to someone else you trust—someone smart, someone who's not involved in all this, and someone you know will believe you. They could get a message to the queen for you at the right time."

I was shaking my head before she even finished. "You credit me with having far more control over this than I actually do."

"Honestly, Will, I don't believe that. I think it's just fear. It feels out of your control. Once you're convinced something is the right thing to do—that it *needs* to be done—you make it happen." She took hold of my hand. "This is something I know a lot about."

I held her hand in both of mine, turning everything over in my mind. She wanted me to follow my instincts, but there were so many variables. One thing was certain, however—what she proposed had the benefit of increasing the odds in our favor. It gave us a chance at two armies instead of one.

I thought about the clock in my head—how it always warned me when I was about to travel. I had conjectured it was somehow tied to fate or a higher power, despite the fact I wasn't sure I believed in either of those things. Might I actually be controlling it without realizing it?

No sooner had that thought process completed, than the clock began *ticking*. I wasn't ready! At this point I trusted Neve's instincts more than my own, yet who could I go to with this errand? Where, and *when*?

The clock ticked louder.

I tightened my grip on Neve's hand, and then—on instinct—let go and moved away from her.

"Will, wait!"

This errand is not for her.

"God in heaven! *Will?* Is that *you*?"

I hunched on a wood floor. I'd lighted on something that was pressing painfully against my hip—I reached under and drew out a woman's shoe.

The room was small, lit by gas lamps, draped in garish fabrics, and furnished with tatty, overstuffed chairs. Cigarette smoke clouded the close, perfumed air, and I coughed. A woman in nothing but a corset and drawers—and heavy stage makeup—had half turned from a dressing table to stare at me.

Someone pounded once on the door. "Twenty minutes to curtain, Miss Gonne."

"Very well," she called out. "Go away!"

She shoved her chair out and stood up, glancing quickly around the room. She yanked a purple dressing gown off a folding screen and draped it around my shoulders. I grabbed the edges of the satin fabric and pulled them tight.

"Naked as the day you were born! What on *earth*, Will?"

Even with the heavy makeup, she was beautiful. Her dark hair was piled on top of her head, wavy tendrils of it hanging loose around her face and neck. Her eyes were bright in the room's low light, and the corset pushed her bosom up and out—and created a tightness at my groin. I had never before seen so much of her flesh. Or any woman's, until about an hour ago.

And she has certainly never seen so much of mine.

"What year is it, Maud?"

She wasn't as surprised to see me as someone else might have been. She knew about my adventures in Faery, and she knew that I had time traveled before the Battle of Knock Ma. In fact, she'd made me tell her the stories several times.

Still, she stared at me with wide eyes. "It's 1887—the first of November."

Exactly one year before the Morrigan's attack on Knock Ma. Three years since the kiss above Dublin Bay, the same day we had parted ways.

Gripping the dressing gown—trying not to imagine how I must look, though out of the corner of my eye I could see my reflection in the large mirror above the vanity—I started to rise from the scuffed wood floor. Maud took hold of my arm and helped me. While I had become accustomed to the dizziness that accompanied this mode of travel, it always took time to adjust. Much like adjusting to walking on land after an ocean voyage.

"Thank you," I said. Rather than slip on the purple gown, I used the sleeves to tie it around my waist—concealing everything below as best I could in the process.

Maud's eyes moved over my chest, causing my flesh to heat. But I took advantage of her distraction to study *her*—and realized that my first glance had missed much. The makeup veiled sunken half circles under her eyes. Excitement had made her eyes appear bright, though in fact they were watery and bloodshot. She'd lost weight, I thought, and as she'd helped me up, I'd smelled whiskey and cigarettes—which wasn't necessarily a cause for concern in itself, as we'd often drunk whiskey together at school, and she had always smoked. The whole picture, however, suggested something amiss. Poor health perhaps, or some kind of emotional strain.

When Maud's inspection of me ended, she steered me to one of the fat, floral-print chairs and pressed me into it. She went to her dressing table, poured me a glass of whiskey, and returned.

Handing me the glass she said, "It's wonderful to see you again, Will. It feels like so long ago since we were both at school." Her tone, which almost always carried at least a hint of sarcasm, sounded earnest and even wistful. "I transform into Lady Macbeth in less than half an hour, and I cannot go on stage until I know what's happened to you. Is that time enough to tell me?"

I laughed. "Hardly. I'll try to give you an abbreviated version. I have quite a large favor to ask."

Dare I trust her with this? Unless I went back to believing in fate or God, I had to assume it was my own decision to come to her. Why? There was *some* sense to the choice, I supposed. This was exactly the kind of excitement she had always craved. Moreover, I did believe she cared for me—had once loved me, even. We had vowed to always remain friends, though I had suspected that once I retired to Connacht I would never see her again.

I swallowed the whiskey for courage and told my tale in as few words as I could manage. It wasn't my way, and after leaving out so many details, I feared she'd never comprehend it all. She sat in the chair opposite me listening attentively—I could tell by the changes in her expression. She did not once interrupt me. By the time I came to the favor regarding the message for the queen, she had folded her arms around herself and doubled over, and her whole body had begun to shake.

"Are you ill?" I asked, alarmed.

She sat up, and I saw tears streaming down her face. Then she erupted into loud laughter.

"To think I spurned you out of fear of *boredom!* Oh Will, you cannot imagine how much good it does me to see you again."

We had little time, but I couldn't let this pass without comment. "Has something happened to you, Maud? You are beautiful as always, yet you seem—forgive me—in low spirits. Though perhaps not at this particular moment."

This elicited another peal of laughter, and I smiled at her.

"Forgive me," she said, wiping more tears from her eyes, "I am well. My path has not led where I expected, and I've wasted some time pitying myself over it. But who *does* choose their path, really?" Her gaze settled on me. "Speaking of which, Will Yeats, I expected you to be a world-famous poet by now. I'm pleased to discover you're very much the same as I remember you."

I opened my mouth to reply, and she waved her hand. "Never mind. We haven't much time, and I have a question or two about this business."

"Of course."

"I know you were endeavoring to be brief . . . I can't help feeling there is some important piece of this story missing. What on earth did the Morrigan want with *you?*"

My instincts—or perhaps cowardice—had led me to leave out everything about Oisin and Niamh, *and* about Neve. Even now I was reluctant to tell her all, yet anything I left out would be information the queen would not have, should Maud agree to help us. So I told her about my connection to the warrior poet, to Borabu, and to the woman from the future.

She stared at me, hands on her knees. "It hardly comes as a surprise to me that you were destined for greatness—god in *heaven*."

There came another sharp knock on the door. "Five minutes, my love." The messenger outside the door was different this time—the voice was deeper, and markedly sterner. "Let us not keep them waiting again."

I raised an eyebrow. She closed her eyes and shook her head. "I'll be ready, Harold."

The party on the other side moved away, and she got up and went behind the screen, pulling down a dress that had been draped over the top of it.

"Harold is my fiancé," she said in a flat tone. "He owns this theater. He has been a great patron of my art. So you see, in the end, I passed over a poet for a businessman. Now it is your turn to laugh."

I cleared my throat quietly. "I would never laugh at your unhappiness. You should know that."

She came out from behind the screen, and I stood up. She wore a medieval gown and a sad smile.

"I know it, my angel. And you may save me yet." She came to me and took my face in her hands. "I will get your message to the queen. We have one more week of the Scottish play, and after that I will deliver it myself. Your name will be enough to gain me an audience with her?"

Breath filled my lungs as relief washed over me. "It should. If you've a pen and paper, I can write the pertinent details down for you before I return."

"There's no need, I always remember everything."

This was true. I knew it was one of the things that had led her to study acting. That, and I think she believed the theater might be the closest thing she would get to the life of excitement she craved.

"You're sure you can't stay?" She smiled. "They say I'm quite good. Harold has theater business after—we could have a late supper."

"I wish I could. Truly. I'm afraid of the possible consequences of spending too much time in my own past."

She bent forward and lightly kissed me on the lips. "Very pragmatic. Take care of yourself, Will. Maybe at the end of this I will see you again."

"I don't know how I can ever thank you, Maud."

Her smile turned mischievous, and again her eyes moved over my chest. "I do. But the audience is waiting."

A final knock came, and she bustled to the door. She turned and blew me a kiss, and then opened the door just enough to pass through. When it closed behind her, I sank back down in the chair.

Seeing her again—so much like her old self and yet so unhappy—had shaken me. I wished that we'd had more time. I vowed to myself I would find her when all of this was over. Seeing me had seemed to help her—maybe there was something more I could do.

I had untied the dressing gown from around my waist and begun turning my thoughts toward the timepiece in my head when a realization stopped me cold.

I had the ability to learn the results of this conversation *now*. Neve had been right about my gift, and she had given me the confidence to more consciously and deliberately use it. Why go back to her now and drag her into an uncertain situation, when I could first discover whether our scheme had been effective? Maud could be unpredictable, and if she broke her promise—or heaven forbid, something happened to her—we would presumably be back where we started and I might find myself needing to quickly enlist the aid of someone else.

After a moment's more consideration, I shook off the idea. I had already made one decision without her, and I sensed she would view me returning to Knock Ma alone as a betrayal. Up to now, we had been equal partners in this, and it felt right to continue that way.

If she *chose* to remain behind, that was another matter.

AN OPEN QUESTION

NEVE

Watching a person disappear—especially one you'd just taken to bed—was unsettling, to say the least. The fact I didn't know where he'd gone, or whether he'd left intentionally, or *why he had left me behind* didn't make it any easier.

But one thing I'd definitely learned from this whole experience was that Will was competent and trustworthy. *Never mind the fact he can be a tad naive.*

I got up and grabbed my clothes—then thought a shower could be an excellent distraction. The prince had probably been sleeping for a couple hours at this point. That had the feel of a thorough nap, though god only knew when he'd last slept.

Slipping on Will's T-shirt because it mostly covered me—and because it already smelled like him—I crept quietly to my bedroom door and pressed my ear to it. All inside was quiet. I took hold of the old doorknob, closing my eyes and turning it as slowly as possible. It gave a rattle and a quiet squeak. Then I carefully pushed the door partway open and stuck my head through—his little body hadn't moved. Which might have worried me, but I could see his chest gently rising and falling. I pulled the door closed again.

I headed to the second bathroom. *This is going to be the best shower of my life.*

I never used Noah's shower, so after I turned on the water I opened a cabinet to look for old shampoo and conditioner bottles. I found them—along with *condoms.*

Steam had filled the bathroom and I hopped in the shower, intending to be quick. Instead I sat under the stream of water thinking about everything that had happened since the last time I was in my apartment. Despite the fact it was now two weeks later, for Will and me it had only been a couple of days. It felt impossible.

Will and me.

I was jolted from my hot-water reverie by the whine of the bathroom door. "Loki?" I squeaked, yanking open the curtain enough to let my head out.

Not Loki—the naked man who'd disappeared from my bed. Relief washed over me.

"Sorry," he said.

I wasn't sure whether he was apologizing for leaving so suddenly or for walking in on me in the shower. At the moment I didn't really care.

"Come here," I said, pushing the curtain open. "You're going to *love* this."

His eyes swept down my naked, wet body and he went instantly hard.

"You're right," he replied, "I do." I'd meant the shower, but whatever. The cleft between my legs grew hot and wetter.

"Come on," I repeated, my voice distinctly huskier this time.

He closed the door and twisted the lock, which got my heart thumping. Then he stepped across the small space and into the tub. I pulled him under the stream of water, and his arms came around me. His erection pushed into my belly and I let out a whimper.

I smeared the droplets of water across his chest with my fingers and then met his gaze—his eyes were honest-to-god sparkling. I reached a hand up to his face, and that was when I noticed he had something on his mouth—*lipstick.*

It sent a dart through my heart, which switched cadence from erotic excitement to free-falling panic.

I forced myself to take a breath and smile, and then I rubbed my thumb across his lips and showed it to him.

His expression would be forever seared into my mind. His eyes went wide as Frisbees, and, as fast as that erection had come on, the color drained from his face even faster.

"That's not—I don't—"

"Remember kissing a woman?"

"No, I *do,*" he sputtered. Then shook his head. "That is, she kissed *me.* I traveled back in time and found Maud. She—she's agreed to help us. She didn't mean anything by it. It's just . . . *Maud.*"

He somehow managed to look both panicked and crestfallen, and I started to laugh. Sure, it smarted, but Will was honest to a fault and I believed him. Besides, I had lectured him about falling in love with me, so it was hardly reasonable for me to start acting like a jealous girlfriend.

He started to speak again, and I put a finger over his lips. "Don't worry about it, it's hot."

I pulled his mouth to mine, kissing him hard and deep—pulling our heads under the water and immediately giving him all of my tongue.

When we came out for air, I said, "Do you want me, Will?" *More than you want that candy-red-lipstick-wearing first love of yours?*

He looked completely confused, but he nodded.

"Good. Show me."

His hands came to my hips and he pulled my body against his. Then his fingers dug into my buttocks and I let out another whimper.

"God," he uttered, "you're so . . ."

Apparently, the poet was at a loss for words—possibly because I had taken him in my hand.

"What shall we do with *this*?"

I ran my hand along the hard length of him and at the end let him spring from my hand. He groaned and curled his hands under my buttocks, lifting me off my feet. For half a heartbeat he looked uncertain—I nodded and wrapped my legs around his waist.

He pulled back the curtain and stepped out of the tub.

"Against the door," I suggested. Then, remembering my recent discovery, I said, "Hang on."

Slipping down to the floor, I tugged open the cabinet, grabbed a condom, and ripped it open with trembling fingers.

Holding up the rubber ring, I said, "I don't know if you have these. It's to keep me from having a baby, okay?"

He nodded quickly. "Okay."

Smiling at his use of my word, I moved closer and pressed the end of the condom over his erection. He throbbed in my hands as I rolled it down, and he let out a loud breath.

He lifted me again, propping my back against the door. Pressing my hands into his shoulders, I maneuvered my body until we had proper alignment, and suddenly, with a gasp, he pushed inside me.

I gave a shuddering moan and locked my legs around him as he began to thrust. The flesh between my legs was already quivering, the muscles inside already clenching—*one, two, three* strokes, and I was lost to shaking, pulsing sensation. My own contractions were just subsiding when he stiffened and came, his hips pinning me to the door panel. My head fell onto his shoulder and I mumbled hoarsely, "*Jesus*, Will."

When his muscles loosened, we melted into a pool of arms and legs on the floor.

We were still catching our breath when my phone chirped. I reached up to the sink and grabbed it—a text from Noah.

Heading back now

I typed: *OK*

I plunked the phone back down and Will stood up. He pulled me to my feet and I helped him off with the condom. Then he wrapped his arms around me, kissing my forehead. I shivered and nuzzled closer.

"Let me explain about earlier," he said.

"Let's get dressed first."

"Is it all right if I . . . ?" He reached for the shower curtain and I laughed.

"Sure, rinse off. Don't get addicted."

When we were dried and dressed, we went back out to the kitchen and I made us both coffee. I fixed mine just the way I liked it, and put out cream and sugar for him. It was my second coffee since coming home—I guess I was making up for lost time. I imagined if a person wasn't always running from the forces of darkness, they could probably find coffee somewhere in Ireland.

After a few seconds I noticed Will was staring at me with sort of an awestruck expression. "I've never experienced anything like that."

I grinned. "I imagine not."

"Thank you."

"You don't have to keep thanking me. You may have noticed it was good for me too."

"I did notice," he said, dropping his gaze to his cup.

Worried I was embarrassing him, I moved on. "What did you think of your first shower? The actual shower part, I mean."

"Wonderfully efficient." He looked at me, a glint in his eye. "The actual shower part, I mean."

The way he was looking at me made me want him to take my clothes off and get me messy again, but we had some unfinished business.

"So, Maud."

Will sighed and sipped his coffee. "Maud."

"Was she surprised to see you?"

"Less than you might have expected."

"You left here kind of abruptly. Did you know where you were going?"

"I think I must have. I was actually thinking about whether you could be right—that I have control over it—when it happened. But I'm not sure that going to Maud was initially a conscious choice."

"You did make a conscious choice to leave me behind though." I sloshed what was left of my coffee around in my cup. "We've kinda been partners up to now."

He chewed his lip. "I know. It was an impulse. I wasn't sure what was going to happen. And it was for the best, really—I mean we had not a stitch of clothing on."

Then he looked like he'd take back that last line if he could.

I smiled. "I bet she enjoyed that."

He cleared his throat. "Indeed, she did seem to."

Poor Will, not a false bone in his body. I had no right to interrogate him.

"Where was she? *How* was she?"

He set his cup down. "In Dublin, I believe. About to go on stage, oddly enough. That's why the . . ." He gestured to his lips.

"Ah. Stage makeup."

"Yes. As to *how* she was—dispirited, unfortunately."

"She was glad to see you, I gather."

"Very much so, I think."

"That doesn't surprise me."

He looked at me. "More importantly, she said she would help us."

"That's great, Will. Do you trust her?"

He nodded. "She's never given me any reason not to. Also, she seemed dissatisfied with her life, and I think my asking lifted her spirits."

"Well, you did say she has a war fetish."

I was dying to know the circumstances of the kiss, but before I could make an even bigger ass of myself, a small voice shouted, "Mama!"

I hurried around the bar and went to the bedroom. "Loki? Hey, kiddo."

The prince was sitting up in the bed, legs still tangled in the blanket I'd put over him, hugging the elephant stuffy to his chest. When he saw me, his bottom lip stuck out and he started to cry. I went to the bed and sat down next to him.

"I want Mama," he said.

"I know, I'm so sorry that she isn't here."

Will stepped into the door frame. We exchanged a worried glance. Had we done the right thing?

In the other room I heard a quiet knock, and Will went to answer the door.

"I know this is really hard," I said, "but Will and I want you to be safe from the monsters, so we brought you here to stay with our friend while we go help your mama. When everything's all safe, we'll come back and take you to her. Does that sound okay?"

He stared at me a moment, sniffling. Then he said, "No more monsters."

"That's right."

Another sniffle. Finally, he nodded. The boy had the most gorgeous dark curls—I allowed myself to brush them once lightly with my hand.

"I bet you're hungry," I said.

A quicker nod this time.

"Let's go to the kitchen. You can bring Mister Boop if you want."

The prince looked down at the stuffy. "He *really* likes kids," I said. "Especially brave ones like you. Do you know what a boop is?"

He shook his head. I tapped the end of his nose. "Boop."

A smile spread over his face and he hugged the stuffy tighter.

I winked at him. "Come on."

I untangled him from the blanket and he hopped down and ran into the other room. The silence was thick out there. Will was fiddling with his coffee cup at the bar, and Noah was standing in front of the living room windows watching him—pretty much as far away from each other as they could get in the small space.

Oh, brother.

"Loki, this is my friend Noah, who was here earlier." Noah walked over to us, kneeling down. "He's going to take very good care of you while we're gone. He's planning all kinds of fun stuff for you to do. We've got some kinds of magic here that I know you've never seen before." *And I'm sure his mother will thank us for introducing him to electronic babysitters.*

"Hi, Loki," said Noah, smiling. The boy offered a shy smile in return.

"I'm thinking he should mostly stay in your apartment," I said. "Who knows what the differences in diseases are between his world and ours, and I'm sure he's never been immunized for anything."

Noah nodded. "I hadn't thought of it, you're right. I can also pick up some masks."

"Good idea."

I walked into the kitchen and put the last sandwich on a plate. Will picked Loki up and set him on a bar stool. Loki proceeded to take the sandwich apart, inspecting each component before dropping it back on the plate, kicking his feet against the bar all the while. Then he started eating the bread. I filled a coffee mug with water and set that in front of him too.

"I'm a big fan of your work," Noah said, and I looked up. *Engaging the enemy.*

"My work?" replied Will, folding his arms.

"Your poetry," said Noah. "I'm sure Neve has told you that in our time—"

"I haven't."

Both men's eyes came to rest on me, and I pursed my lips together. "We've been kind of *busy*." I glanced at Will. "Noah is referring to the fact that you're pretty well known in our time."

Noah's long-suffering expression was almost comic. "I guess that's *one* way of saying he's one of the most recognized and respected poets of all time."

Will's eyes widened, and I sighed. "It's true. I was looking at your typewriter and saw part of a poem that's become such a classic that even I recognized it."

Noah's gaze swung to me. "Which one?"

I winced as I said, "The Stolen Child."

Will still had a stunned look on his face but was clearly suppressing elation. Noah just shook his head in disbelief.

Before Will could snap out of it enough to start asking questions that might trigger time travel ethical dilemmas, I suggested with mock brightness, "Shall we talk about the plan?"

"Why not," replied Noah dryly.

We regrouped in the living room while Loki continued to play with and eat his lunch. I went to one of my worktables and wrote Noah a check to cover Loki's expenses. I thought Noah was going to be weird about taking it, but he folded it and stuck it in a pocket.

Then I explained my idea about going back to warn the queen, and Will recounted his brief visit to the past. The longer we talked, the more worried Noah looked.

"So . . . I have questions." *Great.* Noah loved to play devil's advocate. He'd punch forty-two holes in this plan before he was through, and our options were thin already. "If you do, in fact, manage to fix things back there, is all of *this*"—he made a circular gesture with his finger—"going to have never happened?"

I looked at Will. "Possibly," he said.

"It's kind of unsettling, isn't it?" said Noah. "Of course I hope this works out in everyone's best interests, but I'll have lost a small piece of my life—despite the fact I'll never know about it because it will have never actually happened." He gave his head a shake at the unavoidably contorted logic. "I don't know how I feel about that."

"Me neither," I admitted. Because *some things* had happened between Will and me in the course of this visit. Not inconsequential things.

"Which raises the next question," Noah continued. *Ugh.* "If what you did—or are about to do—actually changed anything, would we even be here having this conversation?"

Will and I exchanged a glance. "Another good point."

How did he sound so calm? *He's Will.*

He rubbed his beard, thinking. Finally he said, "I don't think we can answer the second question, but it does stand to reason that if we are successful in preventing the Morrigan from taking Knock Ma, there will be no need to bring the prince here. It won't have happened."

"But we came up with the plan for you to visit your past

while we were here," I said, "which would be the very thing that prevents the Morrigan's victory. Coming here *has* to happen." My brain was starting to hurt. *I'm an artist, not a scientist, Jim.*

Will frowned and shook his head, giving up.

"And here we have it, folks," said Noah, "the quintessential time travel conundrum. I think it's a good bet the timeline will change, which means you continue to be missing without me ever knowing what happened to you. So I'm helping you on the condition that if you somehow manage to survive—and if you have any memory of this conversation—you'll come back here and let me know you're all right."

"That's fair," I replied. Though I was growing more uneasy about the idea of our memories of this visit vaporizing on our return to Ireland.

I glanced at Will, who by the look on his face was having similar thoughts. But he nodded. "Of course."

"So that's *if*, in fact, you've decided for sure you're doing this. Because at the bakery, it sounded like that was a bit of an open question."

Thanks, Noah.

I looked at Will, and he gave me one of his trademark gentle smiles. This one meant: *It's okay to change your mind.* We were starting to be able to read each other's thoughts.

"This is dangerous, Neve." Noah took a couple steps toward me. "It's messy and uncertain. I *know* you. These are a few of your not-favorite things."

He was right. Or at least if we went back in time a week or two, he would have been right then.

"You said it yourself," I replied. "I've changed. You noticed it before I even did."

"You're *okay* with that?" Noah's gaze flickered between Will and me. "This is what you *want*?"

"Am I okay with not being scared of my own shadow? Am I okay with my worries about things that might never happen not taking up all the space in my head? I am *so* okay with that."

His lips curled down in a gentle rebuke. "I helped with some of that, didn't I? It wasn't all bad."

I sighed. "You know it wasn't. And yes, you were really good to me. I just needed to grow. I don't mean up, but out. Sometimes I made my world so tight I could hardly breathe. I don't know that I ever *would* have if—" *Oh Jesus, Neve, shut up.*

Too late. I saw him finish the sentence in his head before doing it out loud: "If you'd been with *me*."

"I hope you understand that's not on you. It's on me." I groaned inwardly—did I really use a classic breakup line? I guess there was a reason it was a classic.

Technically this wasn't a breakup, it was unfinished business. But it sure felt like one. I hoped he didn't think this was about me choosing someone else. I hoped he wasn't comparing himself to Will—though I knew Noah, and he definitely *was.* I looked for Will, who'd moved away to let us talk—he was trying really hard to pretend he was engrossed in helping Loki tear up his turkey into bite-sized pieces. Will wasn't better than Noah, he just . . .

He'd shown me what a relationship *could* be, without even trying. He had helped me to see what I did and didn't need from another person.

Will gives me the space to become.

WILL

Noah was obviously in love with Neve. I hated myself for it, but I couldn't help wondering whether they had ever shared an experience like the one she and I had. If they had, how much harder it must be for him to let her go.

And how much harder it will be for me, when the time comes.

It was exactly what she had hoped to protect us both from.

Supposing we survived what was to come, I could hardly expect her to start a new life in Drumcliff. She was probably even less likely than Maud to agree to it. Nor could I see myself joining her in this strange future, curious as I might be about a place where you could boil water with the flick of a knob, or indulge in "sex" outside marriage free from consequences.

Nothing is free from consequences.

"Will?"

I turned from Loki, who was making a game of whirling a slice of tomato on one finger. Neve and Noah's discussion had been of such a private nature I'd tried not to hear—it had proven nearly impossible, especially when she started talking about how she'd changed. She was trying to be honest about why she refused to be romantically involved with him, and I admired her for it. She also described a rigidity of her former life that was hard for me to imagine, based on what I knew of her.

"I think it's time to go back," she said.

I smiled down at the boy. His expression was apprehensive. "Are you ready for your next adventure, Your Highness?"

He gave a slow nod, and he reached for the toy elephant that he'd set next to his plate. Then he hopped down from the stool and ran to Neve. She sank down beside him.

"You are so brave that I think your mother and father must be very brave too," she said. "I bet you learned it from them."

"Dada is king of the fairies!" he said, blue eyes wide and bright. "And Mama can *fly*. When I'm big, I can go to Iceland."

"What a lucky boy you are." She put her hand on the toy. "Will you take good care of Mister Boop? He gets scared sometimes, and then you need to give him a squeeze."

The prince tightened his grip on the toy.

"That's right. I'll feel so much better knowing you're looking after him."

She touched the boy's nose and stood. Watching her with him had been a revelation. I hadn't spent much time around children, but she seemed to always know the right thing to say. For the boy's sake, I hoped that we *had* made a change that would mean he never need be parted from his mother. Yet I also desperately hoped that I would retain the memories of this visit.

Noah put his arms around Neve. "Please don't get killed."

"I'll do my best. And I promise I'll do everything in my power to make sure we see each other again."

"As will I," I said.

Noah eyed me before letting her go, and his expression was easy to read: *I'm holding you responsible.* That made two of us.

Noah held out a hand to Loki. Neve touched the boy's hair again, and then walked them to the door. After a final, quiet good-bye, we were alone again.

When she turned from the door, I could see she was worried.

"I want to go soon," she said. "I don't like not knowing whether your visit to Maud made a difference."

"I feel the same." I couldn't help wondering, though, if her sudden urgency was more about being afraid she might change her mind. "Neve, are you certain about this?"

She laughed uneasily. "I wish people would stop asking me that."

"It's just . . . it seems important to be sure."

She nodded, and she studied the inside of her wrist—the clock tattoo. "Did I tell you it's not working anymore?" she said.

"You didn't."

"I can't help wondering if it's because I don't belong here. Because the Morrigan put me in the wrong timeline."

Why these questions now, I wondered? Was she looking for

the certainty that might come with believing in fate? A certainty that could give her the courage to make a hard choice?

"Could be," I said carefully. "Or maybe it has something to do with your magic." *It could mean so many things, or nothing at all.*

She closed her fingers around her wrist. "For as long as I can remember, I've felt like part of me was missing. I saw a therapist for a while who thought it was because of my mother's illness—because we hadn't been able to have a strong bond. And it probably was. But now I wonder if maybe it wasn't the only reason."

Suddenly it dawned on me. She wasn't looking for certainty about returning to my world, she was looking for certainty about *me.* She hadn't wanted to risk falling in love with someone she might lose. The idea of fate taking away your choice in love would disturb some people. Could it be that for Neve there was a sense of safety in something that was meant to be? In the possibility that if our memories of this visit *were* lost, we were destined to find our way to the same intimacy in the new timeline?

Though I wasn't sure where I stood on the question of fate, I wasn't about to say so—especially if her believing in it meant she was less frightened of the idea of *us.*

"I'd say it's worth considering."

She smiled, and how I wished we had more time together.

I reached for her hand. "Shall we go?"

She nodded. "Should we talk about when? It seems pretty important that we don't arrive before we left, and bump into ourselves."

"Agreed."

"It's probably safer to even overshoot by a day or two."

"While taking care not to arrive too late to be of any use to them. Like before."

"Is that kind of precision going to be possible?"

Shrugging, I replied, "Good timing is necessary for us to succeed, so . . ."

"Right. You work well under pressure. It's an excellent life skill."

I bent and picked the horn up off the floor, hanging the strap across my chest. "We have *when*; should we talk about *where?*"

"I think the castle, don't you? The grounds may be overrun, but if your lady friend did what you asked her to, and if it worked . . ."

"The castle, then."

Neve retrieved her spellbook, and I picked up the sword.

"Ready?" I asked.

For an answer, she slipped her arms around me and pressed her cheek against my chest. I wrapped my free arm around her shoulders and closed my eyes, enjoying this closeness in case it was for the last time.

DAMN THE PARLEY

WILL

"The man of the hour is here."

I recognized the voice of Queen Isolde before we'd even managed to regain our bearings.

"Are you all right?" I asked Neve. She was pale, but she smiled and nodded.

We'd arrived back at the great hall. The first thing I noticed was Queen Koli coming toward us. My heart lifted. Her husband wasn't far behind her.

I dared to hope Maud had kept her word, and our plan had *worked*.

To my surprise, Koli came close and embraced me.

"Your Majesty," I said, "I'm very happy to see you here."

"We've been informed that you've witnessed our downfall," broke in Queen Isolde. Her tone managed to be both scolding and gentle. "But you've succeeded, and all of that is no more than a bad dream. Meanwhile we've been waiting on that blasted horn."

"Where's Loki?" asked Neve.

Isolde raised an eyebrow at the impertinence and I had to suppress a grin.

We heard a childish giggle, and the prince popped out of a tent near the fireplace that looked to have been constructed of chairs and tablecloths. Then another child peeked out from the tent—a girl with silver hair. *Lady Alva*. The prince came running over to us and threw his arms around Neve's legs.

"Loki!" scolded his mother. "I'm sorry, Miss Kelly, I don't—"

"It's all right, Your Majesty," said Neve, smiling down at the boy. "Do you know who I am, Your Highness?"

The boy grinned widely. He held out something to her—a wooden toy warrior.

"*Ulf. Frændi,*" he said in his mother's language. Then in English, "Take good care of him."

Neve took the toy, shooting me an incredulous look, and the prince ran back into the tent. *Take good care of him*—Neve had said the same to *him* about a different toy. Was it possible for him to remember something that had never actually happened? Or at least for some part of him to remember it?

I remember. Despite the fact that we had apparently erased the Morrigan's defeat of our friends. We seemed to be forging our own strange timeline between the two worlds.

"We've had the whole story from Isolde," said Queen Koli. There was strain in her voice. "I know that you've saved us all, but my *son* . . ." Her gaze took in Neve as well. "My husband and I will never forget what you've done."

"He's a pretty great little boy," said Neve.

She opened her hand, looking at the toy warrior a moment before holding it out to Koli. The queen smiled and said, "That is Ulf, a close family friend, and my regent in the kingdom of the shadow elves. My son must think very highly of you to give it up." She reached out and closed Neve's fingers over the toy. Ulf, too, had fought alongside Koli and Finvara at the first Battle of Knock Ma.

"I'm sure we're all agreed that the two of you have done very well," said Isolde. "But we are far from out of the woods. Please join us."

I was relieved to see all of the O'Malley cousins were present—plus one guest that I was not prepared for. Maud sat at the great banquet table, at the left hand of the queen. She was beaming at me, eyes bright with excitement. She looked well—kempt and healthy, finely dressed in a military-style jacket patterned after the queen's.

"Maud!" I said, and felt Neve's attention focus.

"Surprised I kept my word?" Maud's tone was teasing.

"Not at all, but grateful for it." I led Neve to the table and we joined the others. "I admit, it didn't occur to me that I might see you, though perhaps it should have."

"Indeed it should," she said with a laugh. "Thought I would let you have all the fun?"

I was heartened by the change in her. Then I remembered she was to have been married. Before I could inquire about her husband, Lord Meath said, "Pardon the interruption, Will, but how did you come by that sword?"

I was setting Great Fury on the bench beside us, next to the satchel with the spellbook. "We found it with Prince Loki, my lord—in the previous timeline. I assumed you'd brought it with you to Knock Ma."

He shook his head. "It vanished after the Battle of Ben Bulben. I have often wondered about it."

"Then I'm pleased to be able to return it to you," I said, raising it again.

"No indeed, it's yours. We are all in your debt, and I have my father's sword. I'm sure that my ancestor would be pleased for his friend Oisin to carry it. And the sword itself does not appear to object."

Diarmuid and Oisin had both been Fianna warriors. In the histories, they had fought side by side many times—including the battle where Oisin and Niamh had lost their lives.

"I'm not sure I quite know what to do with it," I said. "But I am honored, my lord."

"When the need arises," the earl said in a somber tone, "you will know." I waited for him to say more, but he lifted his glass of whiskey to his lips.

Perhaps he was right—it had already happened once.

Koli called one of the servants over to the table, and she asked him to fetch a scabbard for the weapon from the armory. I lifted the strap of Borabu over my head, and Queen Isolde said, "This is it, then?"

I held up the horn for them to see. "It is. Neve found it in the hall of the Horned God."

"The Horned God!" exclaimed Lady Meath. "You've met him then?"

"We have, my lady."

"Is he going to help us?" asked Isolde.

"We asked him, Your Majesty." I exchanged a glance with Neve. "I'm sorry to say that we failed on that point."

"Why do they never meddle when you wish them to?" exclaimed the queen. "Perhaps he might like to know that the Morrigan has burned the forest, and her army of monsters is encamped outside these walls."

So we had prevented the sudden defeat, but not the siege or the fire. In burning the forest, the Morrigan had cut off another potential source of aid, and she well knew it—the goddess was the one who had suggested before the first Battle of Knock Ma that the trees could be an ally.

The queen shook off her annoyance. "At any rate, the only reason we are not sacked already is your cleverness, and Miss Gonne's faithfulness and loyalty to Ireland."

I looked at Maud, and she visibly warmed under the praise. It occurred to me she was exactly where she had always hoped to be. Neve fidgeted in her seat beside me, and I reached for her hand, pulling it into my lap.

"Over the past months," continued Isolde, "I've quietly deployed my army to the neighboring farms and estates. Two nights ago, on Samhain, the Morrigan incinerated the grounds—thanks to you, we were prepared to employ our own magic and survive it. Last night, Far Dorocha led her army of revenants from Faery to march on Knock Ma. Under cover of darkness, our forces flanked them, pinning them down outside the walls by this morning. I believe we are a match for them, and the Morrigan's efforts thus far will have been a drain on her power. Still, we have no way of knowing what else is coming."

Something perplexing occurred to me then. "I'm sorry to interrupt, Your Majesty, but did the two of us come to you here on the day of the Samhain feast, bringing a warning about the Morrigan?"

The queen's eyes fixed on me. "Indeed you *did*, William, and disappeared again before the battle began. Thanks to your emissary's experience on the stage"—she gestured to Maud, who was glowing—"when you first arrived I was able to deliver a performance that convinced everyone I knew nothing of the impending attack. I was afraid if I did not, I might alter the sequence of events in a way that would prevent you from finding the horn, or from time traveling to deliver the message to Miss Gonne."

The queen had known all along? Thinking back to the day we first arrived here, I thought the queen's performance had been extraordinary indeed. *Then* I realized that what was fixed in my memory could be the version of events where she had not yet known about the planned attack.

I looked at Neve, whose eyes were wide. "We are *way* off the map, Will," she whispered. I had to agree.

"A message was brought to us just before you arrived here today," continued the queen. "The Morrigan wishes us to parley with her general, and we have come together to confer. We of course suspect treachery. Needless to say, your timing could not be better, William." Her gaze moved among the others. "What is our next play?"

"Damn the parley and sound the horn," said King Finvara, pounding an empty whiskey glass onto the table.

"Hear, hear," replied Lord Meath. "Let us waste no more breath."

"I'm inclined to agree, but what say you, ladies?"

"For the sake of argument," said Lady Meath, "I would point out that if we corner her, she may unleash everything she has on us. Though that may be a question of *when* rather than if."

Isolde nodded. "Agreed on both counts. Koli?"

Finvara's queen fixed her gaze on Lady Meath. "I think it's time for the children to go."

Lady Meath frowned, but she nodded and rose from the table. Her husband rose too, and the two of them approached the makeshift tent.

"Where will they go?" Neve asked Koli.

"Lady Meath and the keening women will accompany them," said Koli. "The *bean sidhe*. They'll go to Faery, to a location none of us know."

To prevent the Morrigan from getting the information out of anyone. I shuddered.

Lord and Lady Meath were taking leave of each other, and Koli and Finvara got up to say goodbye to their son. Loki was to be separated from his mother again—it would seem some things *were* fated. But at least this time there was hope.

It was a somber moment, and the rest of us tried to give them privacy. As Lady Meath was leaving the hall with the children, Loki broke free and ran back to his mother. Koli turned and caught him in her arms, and the king wrapped his arms around both of them. I heard Neve sniffle beside me, and I pressed her hand in both of mine.

"It won't be for long, son," said the king. I suspected the words of comfort were as much directed at himself and his wife. Finvara drew back and looked at Koli. "Will you not go with him?"

The queen was murmuring a demurral when a servant entered the hall and approached with a scabbard. I got up from the table and belted it around my waist. The sheath was a little wide for the sword, but it was a vast improvement over carrying it.

"We're agreed then," said Queen Isolde. She too rose from her chair as Lady Meath and the children left. "Let us go up."

NEVE

We followed the others to the stairs that ran up one wall of the great hall. A panicky drumbeat started in the middle of my chest as we climbed to the roof.

I thought about the story of Oisin and Niamh—how in the end they had gone to war and died. Was it possible we were doing everything *wrong*? Could we create a different outcome this time, or were we about to repeat a tragic cycle? It was common in mythology, wasn't it? Fate was often cruel.

We popped out on top of the keep and crossed to one end, where a section of the wall was bookended between two towers—I believed we were facing westish. The castle was on a hilltop, and beyond the moat, lower hills rolled away in all directions.

The view was worth five stars on Airbnb—layers of clouds and sky blended into the dark ocean to the west, and the whitecaps seemed to glow.

I didn't spend much time gazing at the scenery, however, for around the castle was a wide ring of felled, charred trees, even wider than the one we'd seen in the previous timeline. There were still isolated pockets of flame and smoke. The enemy was sprawled in a valley, maybe a football field to the southwest, as the crow flew.

The Morrigan's army of the undead.

We could *smell* them from here—the sweet-foul odor of decay. Most of the soldiers were huddled and crouching on the ground, but even at this distance I could feel them watching us—it raised the hairs on the back of my neck. Half a dozen heavily armored figures on horseback—*undead horses?*—rode among them, occasionally barking orders. Now and then a flaming arrow came zipping up from the camp, but the effort seemed half-hearted and the arrows fell pretty far short.

In the center of the camp was a weird kind of . . . *pile.* It was hard to make out from this height, but there seemed to be a structure, and a bunch of the undead guys were crawling around on it. It reminded me of bees on a hive, which somehow made it creepier.

In a half circle beyond the enemy encampment, spread out over the more hilly terrain, we could see and hear the queen's army—armor clanking, green-and-gold standard whipped by the stiff breeze. It lifted my spirits—without Will and me, they wouldn't be here.

"I'm sure someone besides me has thought of this," I murmured to Will, "but wouldn't a few cannons make short work of that camp? The Morrigan burned all their cover and their escape route is cut off. They're just kind of lying there in a heap."

"There are no cannons here," he said. "Gunpowder is tricky

around fairies. Dangerous to leave lying around, and it's also easily disabled by spells. The Morrigan herself disabled firearms in the Battle of Ben Bulben."

"Well, that was . . . an interesting choice."

"Forces both sides onto equal footing, does it not?" Maud had drawn close without me noticing. "She *is* the goddess of war."

Nobody asked you. I had taken an instant dislike to her. Because obviously.

Will was literally surrounded by mysterious and beautiful women. And they were all so damn graceful and competent. The men weren't too shabby either. It felt like hanging out with the Cullens.

"You must be Neve," said the actress, only she used the Niamh pronunciation. Her eyes moved over my Portland clothes in a way that made me want to strangle her. "I'm Maud, but maybe you already know that."

"Hey. How are you?" *That's great, Neve.*

"Very well, thank you—so pleased that this has worked out. The two of you are incredibly brave. And I must say, it's so romantic."

Why was she smiling so much? Why did Will keep going all gawky whenever she looked at him? And why was I not properly grateful that she helped to save Will's friends?

"William." Queen Isolde shot him a stern look. This lady, on the other hand, I was starting to like. "*The horn.*"

"Your Majesty."

Borabu hung at his back, and I lifted and handed it around to him. He raised it to his lips, casting a sidelong glance at me.

"You've got this."

He took a deep breath, and immediately I smashed my hands over my ears—the thing was deep and *loud*, like an emergency beacon. Worse than that, as soon as the call began to sound, the crowd down on the battlefield let loose a bunch of unearthly shrieks.

Will must have sounded the horn for a full ten seconds. When it ended, we all held our breath. I reached for Will's hand, and he raised mine to his lips and kissed the back of it.

Like I was ever going to *not* fall for this guy.

Drums started down in the encampment. The rhythm was low and slow—I could feel it through the stones of the castle. *THUMP-thump, THUMP-thump, THUMP-thump.* Gradually it picked up speed, like a heartbeat. I wasn't sure I'd ever heard anything more chilling. The enemy soldiers began to stir.

"There!" King Finvara shouted, pointing.

Something was definitely moving on the grounds—I realized it was the *ground* itself. A hilltop north of the camp was slowly caving in, swallowing the blackened trees that had stood on its peak. A crater opened up, like a volcano. Then something—or actually a bunch of somethings—started clawing their way out of it. The edges of the crater collapsed under the weight of whatever was frantically digging.

Soon, there were a dozen of them around the perimeter of the hole—they lifted their snouts to the wind and howled.

Wolves.

More were digging out, and the hill continued to crumble. When there were maybe two hundred, they formed a pack at the base of the hill, shaking the dirt from their coats as they continued to yap and howl.

But that wasn't the end of it—some kind of deer was coming out too, tossing enormous antlers that were wide, flat, and smooth like bat wings but with wickedly pointed tips. They were elk the size of horses and they looked like they belonged to another age. Now the officers of both armies were shouting orders, rousing the soldiers and forming lines.

"Is this what you thought would happen?" I asked Will.

His gaze was glued to the action. "Uindos mentioned that

the horn had called his creatures to aid in the Battle of Connacht, but *no*."

"Yeah he made it pretty clear he wasn't interested in helping us again, but maybe what we told him about the Morrigan made a difference. What about the Fianna?"

Will shook his head. "I don't know, maybe they've gone beyond our—"

Lord Meath shouted something in Irish, and I saw *more* things digging themselves out of the crater—these were man-shaped things, and they made a god-awful and very testosterone-inspired racket. Everyone standing at the parapet—royals and guards alike—whooped and shook weapons in the air.

Will's face lit up, and I stood on my toes, curving an arm around his neck and kissing him on the lips. He flung an arm around my waist, lifting me off my feet.

Take that, Will's first love.

Unlike the Irish army, the Fianna were dressed in animal skins and leather armor. They carried wooden shields, long spears, and knives or short swords. Some of them moved among the herd of giant elk, climbing up onto their backs. I thought I saw women among them, though it was hard to be sure from this distance.

The undead army had managed to assemble a shield wall—two shield walls, actually, because the wildlife and the Fianna were about to charge from the north, while the Irish army was lining up to attack from the west. This was definitely not my area of expertise, but it looked like the enemy was pretty badly outnumbered at this point.

"Where is the Morrigan?" called Will over the racket.

"We haven't seen her since she set fire to the trees," replied Maud.

There was a truly wild light in the woman's eyes, and I had to admit it had its appeal. She looked like some kind of sexy war goddess herself, with her military jacket and tailored breastplate, fronds of loose hair whipping around at the base of her neck.

A bunch of shouts fired off in sequence among the armies, and the Irish and the mounted Fianna charged the shield walls. Antlers slashed and canine jaws snapped. Weapons clanged loudly against the Irish army's metal shields. The elk-horses were seriously badass, mowing down three or four of the undead at a time, sometimes flinging them several yards. I had wondered if you could actually *kill* the undead, but soon discovered that once they were crushed they couldn't really get back up—especially if a wolf got hold of an ankle and started pulling them apart.

The *realness* of this battle crept up on me. I'd watched plenty of gory battle scenes on screen—and covered my eyes through the worst of it. I tried squinting, thinking that might somehow make it easier, but the whole gruesome drama was playing out right in front of me.

"Are you all right?" Will had slipped an arm around me.

I nodded. "Yeah. It's just—I guess I'm the virgin now."

I was appalled that I'd said it—I hadn't meant to make a joke of it. It was an easy way of communicating "you may be used to this but I'm not." Will seemed to understand, and he hugged me closer. I turned my face into his shoulder, feeling faintly nauseous and guilty besides. This was about their family and their future, and *they* were watching. I realized I had to stop thinking that way—it had become about my future too. Ever since Will brought me here and we started wreaking havoc on the timeline.

Maybe from the moment Niamh caught Oisin napping in the forest.

There was still a lot of hooting and hollering on the roof, and I caught a snatch of conversation between Finvara and Lord Meath, who were eager to go down and join the fight. Isolde and Maud both stood like statues. I could see the many gears turning behind

Isolde's eyes—hers was the face of a champion chess player. Maud, however, was unfathomable to me. Was she queasy too, and trying to hide it? Was she engrossed in the battle?

"Who is that down there?" I heard Koli ask. "Is it the Morrigan?"

Now that the army of the undead had charged out to meet their enemies, we could see that weird pile *was* a hive-like structure, but made of metal. Next to it stood a lone, dark figure, and next to that a standard flapped in the breeze—a standard with a crow, like the one Will and I had seen on the castle in the original timeline.

"What is happening with my men?" interrupted Isolde. "The fallen soldiers. Finvara, what do you see?"

It was Will who answered. "They don't seem to be . . . staying dead."

I let my eyes graze over the action until settling on a green-coated soldier stretched on the ground, arrows sticking out of his chest. The man slowly got to his feet, and I watched him break off each arrow, slowly and deliberately, leaving the heads lodged in his chest. Then he grabbed a saber from the ground and hacked down a fellow soldier.

"Jesus!" I cried, averting my gaze.

"The fallen are rising," the king confirmed grimly, "and *switching sides*."

"She's using dark magic," muttered his wife.

"It won't matter," said Lord Meath. "She's vastly outnumbered now."

He didn't sound to me like he was convinced.

"I need a messenger," said Isolde.

This got Koli's attention. The younger queen turned, and suddenly a raven *burst right out of her chest*. Thankfully it looked more like a ghost raven than a real one. By the time it swooped around in a circle and alighted on the parapet in front of Isolde, it had taken a more solid form.

"Maud," said Isolde, "take this down."

Will's lady friend drew a small notepad and pencil out of a jacket pocket. "Go ahead, Your Majesty."

"General Varma," began the queen, "please be advised—"

A blast of cold, rotten wind suddenly swept over us. Will and I hunched against each other. There was a loud growling sound that I recognized, and I looked around frantically for the source.

The throat-tunnel. It had opened up in the curving wall of one of the towers, six or eight yards to our right. *Huge* men were running through it. Warriors—they had elf ears like Koli and looked like the toy the prince had given me.

"Shadow elves!" said Will.

Was this good news? I thought Will had said they were allies of Ireland. *But the throat-tunnel.*

There was shouting, grunting, grappling as more warriors charged through and began to clash with the guards. I heard Queen Koli's voice over the others—she was yelling in her own language, and she sounded *pissed.* She'd drawn a wicked-looking knife, and the king and earl had drawn their swords. *Note to self: obtain pointy weapon other than pencil.*

"What's happening?" I asked Will as he drew his sword and moved to stand in front of me.

Before he could answer, one of the elves ran right at us. Will raised Great Fury and the big guy swung a knife like Koli's. The weapons clanged together, the force knocking Will backward into me. He lunged and swung again, blue light dancing along the blade of his sword, making the runes glow. This time, as the weapons clashed the warrior lost his grip and dropped his knife.

Will prepared to swing again, but suddenly hundreds of wildly flapping wings filled the air around us. Enraged ravens dive-bombed the newcomers, their beaks and talons tearing at scalps and arms. But there were *so* many elves—probably fifty warriors on the roof with us now.

A command rang out in a frighteningly familiar voice.

Franken-fae.

The birds were disintegrating, trailing black vapor around us until that too evaporated. With the air cleared, I could see Far Dorocha's hulking form standing next to two elves who were struggling to hold onto Koli. I moved out from behind Will to see her better—she had some kind of chain around her wrists. It was light and silvery and didn't look strong enough to hold *Loki*, let alone his mother. The harder she fought, the more securely the chain seemed to hold her—I could see the links digging into her wrists.

"*Brisingr*," said Will.

Before I could ask him what *that* meant, King Finvara shouted something in Irish, or maybe Elvish. He and the earl were back-to-back against the parapet, brandishing their swords.

Far Dorocha pointed his sword at Queen Koli's belly. "Hold your tongues and drop your weapons—all of you—or I will kill her child."

My heart lurched. Finvara made an anguished sound and threw down his sword—it clanged loudly against the stones. Lord Meath and Will dropped their weapons too.

Far Dorocha lumbered into the midst of his subdued foes, eying us with malice. He was even more terrifying in the natural light, his revenant flesh a sickly gray except for the parts that looked burned. Even if someone managed to raise a weapon, so much of his body was metal it was hard to imagine making a dent.

"Maud," he said, his tone coolly mocking, "take this down."

My eyes darted to the actress—she stood beside Queen Isolde, who was in the grip of two elves. Like Will and me, Maud was apparently not threatening enough to warrant capture. Maybe she had no magic.

But I have magic. Magic I only half knew how to use, and that—my heart plunged into ice water—*that I'd left below in the great hall.* I thought I might be sick. Though I had no idea what I'd have done with a sketchbook right now.

Maud raised the notepad and pencil. Her eyes were bright—but she didn't look afraid. Her imperviousness to mortal peril reminded me of Will's—he had a kind of boundary between himself and what I would consider a natural response to fear. It allowed him to think in a crisis. This woman I could *not* get a read on. If our current circumstances hadn't been so dire, I would have suspected she was enjoying herself.

"To Her Majesty, Queen Isolde of Ireland," began the metallic zombie nightmare, "please be advised that the queen should have accepted the proffered parley, because now we shall be forced to do things the less pleasant way."

Maud looked unsure. Was this just Far Dorocha being an asshole, or was she really supposed to write it down? In the end she did put pencil to paper and scribble. Then she looked at him. "Will your mistress be coming to the castle?"

What are you doing, you weirdo?

"Be silent!" snapped Far Dorocha, turning the milky eye on her. She took a step back. "*I* am the one you serve now."

The color drained from Maud's face and she lowered her notepad.

The monster then looked up at—*Will?* He strode across the rooftop toward us. He didn't slow as he got closer, and panic flared—we were right against the parapet.

"Will!" I cried.

Will gave me a shove toward the king and earl, and I stumbled. Far Dorocha plowed right into Will, gripping around his neck and raising him off his feet. A scream froze in my throat as time stopped. A vision inserted itself between me and Will.

The heavy sword struck, biting deep into his flesh. The beast planted a foot against his chest, kicking him free from the sword.

The vision faded. I screamed as Far Dorocha threw Will over the parapet.

I lurched to the wall, reaching out for him like it would make any difference. Maud was suddenly beside me shouting, "*Will!*"

His body glanced off a buttress and plunged into the moat below.

FOOD FOR THE PIKES

NEVE

"She said you *needed* him!" Maud shouted at Far Dorocha.

I looked at her, tears streaming down my face. "What?" I choked out.

As my gaze moved between them, something clicked—*they know each other.*

A war fetish seems like a total red flag.

She'd betrayed us.

Queen Koli spat something in Elvish, and I looked over and saw the elves wrapping that same flimsy-looking chain around the wrists of everyone on the roof. I thought it must have some power against magic because no one else had cast any spells. But what the hell did I know.

What I know is the person I'd normally ask is dead or dying.

My heart felt shattered. I glanced down at my chest expecting to find I was bleeding. My vision spun and I gripped the parapet. My body heaved as my stomach tried and failed to empty itself.

This isn't happening.

I struggled to follow what was going on. Some of the elves were piling up bodies of the green-coats and the firglas—except for the ones they flung over the parapet.

I have to get to Will. He could be alive.

Far Dorocha, having apparently disposed of his primary target—the one who could time travel and call the Fianna—was now occupied with securing the royals. I took my chance and darted toward the stairs that lead back down to the great hall.

One of the warriors simply turned into my path and I smacked up against him like a wall. He spun me around and pinned down my arms. For a few seconds I saw stars.

"*Why?*" Maud shouted at Far Dorocha. The absurd excitement had finally been wiped off her face. "I *helped* you. You wouldn't have brought reinforcements without my information." She gestured at a cluster of elves.

The monster lifted one wiry eyebrow as his mouth contorted into something like a smile, blackened lips revealing the jagged edges of broken teeth.

"Of course they killed him, you *child*!" I exploded at Maud, pointlessly struggling against the mountain behind me. "He was the biggest threat to their whole plan. What the fuck were you *thinking*? Oh right, you were too busy setting yourself up as junior war goddess to consider the consequences. War is not a *game*, Maud."

She went completely still, her gaze trained on the flagstones. Nobody said anything for a few breaths, and I could hear the sounds of the battle, unaffected by what was happening at the castle. I strained to hear splashing noises, or anything that might give me hope Will had survived.

Finvara muttered something in Irish, and I heard a thump and a groan.

Far Dorocha was watching Maud too, and he looked like he'd taken about as much from her as he was going to. "Will you join the others in bonds?" he asked curtly. "Or perhaps your friend, as food for the pikes?"

Fresh tears started down my face.

Finally Maud raised her head and looked at me, seeming to study me without emotion. Her features had smoothed, though her tears were still drying.

"I serve the Morrigan now. As was agreed."

If we'd just stayed in Portland instead of trying to be heroes. If I'd just listened to Noah.

I'm so sorry, Will.

"Where is Ulf?" Queen Koli snapped at her elf guards. She spoke English—strange, since she was speaking to her own people. But Will and his friends seemed to switch languages as easily as breathing. Then *what* she'd said sank in. *Ulf*—where had I heard that name?

A close family friend, and my regent in the kingdom of the shadow elves.

The prince's toy. Which was also in the great hall, in the satchel with the spellbook that was never supposed to leave my side.

"Likely he has been tossed into a volcano by now," replied Far Dorocha. "How long did you think your people would tolerate a regent? A half-ruler? And a warrior who betrayed his king. You should know them better. I assure you *I* have made it my business to."

I knew from Will that Koli had once been an enemy of Ireland—she was the Elf King's daughter—and she had become queen of both fairies and elves after the first Battle of Knock Ma. I expected a reaction from her to this news of her friend, but she closed her mouth, and she looked directly at *me*.

Will is gone. What does any of this matter?

Of course it did matter to her, and to all of them. Their families were at risk. I could do nothing for them though. Will had been the one with the power to change the future. And the past. I just wanted to go back home where I belonged.

Franken-fae took a few heavy steps toward Queen Isolde, who was captured and bound like the others. So far she had done nothing except watch events unfold. She didn't shrink from him now, and if looks could kill, this whole thing would be over in a heartbeat.

"We would have far preferred this war of unity to remain among family," said Far Dorocha. "But you and your poet couldn't help meddling."

Queen Isolde laughed. *Laughed.* It was the kind of laugh you'd hope to never hear—like a big, buttercream-frosted cupcake that you knew without a doubt was laced with arsenic. I watched for Far Dorocha to flinch because *I* would have crawled into the nearest crack in the wall.

Her laughter faded and the vaporizing expression returned. "War of unity. How charming."

"Perhaps it was for the best. How better to ensure the security of our borders than by making allies of our nearest, most powerful enemies?" Far Dorocha leaned closer, and still the queen didn't flinch. "Of course we would never have been forced to these extremes in the first place had our borders not been breached *twice* on your watch."

Did he mean the battles of Ben Bulben and Knock Ma? If so, he was seriously twisting things around—Will had said Far Dorocha's betrayal caused the first Battle of Knock Ma. After that the elves became allies to Ireland because of Koli's marriage to Finvara.

A cruel smile spread over Isolde's face. "*Do* distort history if you think it will help. Everyone here knows this is nothing more than a naked grab for power."

And that you're a gaslighting asshole.

Far Dorocha turned his back on her. "Take them below."

Maud came toward me and I glared swords, knives, and axes at her. She stopped short, and I congratulated myself. Then she bent and picked up something from the ground. It was one of those chains they'd been using to bind the others.

She came closer, holding it out. *Seriously, bitch?*

It was laughable, really. I had no superpower. The tenpenny magic I did possess I had *forgotten*, leaving it down in the hall where it could help exactly no one.

The elf gripped my forearms painfully, nails digging into my skin, and pushed my hands out to her. I felt her cool fingers against the underside of my wrists as she wrapped them with the chain, fastening it—only that wasn't exactly what happened. There were rings at either end of the chain—they made up the clasp, though I wasn't sure how it worked. Maud's trembling fingers were pressing these rings against the palms of my hands, which were angled toward the ground. On impulse I pressed my pinkie fingers against them, holding them in place, and she pulled her hands away. One ring almost slipped free, but I jerked my hands slightly and secured it.

She didn't fasten the chain.

"You are far from the first to fall under the spell of Far Dorocha," Koli snapped at Maud. The fire that had seemed to go out of her returned. "You will suffer for it in ways you can't yet imagine."

Maud's gaze came to rest on my face, and for about half a second, there was finally an expression I could read . . . *I have already suffered for it.*

She's an actress, I reminded myself. Was she acting now, or had she been acting earlier, when she reasserted her loyalty to the Morrigan?

In my heart I knew the answer. *She's still in love with Will.*

WILL

I struck something hard on the way down. I never had time to feel the pain because next I struck the surface of the water and discovered liquid can become more like a solid with distance and speed. The flesh that had slapped the surface burned, despite the water's frigid temperature.

The light was fading. I tried to swim toward it and discovered my legs no longer obeyed my commands. I stroked my arms frantically—I didn't have the strength to keep it up.

Some claimed this moat was bottomless, but I knew it was a myth. The moat had once been emptied by the very creature who had just killed me—in an ironic attempt to *save* the life of King Finvara. I chuckled, watching my last air bubbles escape toward the surface.

I made a few more strokes with my arms—one more desperate reach for the light. The cold was seeping into my bones. Borabu floated above my head, still tethered to my body.

In my mind's eye, I could see the heroes in Neve's vision, laid upon the blood-soaked ground. *Their* enemies had given them a chance to say goodbye, even if only so they could mock them.

Pushing these images away, I remembered how I'd lain beside Neve and watched her sleep. I remembered her weight on my chest, and how blissful it had felt to be pinned down by her.

I love you.

Why didn't I say it when I had the chance? What would it have cost me? Maybe she would have run from me, but then at least she wouldn't have had to watch me die. What would become of her now?

There was still enough light for me to notice something looming off to my right—it startled me, despite the fact my senses had begun to dull. The body's will to survive was strong.

Abide with me.

Was there a voice, or was it delirium? Maybe my own thoughts had formed the words. They were soothing. They reached down into me. Slowing my heart. Warming my blood. I wished I had a pencil to write them down.

The shadow, I realized, was a tree trunk. I had been floating among the branches for some time now. I reached out and touched the rough bark. Not a hallucination, then. Or if so, a thorough one.

Abide with me.

I caught a limb and curled my fingers around it. Tugging, I drew myself in close like a dance partner. *I know this tree.* I had climbed high into its branches before the first battle of Knock Ma. Then I had watched it take the life of an elf king to protect this place and the people who belong to it—because *I* had asked.

How had it come to be here? Toppled in the enemy's destruction of the forest, perhaps. Yet it was some distance from its original ground. The moat had spared this tree and no other from a fiery death—perhaps that was no accident.

It would still die. *Just like me.*

I wrapped my arms around the trunk.

Abide with me.

TENPENNY MAGIC

NEVE

The elves dragged us down to the great hall. Guards were posted around the entrances. There was some discussion I couldn't understand, but King Finvara told me they'd decided to hold us there until Far Dorocha had secured the castle. Apparently, the elves had once locked Finvara in the prison tower and he had escaped and brought back an army—so this time they intended to keep a closer eye on us.

That was the last chatter among us, because one of the elves punched the king in the mouth for talking to me.

They left everyone's wrists bound, but otherwise we were free to roam around. Finvara and Lord Meath kept eyeing each other until one of the guards yelled at them to knock it off. Then they began pacing, each on opposite sides of the long table.

Queen Isolde stood with her back to the cold fireplace, watching her cousins. At one point her gaze wandered over to me, settling on my face a few moments, and I thought I caught a tiny chink in the grim, calculating facade. I knew Will had been part of her court for a while. Was she grieving for him too?

A tear spilled onto my cheek, and she looked away.

Koli was standing in front of the kids' blanket fort. Hoping they were safe, I imagined, and so did I—especially Loki. Lady Alva was probably a delight, but I had bonded with the prince, even if our time together had never actually happened. It was some small comfort to me that some part of him remembered it too—when he'd given me the toy, I'd felt sure of it.

The toy. My gaze shot to where I'd left my bag, on the bench beside Will . . . the benches and chairs had all been removed.

It's gone.

Though most of the tablecloths had been used to make the fort, I saw that the one at the head of the table remained—and I glimpsed the bag's strap under its edge. My heart jumped; I resisted an urge to run and grab it. It could take me to Will, couldn't it? I'd give it *all* my blood if I had to.

I was trying to figure out how to get the book without the guards noticing when I felt someone's eyes on me and looked around. Koli was staring at me. *Hard.* I could tell that she wanted me to do something, but what?

All I want is to get to Will.

What if Will was dead? I closed my eyes. Wasn't he most likely dead? If he *had* survived, wasn't it better if everyone *thought* he was dead?

I swallowed a sob. Will felt like family to me. These people were family to *him.*

What would *he* want me to do?

Not waste my last trick on trying to save a dead man.

Okay think, Neve. On the roof, Koli had seemed to be calling my attention to Ulf. Why? Apparently, he'd been the elves' chief until Far Dorocha had interfered somehow. That made him the enemy of our enemy. But what use was he to me right now? I wasn't Will. I couldn't travel back in time and make this go away. And how many chances did you get at such a thing, anyway, until the whole timeline exploded?

I thought about the toy again. A likeness had proven to be enough for my magic. In fact, my magic seemed to be *built* on likenesses and symbols. I might be able to use it to bring him here—though unless he had Thor's hammer, I wasn't sure what good that would do us.

Thor's hammer is probably a thing here.

The assurance I was chasing around in my head was not going to be caught. This was going to take a leap of faith.

Gripping the loose rings of my antimagic chain, I walked in what I hoped was a dejected but casual fashion toward the table. When I got there, I plopped down on the floor in front of my bag with a sigh, and one of the guards looked at me. *Smooth.*

Sitting cross-legged, I dropped my supposedly bound hands in my lap and hung my head.

I kept peeking at the guards through strands of my hair until they seemed to have settled into watching the king and the earl, who were still slowly pacing.

My back was to the table, so over the course of the next fifteen minutes—I checked my flesh watch to be sure—I shifted around until the bag was to my left.

Now for the really risky part.

I flinched as someone coughed—Queen Isolde—and the guards looked at her. She coughed again.

Go.

I slipped off the chain and reached quickly under the table.

The queen coughed again. "One of you fools bring us some water," she called out hoarsely.

The bag's flap had thankfully fallen open, and I thrust my fingers inside. *Ow!* Ulf's sword had jabbed the end of my finger.

Ulf's sword jabbed the end of my finger.

I pulled the bag into my lap and one of the guards shouted—they were coming for me. Flipping the book open to a blank page, I dropped the toy into the gutter and smeared the end of my finger on the paper.

Everything blurred out.

"*Augat Óðins!*"

Well *something* had happened. The light was bright and *really* blue—I closed my eyes, trying to regain my equilibrium.

It's freezing in here. Not a volcano, so yay for that.

"Ulf?" I said more out of hope than belief. I wriggled on the odd surface beneath me, and part of it shifted. *Sand? Stones?*

After a few seconds of thick silence punctuated by water dripping somewhere close by, I opened my eyes. My vision had come back into focus but it was still *blindingly* bright in here compared to where I'd been. A blue dome arced overhead, and looking down, I discovered I *was* in fact resting on a mix of sand and small, smooth stones—both black.

I was surrounded by dozens of elves—all of them watching me with their glittering elf eyes. One of them came close and growled some words. My heart hammered. *You can do this.*

"I'm Neve," I said, "a friend of Queen Koli. Do you speak English?"

He grunted. "Only if I must. Koli sent you?"

He looked skeptical. His gaze fell on my bag and spellbook, which still lay in my lap.

"Where did you get that?" he demanded. I flinched as he

crouched and grabbed the elf toy. His fierce expression morphed into something truly frightening.

"Prince Loki gave it to me, I swear! I used it to get here—it's a super long story, and not exactly the most important information I have for you right now."

He narrowed his eyes—he wasn't sure whether to trust me. I didn't blame him.

I studied him right back. The guy had dirty-blond dreads all the way down to his ass, and his eyes were *gold*. He had a tree tattooed on his neck, more metal rings in his ears than I could count, and the most amazing beard I'd ever seen—being from Portland, that was saying a lot. He was scruffily hot, too, but right now he looked like he wanted to tear my head off. Although it seemed like maybe these guys looked like that generally.

"You have to go back and warn her," Ulf said at last, his tone taking on urgency. "The druid is *alive*. He is planning another attack on Knock Ma, and many of our people have joined him."

"Yeah," I said, sighing. "About that."

His frown deepened. "The queen knows?"

"It already happened."

He closed his eyes and muttered something that sounded like the Elvish version of "fuck *me*," and then he conveyed what I'd said to the others. More cursing. More growling.

My teeth had begun to chatter, and I rubbed my arms. "Why is it so cold in here?" Now that my eyes had better adjusted, I looked around again. *Oh, because we're in an ice cave.* The dome above us—I wondered if maybe it was blue (and aqua and cerulean and sapphire) because it was glacier ice. With the light coming through, it was breathtaking.

"Vatnajökull," said Ulf. "Palace of the *íssfólk*. 'Light elves,' outlanders call them."

Light elves? Wasn't version 1.0 of me related to them? I recalled the dream I'd recorded about Niamh and Oisin's first meeting—she carried a sword made for her mother by Icelandic dwarves.

"This is beautiful," I said, "but it doesn't look like a palace."

"*This* is a jail."

Terrific. "Why are you in jail?"

His eyes got even more intense. "Why are *you* in Iceland?"

I DON'T KNOW. How can I do this without you, Will?

The thought made my throat tight, but also reminded me *why* I was doing this. It gave me the strength to get through the complicated story I had to tell.

When I finished, Ulf sat shaking his big head at me. "We cannot help you."

"*Her.* I'm asking you to help *her.* Did you know she's having a baby?"

If I thought his eyes were wide before . . . "I don't mean right *now,*" I said. "But she's with child. Please."

"I will kill him if he hurts her."

"Honestly I hope you'll kill him either way, *but you can't do that from here.*"

He continued to shake his head, disgusted. "We came here to ask for aid from our cousins, to go after the druid and the traitors. We don't like each other, light and shadow, but we like outlanders even less—so we thought they might agree to help us."

"Instead they put you in ice jail?"

He made another grunt.

"Did you tell them *they* might be next if they don't do something?"

"*Ja.* But even if we get out, even if they agreed to help us, would it be in time?"

"How long does it take to get to Ireland from here?"

"By longboat, at least four days."

Four days!

"How did *you* get here?" He looked at the book in my lap.

"Yeah, with that. Magic . . . not big enough magic to transport an army."

And yet . . . *maybe* I didn't actually need big magic.

"Ulf!" The shout came from the mouth of the cave. It was followed by a gruff string of Elvish.

I could see the speaker—another big guy, this one with *white* dreads down to his ass. He was less bulky and . . . kind of tidier? He wore dark leather armor and a long silver cloak.

"Is that one of them? The light elves?"

Ulf nodded. "He wants to know who you are."

I groaned. "Tell him to get his ass in here and find out."

Ulf smirked his approval and yelled something back. The guard moved away from the mouth of the cave.

"Where's he going?"

Ulf shrugged. "I told him you were a sorceress and had demanded an audience with the queen."

"*Their* queen?"

"Ja. Gungnir."

Well, why not. I had some practice with queens at this point.

While we waited, Ulf gave up his cloak for me because my teeth were chattering loud enough for everyone to hear. Instead of unwashed male, which I had expected, it smelled like smoke and a familiar herb. Thyme, maybe?

The guard wasn't gone long—he ordered us to join him at the entrance. *Hopefully a good sign.*

Ulf handed me back mini-Ulf, and I put him and the book back in the bag. Then we went as ordered to the mouth of the cave, where we were immediately joined by a dozen more guards. The closest ones trained crossbows on us—either Ulf had a reputation or the sorceress descriptor had rattled them.

The prison turned out to be part of a whole system of caves

inside a glacier, all with the multifaceted blue ceilings. The natural corridors were lined with silvery black stones, possibly hematite. We wound through them so long I couldn't have said how to get back to the jail. Eventually we entered a much larger cavern that looked like a cathedral, with arches and buttresses and all the other features that made cathedrals so dramatic and impressive. Shafts of green and turquoise light pierced down from the ceiling, leaving circles of color on the floor. Though it was still freezing, there was nothing stark or spare about the chamber. There were rugs, chairs, and sofas, everything impossibly clean and white. The color was all created by the light passing through the ice.

The entire wall at the far end of the chamber was taken up by a throne. Blue and green icicles formed a pattern behind it that reminded me of a peacock tail, while the chair itself was colorless, opaque ice. On it sat a woman. She too had glossy white hair, arranged in a thousand loose braids, and a crown made of gemstones and a silver-white metal. She wore layers of white robes in satin and fur. Her breastplate was also silver-white, and had a mirror finish. A sword carved from ice rested across her knees. In striking contrast to all this—and to her pale blue irises—her skin was a warm brown.

We approached the dais, passing a fire pit that glowed with blue and green flames. Welcome heat radiated from it, but it was cooler than a regular fire. *Magic fire.* One wouldn't want to melt their ice cathedral.

We stopped a respectable distance from the throne, and the queen motioned us forward. When we were a few yards away, two guards stepped in front of us.

The queen's eyes moved over me, and again I regretted not having changed out of my modern clothes. Then she spoke to us in Elvish. I looked at Ulf.

"Gungnir asks if you are really a sorceress."

"Oh." I met her gaze. "Only a minor one."

Ulf opened his mouth to translate, and she waved her hand.

"The prison has ears," she said, switching to English. "We know what it is that you have asked for."

This was a huge relief. I didn't know if I had it in me to tell the story again.

"Then probably you also know that the Irish could *really* use your help, Your Majesty."

"We don't involve ourselves in outlanders' conflicts." She frowned. "Not unless *we* are the ones bringing the conflict."

"I get that," I said, "but I am one hundred percent sure you can think of *something* you want from Queen Isolde. And I also feel pretty confident she'll give you anything short of her country if you help her out of this mess."

Gungnir's eyes widened. I'd gotten her attention.

Everyone has a price.

"The queen is captive?"

"Isolde as well as the king and queen of fairy." Ulf had referenced some kind of light-shadow rivalry, so I decided not to mention Koli specifically. "There are children that have—"

She held up her hand and I shut my mouth. On second thought she didn't really seem the type to be softened by appeals about the children of her enemies.

"Is it true that Queen Isolde is descended from a goddess?"

I looked at Ulf. He lifted his wild eyebrows.

"Something like that, yeah. At least that's what I was told by a friend who once served in her court." My heart gave a heavy throb.

"*Our* mother was descended from the Valkyries."

I took that to be a royal "our." The ice queen had Valkyrie blood—I'd brag about it too.

"I . . . uh . . . Cool. I've read about them." *Good grief.*

"Coincidentally . . . I think one of my ancestors came from the light elves."

Ulf gave me the side-eye, and Gungnir raised her white eyebrows. "Who was this ancestor?" asked the queen.

"I don't actually know," I admitted. "She was the mother of a Faery woman called Niamh."

Crickets.

I was about to back-pedal to the Valkyries when the queen said, "I met Heiðr once."

"You did?" *Immortals*, I kept forgetting.

"Heiðr's mother was a *vǫlva*—a powerful ice witch," replied Gungnir. "I met Niamh once as well. Her mother brought her to court when I was a girl." The queen's gaze lifted as she relived her memory. "She had a beautiful picture book—mostly the flowers of her country, painted in so many vibrant colors. I was very taken with a purple one that looked like little stars. Niamh cut it from her book and gave it to me—it became a living flower right in the palm of my hand."

"Thank you, Your Majesty," I said, meaning it. "I know hardly anything about her."

She smiled. "Now you will demonstrate *your* magic for us, so we will know that your word may be trusted."

Oh. "Your Majesty—" I was about to protest that where I came from, materializing out of thin air was pretty magical, but Ulf slid his big boot against my sneaker, almost knocking me sideways.

I cleared my throat. "What do you want me to do?"

"As you like. We hope you will impress us."

Great. What could possibly impress a hundreds-of-years-old elf queen with an ice cathedral?

Probably not five minutes of standing here scratching my head.

My brain grabbed onto the last thing I'd seen that made an

impression. Because this was Will's world, I didn't have to think back very far. I opened the bag and dug out my book and pencil.

I handed the book to Ulf. "Hold it open like this." For the first time I saw fear flash in his eyes, but to his credit he complied.

I thought about Niamh and her picture book as I started sketching, and it gave me some much-needed courage. After a couple minutes I had a decent likeness. Then I took mini-Ulf out of my bag and prepared to shed my blood again. Suddenly I hated the idea of doing it in front of these people. It made me feel like a circus act, when in fact this was hugely fucking important. Then I heard Will's voice in my head.

You've already given it blood. Absinthe. Symbolic charms. Your artistry. Perhaps now you only need use it.

Maybe what I needed was as much faith in myself as Will had in me. And as I had in *him*. I laid my hand on the sketch and closed my eyes, feeling the tears seeping hotly around the edges of my lids.

I love you, Will.

Ulf gave a shout and the spellbook hit the carpet at our feet. Both of us staggered backward as one of the elk-horses *sprang right out of it.*

The queen shouted too, launching to her feet as she raised her ice-sword. Guards came up from behind and grabbed us.

The elk, however, appeared to be motivated mostly by a desire to get away, and it loped down the long rug between the throne and the entrance, snorting at the air, leaving a trail of steamy breath and muddy hoofprints. A handful of guards ran after it.

Wincing, I glanced up at the queen.

She smiled and sat back down—probably she wouldn't have done either if she planned to slice me in half.

"We will send our warriors back with you on one condition," said the queen.

I held my breath, exchanging a nervous look with Ulf. I didn't have the authority to speak for Queen Isolde. I had no idea what kind of compensation she might be willing and able to offer. All I had was a gut-level feeling that Will would want me to do whatever I had to in order to save his friends. Even if it was too late to save *him*.

"When the battle is won, she must come to us here at Vatnajökull. We—*I*—have a strong desire to know a woman whose people love her so well while she inspires such hatred and terror among her enemies."

So far so good. Isolde was obviously proud, but under the circumstances she could hardly refuse. I waited for Gungnir to continue.

She just sat there on her block of beautiful ice staring at me.

"That—is that *it*, Your Majesty?"

"This is what we require."

Again I looked at Ulf, and he gave me the "what are you waiting for?" eyebrows.

"Done," I said.

SOME MYTHIC HERO

WILL

Blessed lord of the forest. Father of us all.

The line came like a musical shout in my mind, waking me. But not from sleep.

From a kind of sleep.

Was I dead? If I were dead, would I be feeling such an urgent need to breathe?

Don't breathe yet.

I opened my eyes—how they stung! My arms were wrapped around the trunk of a tree—a tree that was submerged in very cold water. The trunk of the tree vibrated, and I heard a deep groaning sound. Then it began to *move*. I anchored myself in the branches. The tree was gliding upward, toward the light. Cold water flowed over my face and limbs.

My heart and lungs made frantic demands. My insides twisted and my vision dimmed.

Not yet. Think about anything but breathing.

A face came into my mind. A smile was really all it was, yet it conveyed a whole person—gentle, kind, funny, skittish. *Neve.* It both lifted and wrung my heart.

Was she still alive?

The trunk heaved out of the water and I gasped, filling my lungs so quickly I breathed in water and began to cough. *Am I really alive?*

Ghosts don't cough.

That sounded like something *she* would have said, and it made me laugh.

The tree was slowly righting itself in a way that would leave me hanging upside-down. I clambered with hands and feet—*my legs move!*—shifting my position like a crab as the trunk swung upward with loud cracking and thumping noises that I could feel under my hands.

The tree, too, was rising from its watery grave. But how? I thought of the Morrigan, and how she was corrupting the natural cycle for her own dark purpose. Was that what was happening to me?

Blessed lord of the forest. Father of us all.

I realized that the great oak had been singing a hymn since I first woke, and the meaning of the words had only now become clear to me.

Not the Morrigan—Uindos.

The tree shivered and groaned as severed trunk and limb were joined again, as roots dug back into the soil. The racket was exhilarating and terrifying. Leaves sprouted from barren limbs—quickening from spring to summer green, then to fiery yellow and orange. The commotion caused them to tremble violently, and already some of them were drifting to the ground.

This was a Faery forest, centuries old, and I was beyond being surprised by anything it did. Still, there must be a reason for the resurrection of a single dead tree that happened to have a dead poet attached to it . . . it felt like a *message.*

End the abomination.

My restored life was a gift—not one that came free from obligation. I shivered at the chilly feathering of those words through my thoughts . . .

End the abomination.

This tree and I had faced an enemy together before. I had traveled back through time to ask it to do something against its nature, and it had answered. What it asked of me now—perhaps what Uindos asked of me—I would willingly give.

I just wasn't sure it was within my power.

The tree had regenerated near the moat, uphill from its original ground. From this vantage, high up in almost the only standing tree for at least a square mile, I had a clear view of the battle raging on the hills below. All the lines had been broken, and it was a tragic, bloody mess. The evil that Far Dorocha and the Morrigan had wrought forced Irishman to fight Irishman, Fianna to fight Fianna. Even the casualties among the fairies and animals who had joined this fight had been transformed into grisly foes.

Our armies were nearly destroyed.

The Morrigan and Far Dorocha stood beside the hive-like structure and the Morrigan's crow standard, watching the battle. The goddess was known for her menacing presence, yet next to her servant she appeared stooped and old.

Could her contact with Far Dorocha somehow be sucking the life out of her?

Then it occurred to me it might be sucking something out of *him* as well. I had not seen him use magic. *He* hadn't taken Knock Ma, the elves had. He hadn't contained the ravens that Koli's magic had unleashed, the elves' brisingr restraint had.

Could it be that he was *controlling* the Morrigan, and that it was taking all his power? He had still been able to transform into the throat-tunnel—he had gotten himself and the elves into the castle. But back in the Morrigan's lair, we had learned that specific ability came to him when he was forced through the Alchemy Gate—like Koli's wings, and the clock that allowed me to time travel. It was part of his physiological makeup now.

I adjusted the strap for Borabu across my chest, and I began climbing down from the tree.

First I had to go back to the castle—I couldn't challenge the enemy without a weapon. And I had to know what happened to Neve. Though I had no idea how I was going to get past the elves inside.

When I reached the drawbridge—which thankfully had been lowered—a voice called, "Will?"

It had come from the gatehouse, and now I heard someone running down the stairs. She burst out of the door—*Maud.*

"You survived!" she said, breathless.

"For all practical purposes."

She laughed, though it had a bitter edge to it. "And you sound like yourself. I'm so relieved, Will, and so sorry for my part in all this. I was envious of your adventures, your importance and *purpose.* And you turned your back on all of it." She shook her head. "You were so stubborn about your 'quiet life,' until you met *her.* Suddenly you were ready to become some mythic hero. When it sank in, I resented you both so much! Can you ever forgive me?"

What on earth is she talking about? "Listen to me, Maud—where are the others? Where is Neve?"

She closed her mouth, sobering a moment. "Confined in the great hall. Though not Miss Kelly. She has disappeared."

My heart flipped over. "*What?*"

"I don't know anything more, Will. I heard the guards talking. I had made sure she was left unbound, and she did something—she got hold of some object—and she disappeared."

Her spellbook! I gripped Maud's shoulders. "Thank you."

She looked like she might cry, but I had no time to get to the bottom of her bizarre confession. I was about to take my leave when I noticed her hands. Releasing her shoulders, I took hold of her wrists, turning her palms up. She gave a little yelp.

"Maud! What in god's name?" The palms of both hands were covered with blisters. Some of them had burst, leaving her skin wet and raw.

"Come," she said, pulling her hands free, "I have something for you."

She hurried inside the gatehouse and I followed, my worries multiplying. Was Neve somewhere safe? How was I ever going to rescue the others or stop Far Dorocha? How many more people would die while I was trying to figure it out?

"I saved this for you, just in case," she said. She squatted on the floor and pulled back the edges of a cloak that was lying there.

Inside the cloak was Great Fury.

My mouth dropped open. "The *sword* did that to your hands."

"I believe it meant for me to know that I am not worthy of wielding it." She gave me a brittle smile. "Which is just as well, since I've only ever wielded dull, wooden ones."

I bent and grabbed the weapon, returning it to its scabbard. "I'm going out there."

"Of course you are. Please be careful."

My first thought was to free the others. What if I was captured in trying? Would that not be the end of hope? And to what end would I free them? Isolde had very little army left to command. The others were skilled fighters, though they would not turn the tide, even with Koli and Finvara's magic. And they had children waiting for them.

Lord Meath trusted the weapon of the Fianna to me.

If I was Oisin, let it be for a reason.

Was I marching to my death? *Probably.* Magic or no magic, there was a good chance Far Dorocha would destroy me. But I had Great Fury, and that had to count for something. Diarmuid had used it to cut down hundreds of enemy warriors in the Battle of Ben Bulben.

And yet it didn't keep Far Dorocha from throwing me off the roof.

The battle was taking place on the very same ground as the first Battle of Knock Ma. I was now crossing the spot where Koli and Finvara had pitted their magic against her father, the Elf King.

I continued my plunge down the slope toward the more level ground to the southwest, where the enemy had camped. The battle lines had pushed out from that area, as the enemy's numbers grew and they drove the queen's forces and the Fianna into the surrounding hills.

The burned trees littering the hillside made the footing treacherous, and I stumbled and slid much of the way down. Scratched and bruised, I reached the base of the hill, and Far Dorocha must have sensed my approach—or perhaps my murderous intention—because he turned from the battle. His lips peeled back in a grotesque parody of a smile.

"I'm so pleased you've finally joined us."

My heart pounded like a war drum and perspiration dripped down my back.

"Call the Fianna," said the monster, "and we'll abbreviate this. I grow weary of waiting."

Seconds slipped by while I tried to make sense of his words. I had *already* called the Fianna. They were out on the field fighting and dying with the others.

Then it dawned on me. I must look frightful—my skin and clothes were filthy with gray-green muck from the moat. I remembered what Maud had said, and how relieved her tone had been: *You sound like yourself.* Far Dorocha killed me, as he had planned to do from the beginning. He thought I was one of *them* now. He had no idea it was Uindos and not the Morrigan's dark magic that had brought me back.

He was ordering me to call what was left of the Fianna to *his* side of the fight.

Assuming his will would be done, he'd already returned his attention to the battle. I studied the hunched back of the Morrigan, beside him. She was silent, and had not even moved while her servant spoke to me. Her war robes pooled on the ground around her feet, like she had shrunk inside them.

I reached for the horn. What was going to happen if I sounded it again? Could it help us? Make things worse? I thought about what Neve might say if she were here.

Things can't really get worse.

I raised Borabu to my lips. As the long call sounded, my eyes moved over the lines—the scattered skirmishes that continued. I detected no change—warriors grappled over the bloodied and torn ground. Battle was horrific enough without being confused about who was friend or foe. With the slow, grim conversion that was happening, I realized this battle would end when all the warriors found themselves fighting for the same side. I shuddered. It was not hard to understand how Knock Ma had been taken so quickly in the original timeline.

We've done nothing but delay it.

Was it possible our actions had even done more harm than good? By asking Maud to give Isolde advance warning, had we not served up the entire Irish army as an offering to the Morrigan? We had not really managed to save *anyone.*

Despair was beginning to weigh down my resolve when I noticed something odd—some of the combatants were dropping suddenly, without seeming to have been struck down. It was happening with the animals—the elk and the wolves. I looked closer for the distinctive leather helms of the Fianna, and saw it was happening to them too. My heart sank—until closer observation helped me understand what was *really* happening. The second call of Borabu had not drawn the surviving Fianna to the side of the enemy, as Far Dorocha had expected. It had released our fallen warriors to their rest, so they could no longer betray their brethren.

A rallying cry went up from what was left of the Irish army and its allies, as they charged the reduced enemy forces.

Far Dorocha turned to me again, this time raising his massive sword. It was a weapon of nightmares, with deeply etched runes and a wide, double-edged blade that was notched on one side. Electricity danced along its length.

"You are more resilient than you appear, poet."

The monster lurched toward me and I raised Great Fury barely in time to block the first strike. Blue light flashed and sparks flew as the weapons clashed together—the heavy blow knocked me to the blood-fouled ground. I squirmed in the muck, trying to get my feet under me.

I am alone in this, I realized. *Merely mortal.*

When Lord Meath had wielded Great Fury against the Fomorians at Ben Bulben, his ancestor Diarmuid had worked through him. Oisin was not my ancestor, he was *me*. In this new life, I had retrained myself to be a poet, but I had turned my back on the warrior.

Again I heard Neve's voice in my thoughts: *Tell that to those three firglas revenants you cut down.*

I scrambled to my feet, raising the sword and managing another block—this time I kept my footing.

His attack was shambling, his new body with its metal components heavier and perhaps less responsive than the old—I was able to dance away and rest a moment before he came at me again.

I recalled the memory of Oisin's that had saved us from the firglas—I had thought I was facing a hundred foes, and I'd managed to draw strength from Diarmuid's ancient weapon.

As Far Dorocha drove forward, I thought about the people I had come back from the dead to save, and I swung the blade as hard as I could.

Blue flame arced out toward my enemy. He caught it against the blade of his sword. Great Fury's energy flashed and popped, forcing him back—one, two, three steps. When I thought he would fall, he closed his eyes, and I watched the blue flame that had enveloped his blade turn *white*.

I tightened my grip on my weapon, which had started to vibrate. My forearms burned, and perspiration dripped down my forehead.

A slight movement behind Far Dorocha caught my eye—the Morrigan, who had not moved even as our swords clashed loudly behind her, had turned to face us. She was pallid and gaunt, but her dark eyes glittered.

Was Far Dorocha using *magic*? Had it caused him to lose his hold on her?

The white light surged like lightning, chasing Great Fury's blue flame back toward me. A fiery pain cut into my arms and I dropped the sword.

Far Dorocha murmured darkly and flicked his hand. Great Fury spun out of my reach and the monster raised his blade to finish me.

THE PEN AND THE SWORD

NEVE

Ulf and I stood on the glacier in the blazing sun. I wasn't cold anymore. Fifty loyal shadow elves, freed from ice jail, and two hundred light elves formed lines before us, awaiting Ulf's signal. Behind us was a vertical pillar of ice probably thirty feet tall.

Ulf was waiting on *me*, but I allowed myself a moment to take it all in—rows of silvery plate armor, glittering in the sun, the white wolf standard of the light elves and the shadow elves' raven, both rippling in the breeze. All eyes on me, and the strange calm-before-the-storm quiet, like everyone was holding their breath.

You've got this.

I looked at Ulf. "Ready?"

He grinned and raised his wicked-looking elf knife—a scramasax, Queen Gungnir had called it.

I opened my spellbook to the drawing of the throat-tunnel,

with its blood and absinthe stains. The throat-tunnel that was a *living* Gap gate—Far Dorocha's superpower gift from his revenge march through the Alchemy Gate.

Turning to the ice pillar, I closed my eyes and thought about Will. Quiet country life aspirations aside, he would have *loved* to be here for this.

I held the spellbook out in front of me.

Come on, asshole.

The book flew from my fingers, somersaulted a couple times, pages flapping wildly, and plastered itself against the ice pillar. The drawing howled like a demon and began to stretch and contort, until once again I was staring into the angry maw of the throat-tunnel.

Exclamations went up among the elves behind us. I looked at Ulf and saw the fear in his eyes. But he was still grinning like a man possessed. He raised his scramasax higher and yelled in Elvish—it must have been something like "let's go, guys," because a loud cheer went up from the warriors. At first it was only the shadow elves, and then the others joined in. They raised shields and weapons in the air.

There's definitely something wrong with these people.

Yeah, but they're my people now.

Ulf ran for the opening, swearing in Elvish at the top of his lungs. The rest of the shadow elves took up the charge after him. When he got to the gate, it sucked him in and swallowed his yell. Then his countrymen got sucked in after him.

The light elves froze in shock, and I held my breath. *Please don't lose your nerve.*

Queen Gungnir's general shouted an order, and he began the charge. The light elves followed with a bone-jarring battle cry.

I watched them go, hoping I wasn't sending them to their deaths.

When the last of the elves were almost through the gate, I jogged after them, holding my breath as Far Dorocha's big mouth sucked me up too.

I found myself ripping through the tunnel alone, and panic surged. What the hell happened to my army? What if we ended up scattered across dimensions?

It will work—just like before. We'll all end up wherever Far Dorocha is.

Just like Will and I had, back at the start of all this.

I popped out on slick ground. Mud, but not dirt and water. *Blood and ash.*

The hard landing knocked the breath out of me. I crouched on the ground, getting my bearings—I'd been spit out right in the middle of the action.

Actually, you brought the action with you.

I had roaring elves on all sides of me, except for where the throat-tunnel made a crater in the ground. Its chthonic screech was fading—it was slowly closing.

My muddied, brilliant spellbook lay beside me—I snatched it up and looked frantically around. I glimpsed Ulf—he and the rest of the shadow elves were scrambling up the hill toward the castle. There would have been no talking him out of rescuing Queen Koli before anything else, even had I wanted to.

It was fine, Queen Gungnir's warriors were going after the revenants—and it looked like there were a *lot* less of them than when I left. I searched for her general through the chaos of arms, legs, swords, beards . . . and saw something that stopped my heart . . . and time itself.

Will was on his knees on the opposite side of the throat-tunnel. He had the hilt of his sword in one hand, its tip on the ground like he'd been dragging it. His eyes were moving everywhere.

But *was* it Will? If he was dead before and alive *now* . . . I thought about Finvara's father.

Oh god.

"Will!" I screamed.

His eyes found me—his face lit up like Christmas.

He scrambled around the throat-tunnel toward me—he didn't have far to go; it had almost sealed.

Any second, Franken-fae will have arms and legs again. Then what?

An idea exploded in my brain.

Will reached me and I yelled over the battle noise—it was like one of those dreams where you're running but going nowhere—I couldn't get the words out fast or loud enough.

"The sword! Hurry!"

I opened my book to the tunnel drawing, laid it down in the muck, and backed away.

"There!" I shouted. "Stab it!"

He looked at me, questioning. Did I really want him to kill the spellbook?

I nodded exaggeratedly. "Yes, do it!"

He raised the sword and I closed my eyes. "One final spell, *please.*" I thought to call on Niamh's grandmother, the ice witch, in case it might help me. Instead, I thought of my *own* mother—the smile on her face the first time I rode my bike by myself. *That was a good day.*

I opened my eyes and down the sword plunged, right through the gutter of the book. A sudden rumble and flash knocked Will backward and the book burst into flames.

The familiar ghastly howl erupted from the crater, and Will crawled to me and pulled me back from it. The hole was stretching open again, dark smoke billowing out. We ducked close to the ground and scooted farther away.

The sound cut off sharply and the smoke began to thin.

Then the crater was shrinking again—it stopped at maybe eighteen inches across. The rocky rim had been blackened by smoke, and a sickly gray color replaced the raw red of the tissue inside. Destroying the drawing of the throat-tunnel had destroyed the *actual* throat-tunnel—and the rest of Far Dorocha along with it.

It was a literal manhole.

Now we just need a cover.

Will pulled me hard into his arms, almost smothering me. I managed to croak, "You didn't die!"

He drew back, taking my face in his hands. "I may have, actually, but I feel much better now."

I put my hands over his and started laughing through tears. "I might need you to explain that."

He grinned. "I promise I will." Then he kissed me. Feeling the lips of someone you thought you had lost . . . it's the best feeling there is.

With his mouth on mine, and the gentle pressure of his thumbs against my cheeks, it was hard to remember the important thing I had tucked away in case I ever saw him again. Suddenly I did.

"Wait, Will."

He drew back, his eyes searching mine.

"Before anything else tries to kill us, I need to tell you something."

He raised his eyebrows, waiting.

"I love you. I was furious with myself for being too scared to say it before you died."

A smile spread over his face and he pulled me close. "You are so much braver than you think you are. I love you too."

My throat tightened even as a tickle moved down my spine. I pressed my cheek against his chest, and low in my belly everything went suddenly warm and wishful.

Then I saw something weird. A boulder was rolling over the

ground toward the manhole. In context, it wasn't *that* weird—until I saw there was another one behind it. And another one.

I gave Will's arm a tug and we moved out of the danger zone. The first boulder rolled over the manhole, covering it. The second and then the third rolled on top of it, forming a small cairn.

Looking around, I discovered the battle had paused like a creepy tableau. Combatants were stuck in strange and awful poses, defying physics and every other natural law. Literally nothing was moving—except rocks. They were coming from every direction now, rolling and bouncing from the hills around us. Boulders from the burned forest, most of them covered in moss and lichen, charred in places.

Somebody was using powerful magic.

WILL

It ended when the pile of stones had reached about twelve feet high. The eerie silence of the battlefield was now unbroken.

A few yards away from the new monument was the hive structure—or what was left of it. It had been reduced to a mass of melted, twisted metal. The Morrigan stood beside it, her dark, sunken eyes fixed on *us*.

She began walking toward us, the tip of her bone staff dragging over the ground as if it had grown too heavy to lift. I felt a strong impulse to run, and yet how could we escape a goddess?

We did it once before.

We had Neve's spellbook then.

Anyone who might help us—Fianna, firglas, Irish soldiers—seemed to be under some kind of enchantment. We had no choice but to face her alone.

Neve and I exchanged a tense glance. I reached for her hand and pulled her closer.

The Morrigan moved to stand in front of the cairn. She looked small and frail against it. Yet I had no doubt she could reduce us to ash if she chose to.

I remembered the lovers on the battlefield—how they'd died side by side under the eyes of their enemy. Was it *fated* to be our end? Was it a cycle, like life and death, that could not be defeated?

"One more task, poet." The Morrigan's voice was like winter leaves crumbling underfoot. Her watery eyes found my sword on the nearby ground.

"I won't help you take the crown," I said, my voice trembling. "I'll die if I have to."

She lifted a thin eyebrow, and I thought she might laugh. Instead, she raised a long finger, pointing at Great Fury. "The druid has corrupted this body with his whispered lies and magical snares. While it lives, the wheel is broken."

Her gaze moved over the field and hills, strewn with the bodies of the dead and the paralyzed forms of the living. I followed with my own eyes, sickened by the sight of men frozen in the act of murdering each other, their eyes lit with fear and fury. What did she see, I wondered? I knew that war and violence did not trouble her.

The wheel is broken. It wasn't the battle. It was the desecration and corruption of the natural cycle.

A thought came to me then . . . had the Morrigan granted Niamh's wish for rebirth in the way she had—suppressed memories, far-flung timelines—to make a *point*?

Everyone gets one turn on the wheel.

"You must destroy this body," said the goddess, her eyes fixed on me again. "It is the will of Dana."

I stared at her. Dana, the mother goddess of the Tuatha De Danaan—of the Morrigan herself, and of Uindos—wanted *me* to strike down the goddess of war? Could it be some kind of trick?

She could have easily killed us by now.

I looked at Neve. Her eyes were wide, and she shook her head helplessly.

My decision.

Letting go of Neve's hand, I walked over and picked up the sword. It felt heavier now.

I raised the blade, my whole body shaking.

The goddess nodded and closed her eyes.

I looked once more at Neve. She formed silent words: *You've got this.*

I held my breath and swung.

REBIRTH

WILL

When I woke, I found Neve lying beside me. I bent my cheek to her lips—*breathing, alive*. She began to stir.

Then I heard laughter and rose to my feet.

A young, black-haired girl stood where the crone had. She held the bone staff, though it was several feet taller than she was. She smiled at me—it was an unsettling smile, neither happy nor childish—and she walked toward the nearest cluster of combatants. As she walked, she clutched the edges of her too-large garments with one hand. They dragged heavily along the ground behind her, leaving a trail in the muck.

When she reached the fighters, most of them straightened, lowering their weapons and looking around in confusion. Two crumbled to dust. She continued to wind through the field of battle, and in her wake, many of the *slain* began to stir as well. It wasn't the same as before, though. Fianna, wolves and elk, soldiers of Ireland, firglas, even the shadow elves who had joined Far Dorocha—all were made whole again. They weren't revenants or risen corpses. They were *living.*

I had to watch for some time before I really understood it—the Morrigan was turning back the clock, in a sense. Reversing the carnage wrought by her servant. The only ones left to sink into the battle-riven earth were the ones who should never have been raised—Far Dorocha's original army of revenants.

Neve had revived, and she stood up. I slipped an arm around her, and we watched the goddess until she'd completed her circuit of the battlefield. Then she continued into the hills to the west, where the sun was sinking toward the Atlantic.

Those around us began helping others to their feet, all of them still struck with confusion and wonder. Armor and weapons clanked, but for a while, no one spoke.

I looked at Neve, and she smiled. "We're alive."

I pulled her into my arms. "Very much so."

We did hear voices then, drifting down from the castle. We watched a line of people cross the drawbridge and cluster near the gatehouse. I took Neve's hand and we made our way toward them.

When we reached the gatehouse, I saw that the whole family was accounted for—Queen Isolde, Koli and Finvara, Lord and Lady Meath, the children. Ulf was there too, along with Maud. She was bruised and scraped and her hands were thickly wrapped in bandages—I didn't think I had ever seen her look more pleased.

Neve squeezed my hand as Isolde stepped forward to meet us. She gave us a queenly nod.

"Mr. Yeats and Miss Kelly. *Huzzah.*"

NEVE

After answering a million questions from the royals at the gatehouse, they finally let us go back to the castle to get cleaned up.

The place was a disaster—apparently, the shadow elves had all been fighting each other in the corridors. The traitors had been locked in various towers, their fate—along with the fate of the others down on the battlefield—as of yet undetermined.

Upstairs, I peeled off Will's filthy clothes and educated him about how much fun two people could have in a small brass bathtub. Clean, dressed, and blessedly warm, we stood together at the window and watched *the forest growing back.*

I'm in Will's world now.

But for how long? That hadn't exactly been settled yet, and I was trying not to think about it. The discussion would have to wait, anyway, because everyone was expecting us in the courtyard for a makeshift feast—*and* for the redo of the Samhain bonfire, being held in honor of the victory. Also because the first one had been canceled when the Morrigan started raining down fire on the grounds, rendering it redundant.

We found the royals sitting in fancy chairs in front of the Victorian conservatory, watching the fairies cavorting around the bonfire.

Queen Koli led us to the bench that had been saved for us—they'd placed it in the center of the row of chairs, seats of honor. Servants brought glasses of a sweet, honey-smelling wine.

"Miss Kelly," began Queen Isolde in that tone that made me feel like a dog caught counter-surfing, "Ulf tells me you have conducted unsanctioned diplomacy on my behalf."

Koli's elf friend was standing nearby holding a tankard as big as his head. Before I could find my tongue, he said, "I told her she *ought* to be thanking you, because Gungnir could easily have asked for the Irish fleet."

I could not imagine *anyone* speaking to Isolde like this. Half that tankard must be empty.

Ulf momentarily became the object of queenly scrutiny, and I nudged myself to take a breath.

"Right you are," Isolde said. Her gaze came back to me. "Thank you, Miss Kelly, for your efforts on behalf of Ireland. I am happy to report that the newly appointed king of the shadow elves will be accompanying me on my diplomatic visit to Vatnajökull."

By the look on his face, this was news to the newly appointed king of the shadow elves. His wide eyes drew a peal of laughter from Koli, and it was impossible not to join in. Even Isolde cracked a smile.

Koli had, apparently, given Ulf a promotion. She agreed with Franken-fae that the shadow elves could not be expected to respect a regent. They needed an on-site monarch, whom they could occasionally try to murder to convince themselves he or she was worthy. So Koli was cutting her official ties with her homeland and casting her lot with the Irish.

I could imagine how hard a decision that must have been.

"Isolde adores you," Will said close to my ear.

I laughed at that. "You think so, do you? You're pretty transparent, my friend."

He gave me a half-squinting smile. "They *all* adore you."

"And how about you?"

"I don't adore you."

"No?"

He moved closer. "I love, desire, worship, *and* adore you."

"You're not going to make this easy, are you."

He grinned and pulled my mouth to his.

When he let go, I'd practically forgotten who I was.

His lips came again to my ear. "We belong together and both of us know it. What do you say?"

ONE YEAR LATER

NEVE

Portland, Oregon

I told Will that I'd miss pumpkin spice lattes too much, and that I wanted to keep my options open. I think he maybe almost believed me, because I had flat out refused to marry him.

Then I kept my promise to Noah and went home. He had remembered nothing of our trip to Portland with the prince, just as he'd feared would happen if we changed the timeline. I'd had to go through the entire thing with him, and when he got over *that*, I told him what my plan for the future was. He took it all about as well as last time. But he got over it, and even let us crash on his futon when we visited.

Yep, in the end, I did officially quit my job and let my apartment go. I refused to give up Portland, though . . . and especially the French bakery.

They were busy today, and our order was taking forever. I sat fiddling with my heart locket, wondering what my mother would have thought of this strange life of mine. Then I added a few more lines to the sketch on the table in front of me.

"What are you working on?"

Will was looking at me over the top of his new reading glasses, and *oh my god* it made me wish we still had a bedroom in this time zone. Since we spent most of our time in Drumcliff, really it made no sense. We were never here more than a day or two before I started missing our hygge paradise.

"Just my sketch journal," I replied.

I glanced up as the waiter visited our table and plunked down our coffee and croissants. They were amazing, and the only thing in this space-time I would accept as a substitute for Mrs. Tobin's scones.

"You still working on the ballad of Will and Neve?"

He laughed. "Something like that."

I teased him for writing about us, though secretly I loved it. The irony of this whole picture was that *I* was using an Icelandic charcoal pencil made from a bone, and he was using my laptop.

"Can I see?" he asked.

I sipped my latte, considering.

He smiled. "Please?"

Melt.

"If I let you, do we get to do Halloween here?"

Will smirked. He had picked up a few modern mannerisms of which I was not exactly a fan. Good thing for him he was adorable in every other way. "You're not afraid of the ghosts anymore, are you?"

I tossed my napkin and hit him in the chest. "Damn right I am."

"You know Mrs. Marsh is expecting us for the few days before. We might as *well* spend Samhain at Knock Ma. Koli said the prince is asking every day . . ."

"So. Not. Fair." He knew how to get me. I was practically calling Mrs. Marsh "Mom" at this point, and to Loki I was "Auntie Neve."

He pushed a hand through his hair and grinned.

"Okay, *fine*," I groaned.

"Fine to which part?"

"All of it, you jerk."

I spun the journal to show him the sketch I'd made of him standing in the field behind his house. *Will in his natural habitat.* Proud as I was of everything we'd accomplished together, I preferred sketching him acting like a normal guy. Like the guy he wanted to be.

His face softened as he studied the drawing. His eyes lifted to mine.

"I love it."

Okay, yeah, I was definitely going to marry him someday.

ACKNOWLEDGMENTS

The Faery Rehistory series was inspired by a lifetime interest in fairies and a large number of books on the subject that I collected over the years. One of the more important and influential of these was a book on Irish folklore called *The Celtic Twilight*, written by Irish poet W. B. Yeats. Yeats was a student of folklore and mysticism, and he had magic in his soul. He brought Ireland's mythic heroes to life. As an author inspired by him, transforming Yeats into an Irish warrior poet for the final book in this series felt like the most natural thing in the world.

I've included lines from several of Yeats's poems in *The Warrior Poet*: "Anashuya and Vijaya" at the beginning of the book, "The Stolen Child" in the chapter "Human Child," and "The Two Trees" in the chapter "Spellwork." I also wrote a few lines of poetry inspired by Yeats, and included them as the thoughts of my fictional Yeats—you'll find those in the chapters "Under Ben Bulben" and "A Delicate Matter."

There are also lots of *living* people who helped make this book, and this series, possible. A huge thank you, as always, to my indispensable agent, Robin Rue, and her assistant, agent Beth Miller (who reads early drafts without complaint and then makes them better).

All the great folks at Blackstone I've had the pleasure of working with along the way. I simply adore Corinna Barsan, my editor for *The Warrior Poet* (and *The Raven Lady*), who just *gets* me. Ember Hood, my wonderfully smart and kind copyeditor, who has been with me for this whole journey. Cover designer Kurt Jones, who came up with the look and feel for the series, and Mandy Earles, who has been fabulous to work with on marketing. Josie Woodbridge and Rick Bleiweiss for loving the books and being amazing people. My heart was broken last year when some of the folks at Blackstone were hit hard by the Oregon wildfires—in the midst of a global pandemic, no less.

I've been blessed with fantastic narrators for this series: Alison McKenna and Alan Smyth. I have a terrific language consultant I've worked with on all three books: Jeff Lilly. Thanks so much for your support, local booksellers Annie Carl (The Neverending Bookshop) and Jim Tinney (Kiss the Sky Books). And also book bloggers Tammy Sparks (*Books, Bones & Buffy*), Justine Bergman (*Whispers & Wonder*), and Has Saadani (*The Book Pushers*), along with the fabulous Instagram book reviewer community. Thanks, too, to the Pacific Northwest Booksellers Association for all they do to support local authors.

In *The Warrior Poet*, I describe an image of a man and woman pointing an arrow at the sky—an image that Will and Neve both sketched in their notes about their dreams. That image was described to me years ago in a reading done for me by Robert Alan Hager.

My love and heartfelt thanks to the usual suspects: my incredibly supportive husband, Jason Knox; my fabulous girls, Selah and Talia; and my indispensable beta (and theta and zeta) reader and dear friend, Debbi Murray.

The fact that a book was able to come together *at all* with everything that came at us over the last year is nothing short of a miracle, so way to go, us, and thank you, universe.